I0722784

SILENT BORDERS

SILENT BORDERS

ALEXANDRA RYDER

Translated from French
by Sandra Lazar

In memory of my mother
who passed on to me her love of books

« The day the power of love overrules the love of power, the world will know peace ».
—Mahatma Gandhi

CHAPTER 1

The Black Sea Beach looked like any other modern beach, where people with sunscreen-covered bodies spent their holidays beneath the blinding sunlight. Miles of white sand lined with hotels, restaurants, and amusement parks had attracted millions of foreign tourists for many years, but that was no longer true.

The economic policy of the regime had plunged the country into poverty. Poverty and the suppression of freedom of speech had triggered public discontent. The number of those who wanted to flee abroad had increased despite being aware that they risked imprisonment or death.

The government had made decisions; well-dressed tourists spending carelessly were no longer welcome. The millions of dollars they spent at the Black Sea were less important than the total submission of the population. The surveillance of people who came into contact with foreigners became tighter. The greenery was no longer maintained, and the hotels began to look pitiful without renovation.

Apart from the crowds, there were villas made up of luxurious rooms, with well-maintained gardens and beaches cleaned every day. In their restaurants, you could taste the best caviar and champagne.

Only the most loyal members of the Communist Party had access to the villas. My name is Ana Zaicovich, and I am one of those privileged people. But for how much longer? The night before my vacation, I overheard George, my handler, and Avram, the man I trusted like a father, revealing the truth: the Romanian secret police, the Securitate, had manipulated my entire life. They'd killed my family and placed me in an institution, grooming me into a top-tier spy. Now, I know that my supposed allies are my deadliest foes. Heartbroken, I retreated into solitude, grappling with the betrayal.

As I waded into the water on my final vacation day, I knew I was alone, betrayed by those I once trusted. I took off my hat and crept slowly into the water. Soon, I heard nothing but the squeal of my hands in the salt water of the sea. I pressed my arms against my chest to control my rising anger. Burning tears were running down my cheeks.

I wondered how many happy and innocent children had become orphans with lonely souls. I'll probably never know. For the time being, I learned I was one of those children and had only one desire: revenge. I had no idea my desire would begin to fulfill the latter night.

The sun's heat dried my tears, and a wet breeze tickled my face.

My gaze embraced the horizon at the place where the sea meets the sky. A gust of wind agitated the sea's water, and a shadow obscured the sun's light. *The storm is rising. I'd better go back to the villa,* I thought. I swam long strokes towards the beach. Other latecomers were picking up their things so they wouldn't get wet. In a few minutes, the beach was empty.

I wrapped my shoulders in the beach towel and walked down the path, which was adorned with flowery bushes that zigzagged among the villas.

A delicious smell from the restaurant kitchen reached my nostrils, but I wasn't hungry. I rushed into my room, threw my things on the bed, went into the bathroom and let the shower run over my skin.

After applying an after-sun lotion, I approached the window.

A supernatural calm had settled as if the atmosphere held its breath before the thunderstorm broke. Large clusters of clouds obscured the sky. Huddled in the bed, I listened to the sea rise and the wind howl. My eyes were heavy, and I fell into a sleep haunted by nightmares.

When I awoke, a groan stuck in my throat, the alarm clock read two twenty-five in the morning.

The rain was drumming slightly on the windows. I wiped up the sweat covering my face, wondering if I was doomed to live haunted, night after night and waking up startled at the beating heart and blood pounding under my skull.

With sudden gestures, I took off my wet nightgown and threw it on the bed, put on a sports outfit and running shoes, put my hair under a cap and went out into the hallway.

Instinctively, I moved without making any noise. To avoid unwanted encounters, I went opposite the main door and left the villa through the emergency exit, ensuring the door remained unlocked.

My eyes searched the darkness of the night. The rain was pouring, but the lightning had calmed down, and the thunderbolts that sounded earlier were silent. I walked towards the beach.

Arriving at the water's edge, I sped up and soon began to run, exposing my face to the rain and trying to free myself from the flood of emotions that tormented me.

The beach became narrower and narrower, and I had to stop after a few hundred meters. A stone wall, built to prevent tourists from reaching the shores of the villas, cut me off. I leaned against the wall and looked around. I had completely forgotten about the existence of this wall.

A lovely villa was almost invisible near the wall, thanks to the density of trees and shrubs planted around it. A faint light shone through its windows, and laughter resonated from inside. The rain hasn't relented at all and the night was pitch black.

Screams suddenly filled the darkness. Alert, I listened

intently. The sound died down, and the night became silent. The rain continued to fall, dripping down my body. It was time to leave before someone on the inside spotted me and thought I was spying on them.

My thoughts were interrupted as the door of the villa opened, and a completely naked woman ran out, followed by two men who caught her without trouble. As she tried to free herself, the woman screamed, squirming around in desperation.

Slowly, the screams turned into groans of pain as if terror were crushing her throat. Through the thin rays of light past the door's opening, I saw the two men pull the women back inside the villa. The door closed with a loud blow, and complete silence set in.

It took me nearly a full minute to absorb what I saw and shake off my disbelief. The groans of pain still echoed in my head, and I let the rain flow down my face as if to wash away the bitter guilt that had taken over.

I remained motionless in the heavy feeling air, unable to leave. Finally, I faced the facts: I could not turn my back and forget what I just saw.

After a moment of hesitation, I approached the villa and climbed the stairs to a terrace adorned with stone slabs made slippery by the rain. With my back hunched, I moved forward to pass unnoticed. When I got to the window, I stopped and looked around. My instincts told me no one was there, but I wanted to ensure.

I inched my face to the glass and, for a moment, stopped breathing and stared helplessly. Two completely naked men were sexually assaulting the woman. Blood flowed down her legs, and a reddish circle formed on the floor. She had her hands and feet tied to four metal rings, anchored to the wall opposite the window so that she could not make any movement. A plastic restraint covered her mouth as she bled from her nose.

It was clear that this was not the two men's first experience of this kind: the metal rings attached to the wall, and other objects used in sexual debauchery combined with their casual attitude in a situation that would have frozen the blood of any average person proved that.

I shook my head in disbelief, quivering from disgust and rage. My first impulse was to enter and free the woman. My fingers were curled around the handle, ready to open the door, when I realized the gravity of the situation. I knew I had to act, but it would be wiser to notify the police. And I have to hurry.

I took one last look inside. The two men had changed positions, and I could see their faces. A shiver ran down my spine. I couldn't believe it. I knew those faces; I knew those men! They were essential government members; men used to command and to power. They also knew me because I had dealt with them a few times.

A surge of anxiety hit me, but I quickly pushed it aside. Just moments ago, I had considered contacting the police. Now that I understood the forces at play, I knew better. The police wouldn't help the girl. They'd launch an investigation, write their reports filled with convenient half-truths, and let the case disappear into the hands of powerful men. The inquiry would be quietly closed, and the girl would be forgotten.

That wasn't going to happen. Not on my watch.

My pulse quickened, and anger sharpened my senses. A plan formed in my mind: no more waiting or following rules that worked for everyone but the innocent. This time, I'd make my own rules. I tugged my cap down to shadow my face, steeling myself. With a deliberate movement, I raised my hand and knocked on the window. It was more than just a knock; it was the start of a fight on my terms. After several firm taps, the taller men finally opened the door.

"Who's there?" he screamed, his voice sharp with panic. "Who the hell is there?"

I knocked again, deliberately. The repeated sound grated on his nerves, and I could hear the frustration boiling over. After a moment, there was a flurry of movement inside. He hurriedly threw on a pair of shorts, stomping toward the door, his rage building with every step. When he flung it open, his breath caught as he noticed the figure of a woman standing outside.

I stayed in the shadows, ensuring he couldn't see my face.

"Who are you? What makes you think it's okay to disturb people at this hour?" he barked, the stench of sweat and whiskey rolling off him in waves.

"Where did you learn to treat people like that?" I shot back, my voice calm but cold.

He sneered. "Maybe you need a lesson too, huh?"

"Let's just say it's not your lucky day," I replied, the edge in my voice unmissable.

Without warning, he swung, aiming to slap me across the face. But I was faster. I ducked to my left, dropped low, and drove my shoulder into his gut with force. He stumbled back toward the steps, gasping for breath. For a moment, he seemed winded, but then, with a furious growl, he regained his footing and rushed at me, his eyes wild with fury.

As he lunged, I moved on instinct. My body flowed into motion, muscles coiling with precision. I dropped to the floor and, with a powerful kick, I slammed both feet into his lower back. The force sent him flying over the railing of the terrace. There was a dull thud as his body hit the sand below, unmoving.

I didn't hesitate. My feet were already moving down the stairs toward him, ready to strike again if needed. But as I neared his body, I stopped. The man wasn't moving. A dark pool of blood spread around his head, the jagged rock he had fallen on unmistakable.

I froze.

I hadn't planned on killing him. My mind raced, grasping for the next step. Things had just gone terribly wrong.

A noise from the terrace broke through the haze. I glanced up. The second man had turned on the outside light, and the harsh glow illuminated the scene. His eyes flicked from his friend's lifeless body to the shadow of me on the sand below. In his right hand, a gun gleamed under the light.

He raised it, and I knew he wasn't hesitating in that instant.

"What the hell is going on? Who are you?" he screamed, disoriented because he couldn't see my face.

I realized I had no choice but to eliminate the second man.

"It doesn't matter who I am," I answered. "Your game is about to end. Soon you'll be in hell."

An urgent thought crossed my mind: time was running out. I must act quickly before sunrise; otherwise, I'm in danger of being seen.

I exited the darkness, climbed the stairs and walked straight towards him. The light fell on my face. He recognized me and exclaimed in surprise.

"Ana! Is it you? Have you gone mad?"

"Mad! No way. I just barely started seeing things the way they are. Understanding that the so-called protectors of the people are nothing but scum like you."

The man watched me move forward like a wild-eyed jungle predator crazed by bloodlust. The panic stopped him, and he froze on the spot, his normal split-second reaction dulled by disbelief.

"Ana! You can't do that! I have a gun! Think!"

Then, recovering his composure, he aimed his gun directly at me and fired. Suspecting his intention, I leaped quickly to the right, rapidly changing directions to the left and disappearing below the terrace. The man took a few steps toward where he last saw me, slipped on the stone slabs, and fired twice. Lying in the dark, I counted his shots.

"I'll kill you, Ana!"

"You have already tried," I replied while moving around. I knew he wanted to make me talk to find out where I was hiding.

Three shots erupted from the shadows, the bullets embedding themselves in the staircase above me. Then I heard the click of the empty gun; he ran out of bullets.

When he understood the trap, it was too late. His mind exploded in anger, and he lost control of himself. He moved in the direction he thought I was hiding, ready to pounce.

I lunged from the shadows, a sardonic smile twisting my face. I had absolute control over my body, moving with the fluidity and confidence of a panther ready to pounce on her prey. My fierce determination made him shiver. Mid howl, he was about to cross the dark threshold when I applied a terrible blow to his nose. Blood gushed out, and shaken by pain and shock, he tried to regain a clearer vision.

The situation appeared to him in all its horror. He has to neutralize me, or he'll end up dead. With his arms outstretched, he moved forward and was about to attack when I stopped him with an impressive kick. He wavered, his knees bent, but he refused to fall. I gripped my arm around his neck when he wanted to get up.

I felt brutally strong, and I fought with a ferocity I had never felt before. I kept the pressure on his larynx, preventing him from breathing. I heard cartilage cracking, and he collapsed.

I pulled his body towards the sea. A few seconds later, I heard the sound of crushed waves, which tipped him over into the darkness of the sea. He fought with all his power, desperately trying to regain the surface. Despite all his efforts, the current pulled him towards the bottom of the sea. The black water closed over him and filled his lungs.

I made my way through the great waves of water that smashed on the beach, pulled the other man's body out and pushed him into the depths of the sea. I watched the two bodies float and get tossed around by the waves without feeling any remorse.

The rain fell relentlessly, and my clothes were completely wet. I took a deep breath and relaxed my muscles. The horizon's light was reddish, piercing through the heavy, oppressive clouds. Sunrise was approaching, making it urgent to leave the area immediately.

Back inside the villa, I found the women half-conscious, barely clinging to reality. Her wrists were raw from the restraints, her body limp. Gently, I loosened the bindings that had dug into her skin and helped her into a dress. Her breathing was shallow, her body bruised and weak, but there was still life in her.

Supporting her weight, I led her outside to the shoreline, where the cool night air and the steady rhythm of the waves greeted us. As I guided her toward the water, the salty sea breeze filled the space around us. Kneeling by the shore, I let the waves lap over her bruised body, washing away the grime and blood, small mercy amid her suffering.

The sudden cold of the water brought her back to consciousness. She opened her eyes wide with fear and confusion flashing across her face. She flinched at the water's touch but remained still, too weak to resist. "Don't be afraid," I whispered, my face hidden in the shadows of the night. "You're safe now. I was able to help you."

My voice softened as I continued, knowing the gravity of what I was about to tell her.

"I can't explain everything now, but you'll understand when you read the papers in the next few days. What's important is that you get home now."

Her eyes searched mine, filled with questions, but I pressed on.

"Listen carefully: Don't tell anyone what happened tonight. Your life depends on your silence. The law won't protect you here, you know that. Get out while you still can."

The weight of my words settled in her mind. She nodded, shivering, her wet dress clinging to her skin. Slowly, unsteadily, she began to walk along the beach, her movements shaky but determined to leave.

I watched her go until she disappeared into the night, then turned back toward the villa. There was no time to waste. Inside, I erased every trace she might have left, and finally, I turned on the taps in the bathroom, letting the water flood the floor. The scene would look chaotic, but with any luck, there would be no proof of the young woman ever being there.

I cast a last glance toward the sea, telling myself that during such lousy weather, accidents happen a lot easier, especially after a substantial consumption of alcohol. The sea's big waves and the rocks will take care of the rest; the two bodies will be unrecognizable after a few hours. When they are identified, the conclusion will be that they drowned due to an excessive consumption of alcohol.

As if it had decided to be my ally, the sea had washed away all traces of steps on the beach. The sky was getting brighter and brighter. I have to live before somebody sees me and make a connection with what happened.

Stretching my muscles, I ran along the water and approached the villa where I stayed. Arriving at the alley, I began to walk normally, struck by the cold. Then I went around the villa and approached the exit door through which I had left a few hours earlier. I held my breath to detect the slightest noise as I walked into the hall, leaving traces of water on the polished wood.

The hall was silent. Relieved, I opened the door to my room. I went into the bathroom, undressed, and threw all my clothes in the bathtub. After rubbing my body and hair with a towel, I put on a robe, went out into the hallway, and removed all the watermarks I had left on my way in. I was determined to cover my tracks.

The alarm clock read six thirty-three in the morning when I began to clean my wet clothes, removing all traces of sand. When I finished my shower, a cloud of steam was floating inside the room. I slipped between the sheets and fell into a deep sleep without thinking about the events unfolding.

I woke up three hours later, but I lay still for a long time with my eyes open. I thought of my family and the woman I had just rescued and the sad history of my people. So much bloodshed, so many lives stolen.

I wasn't proud of the previous night's events. But now I know there was no other way to fight against the paranoia and the intrinsic violence of the people devoted to the Ceausescu government.

Completely naked, I walked towards the bathroom and examined myself critically in the mirror. There were no scratches. My face looked rested; nothing showed the exhaustion I was feeling.

I got dressed and left the villa. I needed caffeine and protein to overcome my exhaustion. The sky was apparent in the nascent daylight, but the temperature had dropped sharply.

There were few people in the restaurant, so I was served quickly. After swallowing three cups of coffee, I felt better. On the other side of the window, people were hanging around, gathered in small groups, discussing and analyzing the damage caused by the storm and deploring the abrupt temperature change.

I finished eating, left the restaurant and went back to my room. The damp clothes hanging in the bathroom evoked the events of the last night. I picked up the clothes, packed them in a plastic bag, placed them at the bottom of my travel bag, stuffed the other clothes over them and left the room.

The parking lot was littered with debris reminiscent of the storm. Fortunately, my car was not damaged. I started the car and exited the parking lot, feeling the engine responding nervously to my demands.

Bent over the steering wheel, I drove towards the highway entrance, lowered the window, and stepped on the acceleration pedal. The car cut through the curtain of humidity, creating a wind with its momentum.

CHAPTER 2

A grim day flooded the ranch valley. The air was thick with humidity. The sky carried heavy black clouds, and the atmosphere was filled with bad omens. Lying by the pool, Matt O'Connor watched his brother, Ryan, bring the horses into the stables. He felt good here. The nature, the honest people, the tender looks of his parents... there was nothing to do but enjoy each day. He had left this oasis of peace years before, driven by the craving for adventure and the desire to do extraordinary things.

The excitement of risk had plunged him into a world torn apart by wars and terrorist attacks, where industrial espionage, arms trafficking and hostage-taking were commonplace, a world where terrorists killed innocent people at the slightest threat. Officially, he was the Chief of Security at the American Embassy in Bonn. In reality, he was what a regular person would call a spy.

After years of training and missions where he nearly died, Matt needed a vacation like this to prove that all the risks he was taking were for a good reason: to protect oases of peace like this one. His friends did not know precisely what he was doing. They thought he was lucky because he got a job with the government.

His parents had been very disappointed. For generations, no O'Connor had done anything but follow the family tradition of breeding and training elite horses. It was supposed to be the same for Matt.

Gripped by his thoughts, he looked at the sky, strangely beautiful despite its threatening appearance. A sudden crack of thunder made him jump, and a violent wind seized the valley, raising pieces of wood and dried plants very high in the air.

Ryan was still in the stables, and Matt decided to join him. The air was as thick as blood, and he had trouble moving forward.

As he passed the stables, which were excellently maintained and housed the most beautiful breeds of horses, he listened to the nervous scratching of the mares caused by the bad weather.

He found Ryan in a remote area, trying to appease a young mare panicked by the force of the thunder. He touched the animal's skin with expert movements until he stopped shaking. Looking at the scene, Matt thought about how he'd never been able to share Ryan's passion for horses. Deep down, within the confines of his conscience, he resented himself for involving his brother in his work. If things turned sour, he could never forgive himself. But he had no other choice.

"You're very talented and patient, brother! Let's sit by the pool. I need to talk to you."

Ryan gazed at him.

"You look concerned, brother; what is it? Nothing serious, I hope?"

"No. Nothing serious. The Agency needs your help, but don't worry; the risk percentage is meagre. I'd say it's pretty lame."

"You told me the same thing last time, and I almost died. But if the Secret Service needs me, I have no choice but to accept," Ryan replied with a flash of amusement.

Goddamn it! thought Matt. *He accepts before he even knows what it is!* thought Matt. *We are indeed of the same gene. Our nostrils expand when we catch the scent of adventure and danger, the thrill of the unknown calling to us.*

Ryan caught his expression and burst into laughter. They leisurely made their way to the swimming pool, unconcerned about getting wet. The once menacing clouds had now transformed into a gentle, regular rain, as if they had exhausted their fury and were now just a drizzle.

Matt looked at his brother's athletic and confident look as he followed him to the pool. Memories of the last mission resurfaced. He saw his brother lying on the hospital bed with a black eye and a chest covered with three layers of bandages.

He had called his father to explain that Ryan had been in a car accident and was going to stay in Germany for a while. His father's anxious voice still echoed in his mind.

I warned him that this would happen to him one day. He drives like a madman, his father had said, trying to hide his bitterness.

Feeling guilty for lying to his parents about his brother's condition, he decided not to let it happen again. But, despite all his efforts, the Director of the Agency at Langley was very firm in his decision: "Matt, I don't mean to be rude, but my answer remains the same. We've been over this. Maybe you've forgotten what's at stake. That son of a bitch, Carlos, has unleashed a series of attacks and murders all over the world that we can no longer stop! His men are fanatics who are capable of blowing up the planet."

"Exactly, Sir," Matt had answered. "These people are too dangerous. You know well what happened the last time we've got my brother involved."

"Langley's order is clear, Matt. We must act immediately without anyone thinking we are responsible. The resemblance to your twin brother is the perfect cover. In addition, he is not in any danger this time. Many people are risking much more than him to keep our country safe. Make sure that everything will go as planned. Can I count on you?"

"Yes, sir."

"I'm glad to hear that," said the Director as he rose, signaling that the meeting was over.

Matt did not share the view of his superior. In the

field, perfectly planned traps in an office can close in on you and put you in danger. But that never stops him from carrying out an assignment. He had been training to such a degree that he could adapt and overcome no matter what obstacles he encountered.

On the other hand, it was a hazardous operation for his brother. Even if they have the same physical strength, Ryan must learn how to react in a critical situation.

He decided that this time, he would make sure nothing happened to his brother.

The rain stopped abruptly and gave way to a hazy heat that prevented nature from breathing. Matt went to get two beers and sat next to Ryan.

"So, do I get a summary of what I must do in my future role as a spy?" Ryan began.

"First, I want you to know it wasn't my decision. I did everything possible to keep you from this mission, but…"

"Let me guess," Ryan interrupted with a mocking smile. "Langley sent the order down through your superior. Look, buddy, I understand the situation perfectly. So, will you tell me what this is all about?"

"You'll take my place at an annual embassy reception."

"Oh, that sounds simple! We just need to swap shirts. What colour do you usually wear for your *official outings?*"

"Listen, Cowboy! Cut the crap! You have to promise me you'll be more careful this time. Always be prepared for the unexpected."

"I get it. You can count on me this time. What exactly is the plan?"

"You'll need to be in Bonn exactly one week after I leave here," Matt instructed, his voice calm but firm. "You'll travel using my passport. We look so much alike that no one will suspect a thing. It'll seem like I'm returning from a short vacation to everyone else. Once you arrive, someone will meet you at the airport and take you to my summer house. I'll already be there, ready to brief you on everything. Your main role will be to take my place at the embassy reception."

"I get it," Ryan replied thoughtfully. "You need an alibi; you can't be in two places simultaneously, just like last time. But why must I use your passport if you will be in Bonn when I arrive?"

Matt leaned forward, lowering his voice.

"Because I have some business to handle in London before the reception. If something goes wrong and our switch is discovered, we must ensure you have an airtight alibi. Tomorrow, I'll travel to London using your passport, making it seem like you've been there the entire time. It's the only way to guarantee you're never linked to Bonn."

"And how will you get from London to your summer house in Bonn?" Ryan pressed, frowning.

"I understand your concerns, Ryan. But trust me, this is the best way to ensure our plan's success. You'll be briefed on everything once you arrive at the summer house. Your main role will be to take my place at the embassy reception. And don't worry, we've taken every precaution to ensure your safety."

Ryan nodded but didn't seem entirely convinced.

"I hope you'll give me more information this time than last. If I'm risking my neck for you, I'd at least like to know why."

Instead of answering, Matt dove into the pool. For the few hours he had left, he wanted to forget everything and soak in the peace around him.

CHAPTER 3

The aircraft was on the runway. A fuel truck filled the tanks while a maintenance crew checked the engines. They had left the United States last night and had just landed in Frankfurt, the destination of most of the passengers.

Ryan beckoned the waiter to pour him another cup of coffee. Time was passing too slowly for his taste. Finally, a voice announced the flight to Bonn. Ryan asked for the bill and, without paying any attention to the glances the women gave him, he quickly boarded the plane.

Relieved to escape from the airport's atmosphere filled with people, he crashed into the comfortable first-class chair and closed his eyes. Usually, it only took a few minutes for him to start dreaming, but exceptionally not this time.

He looked carelessly through a few newspapers, then closed his eyes and tried to relax. His thoughts wandered to what was waiting for him in Bonn, a mix of anticipation and uncertainty filling his mind.

From there, his mind drifted to other things, and five minutes later, he fell into a deep sleep.

"Ladies and gentlemen, this is the captain speaking."

Ryan awoke slowly, aching all over, and straightened out of his seat. The flight had been very short, and he felt more tired than before falling asleep.

Through the portholes, white clouds floated around the aircraft. The engine made a loud noise, and the plane struck the ground at the airport with a squeak of brakes.

Ryan picked up his luggage and followed the other passengers to the exit. A beautiful blonde with a Marilyn Monroe look gave him a big smile and approached him.

"Welcome to Bonn! You must be Ryan! The resemblance to your brother is amazing!"

"You guessed right!"

"My name is Gertrude. I work with your brother. Please follow me."

A few minutes later, she opened the trunk of a black BMW, and Ryan put his suitcase inside.

The uniform purring of the engine and the comfort of the new leather seat drove Ryan into a pleasant lethargy. Gertrude tried to engage in conversation with him, but, at risk of being rude, he wanted to make her understand that he did not wish to entertain her. As a result, he only responded using monosyllables.

Instinctively, Ryan realized that she was more surprised than hurt by his silence. She wasn't used to it. Any man should have been drawn to Gertrude. Confused, he wondered if his excess had not led him to indifference towards women to the point where he could not even pretend to care. He allowed his gaze to drift towards the window, pretending to be mesmerized by the landscape.

"I'm not your type?" Gertrude's voice held a note of surprise.

Gertrude's direct question left him helpless for a moment. *She's got a lot of nerve*, he thought. Her boldness was unmistakable, and it left Ryan momentarily speechless. But he decided to and make an effort.

"You're a beautiful woman, Gertrude, and you know it. I don't mean to be rude; I'm just exhausted."

The BMW engine ran at full speed from the moment they left the big city until they arrived at a charming little village surrounded by emerald-green hills.

After crossing a small bridge over a river, the road bifurcated into a large driveway that led to a stone house. The house was modest in size by some standards, but Ryan found it very charming. The surrounding land was covered with a profusion of roses and hydrangeas that filled the air with a sweet scent, enhancing the beauty of the landscape. A curtain of trees surrounded the ground, making it invisible to passers-by.

Gertrude parked the car next to a black Mercedes in front of the house.

"Here we are!" said Gertrude. "Do you need help with your luggage?"

"No, thanks, I got it."

"As you wish," she said, going to sit on a chair by the pool."

Ryan sensed a touch of weariness mixed with wounded pride in her voice. He almost answered, but he changed his mind. He was too tired to engage in a discussion based on unnecessary compliments.

"Welcome to my country house, cowboy."

His brother Matt walked towards him briskly and hugged him.

"I'll give you time to shower while I make some coffee. I need to give you some information, and I don't have much time."

"Couldn't it wait until tomorrow? I'm having a little trouble concentrating after this long journey!"

"Sorry, buddy, but I need you tomorrow night, and I want you to be more informed this time. I don't understand why you're so tired; you're used to travelling and falling asleep like a stump on an airplane!"

"Not this time."

"After a reenergizing coffee and a brisk shower, you'll be as good as new."

He disappeared into the house, and Ryan had no choice but to follow him.

The house's interior was more decadent than its exterior, with dark wooden furniture, delicate fabrics, and heavy half-drawn curtains. The tranquility of the place invited relaxation. With a weary gesture, Ryan took his suitcase and entered the bathroom.

Fifteen minutes later, Matt watched his brother leave the bathroom. Looking at his brother's face was always a strange experience; it was like looking at himself in a mirror. He was almost baffled to see how much he had missed his brother.

"I'm sorry, Cowboy, but I must return to the embassy soon. You can relax after I give you some information. I'm not the one who makes the decisions."

Seeing the serious look on his brother's face, Ryan burst out laughing.

"Oh! Shut up," said Matt. "You will always be an idiot," he exclaimed.

The silence lasted precisely two seconds, during which their eyes crossed paths. They burst out laughing, forgetting for a moment why they were reunited.

"We'll be further along when you start to enlighten me on what I must do," said Ryan.

"All right. In two days, there will be a reception at the Romanian embassy. As we decided, you'll go instead of me. I'll let you have the BMW. For starters, I'll tell you briefly what I did in London pretending to be you."

They talked until Ryan knew everything he needed to learn. Then Matt opened a drawer on the coffee table, pulled out a disc, and placed it on it.

"I have the photos of the ambassador and his guests on this disc. I also have various conversations between them; this will give you a good idea of how to start a discussion, if necessary. Gertrude will go with you. She knows everyone, and she'll intervene if you're in trouble. She's pretty enough and knows how to draw attention to herself. Five hundred meters from the embassy, there's a hotel under renovation; you can't miss it. You can park the BMW on the street. Please stay in the car; Gertrude will pick you up with a vehicle from our embassy around seven o'clock."

"Until what time do I have to stay at the Romanian Embassy?"

"Try to impersonate me until nine o'clock. At precisely nine o'clock, you have to devise an excellent reason to sneak out of the embassy and meet me near the right corner of the building. You'll have a few minutes to update me on the progress of the evening so I can replace you at the reception. At that point, your mission will be over. You'll find the BMW where you left it and come back here. Gertrude and I will come back later."

"I suppose you don't intend to tell me what you will do during that time?"

"You guessed right. Knowing that could only hurt you if things go wrong. This time, the people involved are perilous."

"More dangerous than the ones who hurt me last time?"

"Far more dangerous! This is all the more reason to stick to the plan. Now you can get some rest. You can take any room in the house; the fridge is full. I'll be back tomorrow around noon. Until then, you'll have time to study the disc. Good night, Cowboy!"

The Mercedes driving further away echoed through the park for a few moments, and then the noise settled, broken intermittently by the tinkling of a pendulum. Ryan opened the first door next to the bathroom, climbed into bed, and fell dreamily asleep.

CHAPTER 4

The unforgivable heat of the sun was beaming over the city, and a smell of melted asphalt mixed with BBQ smoke and sweat was floating in the air. Protecting their eyes with their hands, the pedestrians looked to the sky for a sign of rain. The traffic was heavy and crowded with taxis.

I was impatient to get home and shot from lane to lane without paying attention to the speed limit. Many drivers leaned on their horns and gave me the finger, but I never let their hatred get the better of me.

When I arrived at my apartment, it was almost two o'clock in the afternoon. During the trip back, I realized that if I acted alone against the sprawling power of the Securitate, I would have little leeway. Accompanied by

George, my trusted friend and former lover, and Avram, my chances of success would increase.

Without hesitation, I picked up the handset and dialed George's number. He answered after the first ring.

"Hello!"

"Hey, George!"

"Ana, what a nice surprise! How was your holiday?"

"Wonderful."

"Better than last year?"

Images of my last year's holiday with George crossed my mind.

"Not really. I missed you," I lied, my heart heavy with guilt for deceiving him.

George kept quiet for a moment, stunned, before answering.

"I missed you too!"

"Let's meet, George. What are you doing tonight?"

"Nothing that can't wait!"

"Then I'll see you at my place."

I hated myself because I played with George's feelings but didn't trust the Securitate, a powerful and secretive organization that operated with an inescapable surveillance system. Even if I knew my superiors trusted me, I had no evidence that I wasn't under surveillance. I had to pretend I wanted to renew my love relationship with George if they listened to my phone conversation.

George arrived a few hours later.

"It's good to see you again!" he said. "You're still as beautiful as ever."

Then, slowly, he drew me to him. I moved away, feeling guilty.

"George, our relationship has given way to a beautiful friendship, and I'd like to keep it that way. But you know as well as I do that our phones can be tapped. That's why I have to pretend. I'm sorry. But at this point in my life, you are the only one I can trust. And I need your help."

I felt George's body stiffen, but he made no comments.

"Something to drink?" I asked.

"What do you have?"

"Coffee or water."

"I'll have a coffee."

While making coffee, I felt George's eyes studying me, his curiosity barely concealed. It was time to get to the point. Over the next hour, I brought him up to speed, recounting everything, beginning with overhearing his conversation with Avram and ending with what I did at the Black Sea.

"Before heading to the Black Sea," I began, setting the coffee cup before him, "I decided to visit Avram and Anastasia. They were like the parents I never had. I wanted it to be a surprise visit, to see them before they knew I was coming. But when I got there, I overheard Avram talking to you. That's when I first heard him reveal that the Securitate had killed my family. He said they had transformed me into one of their best agents without me even knowing my true past."

George's face paled. He glanced down, clearly unsettled.

"I had no idea, Ana. As far as I know, you were just

another orphan trained by the Securitate to serve their interests. But Avram explained everything: your father's role as a university professor who dared to speak out against Ceausescu's regime, how he inspired his students to resist, and how that act of defiance cost him his life, along with your mother's and your grandparents'. He told me the Securitate eliminated them to send a message, but they spared you, planning to mold you into one of their own."

"Did you believe Avram?"

"I struggled to accept it at first," he admitted, his voice tightening. "But Avram had proof. Later, he showed me old photographs of your father's protests, the secret reports the Securitate kept on him, and even the file documenting their plan to execute your family. It was all there in black and white."

George swallowed hard.

"What finally convinced you that Avram was telling the truth?"

I took a breath, feeling the sting of those memories. "I've had nightmares my entire life, horrible, fragmented images of violence and fear, but I could never make sense of them. Avram told you that I was there that night, that I saw my family being murdered. He said that the trauma was so intense that I blocked it out completely. But when he said it, those nightmare images started to make sense. It was as if a locked door in my mind had suddenly burst open, and I could finally understand what I'd been seeing all these years. I was there, George. I saw everything."

George's eyes searched mine, filled with sympathy and

fear.

"And now what? What do you plan to do?"

I leaned in, my voice low and cold.

"I want to make them pay. Every single one of them. I want them to feel the fear and pain they inflicted on my family. And when they've suffered enough, I'll kill them."

"It seemed like a suicide mission to me," George concluded.

"It doesn't matter what lay ahead. I want revenge."

"I understand your desire for revenge," George said very quietly. "But to do that, you'll have to play both sides. Like I do. It's a dangerous game."

"I'm willing to take the risk."

"Very good. Avram and I are part of the Organization. To date, we are counting on thousands of members who, like us, want to overthrow the dictatorship of this Government. I'll be the contact between you and the Organization. No one will suspect anything. We can pretend we're back in love."

"Do you want to tell me more about the Organization? The few words you exchanged with Avram while I was listening are insufficient for me to understand her role."

"It has existed for several years, and we have representatives in every corner of the country and several Western countries. Our goal is to overthrow the Government. Hiring new members takes a long time. We must be cautious; one mistake and we'd all get shot. Some members occupy critical positions in the Government and the Securitate. They provide information and are known only to a few Organization members. I count myself among them.

"How do you have access to information?"

"I set up a listening and recording station in my office. It's well hidden. I connected it to Popescu's office."

"Recording the conversations of the head of The Securitate is extremely dangerous!"

"I'm aware of that. But it's the only way I can help the Organization. Unlike field agents like yourself, who have much greater scope and latitude for obtaining overwhelming evidence."

"I don't understand! You don't need to pile up evidence against the Government to start a revolution! What you need is the collaboration of the people!"

"It's not that simple. You have to understand that we will only succeed with help from outside the country. The communist regime was implemented by intelligent, cold and unempathetic people with immense power. They decide whether the time has come to change a regime, not the people guided by their emotions. But we also know that the great powers favor change. And the evidence we've accumulated can precipitate that change."

"I still don't understand."

"As a result of the manipulation to which you have been subjected for all these years, you know very little about the cult of the personality of Ceausescu and those who are faithful to him. Compared with the other presidents of the Eastern European countries, he chose an independent policy. He made constant and elaborate efforts to gain the support of Western nations while our industrial espionage companies stole their secrets. At the same time, he maintained a close partnership with Arab terrorists who were feeding money into his bank accounts."

"You mean…you have evidence implicating our government?"

"The Securitate and implicitly the government. I recorded a conversation that incriminates them without a shadow of a doubt. Arms and explosives are being smuggled through our embassy in Bonn, Germany."

"They can deny it."

"Not this time. The Israeli secret service, Mossad, uncovered the operation and contacted Popescu last week. They showed him a document with information classified as top-secret by our government.

The document also contains the names of the three people responsible for the operation, Popescu and two of his deputies, Sorel Dimitriu and David Chirileanu, as well as the names of the participating agents. They told him to immediately stop the relations with the terrorist Carlos, who is Israel and the West's greatest enemy. Otherwise, they would notify the countries concerned.

The good news is that Popescu and his deputies are willing to continue filling their bank accounts. They're eager to take risks and complete a final deal with Carlos."

"In other words, they are ready to risk triggering an international scandal! But why is that good news?"

"If that happens, our government will be compromised, and the Russians will have no choice but to intervene.

That's the moment we are waiting for."

"You know, as well as I do, that they can make one last transaction. Popescu's smart enough to beat the surveillance. Without the Mossad document, you will have no proof. It takes more than a record to accuse a government.

"That's right. That is why we need the Mossad document."

"If you could get your hands on this document, what would happen?"

"We will make sure that copies of the document get into the possession of the KGB."

"KGB! But ... I'm sure the KGB knows, and they approve of Carlos's actions! Even if they let him appear silently responsible. It's a politically motivated gesture. The Moscow apparatus continued its work with caution and discretion."

"Of course, Moscow approves!"

"Then everything is for nothing!"

"Is not. What the Russians don't approve of is losing control. For many years, the Russians tried to prove that the communist system represented an ideal world system. To achieve their objectives, they installed loyal subjects to Moscow at the head of each Eastern country, whom they have constantly monitored. Obedience is paramount for the Russians. Those who fail to obey are sacrificed. I have to tell you that they are skeptical about our president in Moscow. They are concerned that he has become a fanatic, completely ignoring the vulnerable situation in the country and the principles imposed by Russia."

"And you want to accentuate their skepticism!"

"We aim to increase Russian discontent with him and convince them that his replacement is inevitable. This is a hazardous project which requires extreme caution. To succeed, there must be absolutely nothing incriminating that can trace them back to us. We must convince the Russians that the information is not coming from this side of the Iron Curtain."

"You will convince them with clear evidence and the required contacts."

"We've come to the same conclusion, but the task will not be easy. Ceausescu's followers are ready for anything to protect their comfortable lives."

"Do you have any idea how the Russians will proceed?"

"We have yet to determine how the Russians will proceed, but we will know when the time comes, thanks to our contacts. If we succeed in triggering a revolution that coincides with their actions, we will be able to defeat the Russians and install a democratic system."

"It's a brave but dangerous move," I said. You don't have to underestimate the KGB. They're unbeatable at this little game."

"I know. They manipulated the governments of the Eastern countries like pawns on a board. That's why we calculated it all. We will move the masses and take them by surprise."

"It's not just about moving the masses," I added. "It is also necessary to determine who will be the new president. Otherwise, there will be chaos."

"Trust me, we'll be ready."

"What can I do to help?"

"So far, nothing. Give me time, and we'll see."

He hesitated momentarily, then said, "You will be leaving for Bonn very soon. Popescu is convinced that a mole in the Bonn embassy would have given Mossad the information. He'll send you there to find out who it could be."

"Why me?" I asked.

"He trusts you."

"Of course, he does. He played me like a puppet, but not anymore."

"It's late," said George, glancing at his watch. "We'll talk again tomorrow."

"Just one more question. Does Popescu have a camera installed in his office?"

"Not! I would have known if there was one. Why?"

"Because I want to know."

"Ana! Don't do anything stupid!"

"Don't worry about a thing. I'll see you tomorrow."

I accompanied him to the door and wished him good night. As I did, my mind drifted to George's plan; even with the Mossad document, it was still a long shot.

Compared to George, I never allowed myself to underestimate the capabilities of my enemies. All I knew was that I wouldn't stop. I will avenge my family. No matter how dire the situation, failure was not an option. My determination to bring justice to my family was unwavering.

Staring out the window, I saw my reflection; I looked drained. I needed to escape this constant tension and fall into the comfort of sleep, but I also knew that I would wake up ready to face the next day's challenges.

CHAPTER 5

I awoke, consumed by a devastating sense of loss, aching with an insatiable thirst for justice. The apartment, still veiled in darkness, offered no solace. I mechanically donned my sportswear and running shoes, stepping out into the night without bothering to lock the door.

It was very early, and no one was in the elevator when I went to the garage. Ten minutes after leaving the garage, I arrived at the Securitate sports field.

The morning air was crisp, and I wasted no time. I began my ritualistic run around the field, the cement walls serving as my silent companions. I started slowly, gradually picking up the pace until my muscles protested. An hour later, I retreated to the weight room, my body a testament to my unwavering commitment.

Back in my apartment, I took a refreshing shower and had a hearty breakfast. The phone rang as I was preparing a second cup of coffee. I had no desire to answer, but I picked up the receiver after a few rings.

"Hello!"

"Comrade Ana! I'll be waiting for you in my office in half an hour," ordered Popescu's voice.

"I'll be there," I answered, but Popescu had hung up before I finished my sentence.

I dried up my wet hair and tied it up in a ponytail. Dressed in safari pants and a black T-shirt, I left the apartment. Neighbors I'd never met greeted me in passing. Twenty-five minutes later, I was in the anteroom of my superior's office. The secretary beckoned me to follow immediately.

Popescu's tired features surprised me. I'd never seen him looking like that. *George is right*, I thought. *He is under a lot of stress. But it's nothing compared to what I'm planning for him. Payback is coming.*

Popescu's dry voice interrupted my thoughts.

"Comrade Ana! You look rested and in great shape! That's perfect because you'll need it for your next assignment. You have never disappointed me and must not disappoint me this time. Tomorrow, you'll fly to Bonn."

This is not good, I thought, panic gripping me. I need more time to strategize with George. I must find a way to outsmart this situation.

Popescu spoke for a long time, explaining what he expected of me.

"The task will be unlike anything you've faced before, shrouded in secrecy and danger. We suspect a mole in the Bonn Embassy, a traitor selling our secrets to the highest bidder. They believe the mind is impenetrable, but I refuse to accept that. Guilt leaves a trace. I trust you to uncover the traitor. Take all the time you need; I'll ensure your presence in the Embassy is justified."

The phone on the desk started to ring, and Popescu picked up the receiver with an irritated gesture.

"I asked not to be disturbed!" he exclaimed. "What is it so important?"

I didn't understand what the voice was saying on the other end of the line, but the expression on my superior's face did not seem happy. He listened for a while, then closed the line and got up from his chair.

"I'll be back in a few minutes," he told me, leaving the office.

I looked around the luxuriously furnished office. My eyes landed on a wooden panel. George told me that a wooden panel had concealed the safe where Popescu had kept documents before placing them in the agency safe. I was sure that he had no intention of putting the highly incriminating Mossad document in the agency safe and taking the risk of someone seeing it. The document, potentially bringing down the entire operation, should be here.

Silently, I rose from my seat, my heart pounding. I cautiously approached the panel, and my every move was calculated. As I slid the wooden panel, my eyes widened in surprise. The safe was open, a sign of a potential trap. Adrenaline surged through my veins, my senses on high alert.

I held my breath and carefully removed the envelopes, my hands trembling slightly. The Mossad document was my target, and I had to find it swiftly.

I thought it would be too risky to keep it, and I would be the only one to blame. I have to find another way to take possession of the document. The safe is an old model; opening it will be child's play.

I put the wooden panel back in the same position as I had found it and went to sit on the chair. Less than two minutes later, Popescu was back.

He opened a connecting door without a preamble and signaled me to follow him into the next office. The room was dimly lit, the air heavy with the scent of old books and secrecy. He switched on a projector on a small table in the middle of the room and lowered the blinds. In the bright square projected on the wall, I recognized the building of the Romanian Embassy in Bonn.

"Take as much time as you need to analyze the building plans and the photos of all our agents working there. Use your photographic memory because the answers will be only in your memory if you need them once in the Embassy. I expect you tomorrow morning at nine o'clock to finalize the details."

Without adding anything, he left the room.

I leaned back in the chair, my mind whirling with conflicting emotions. Being in this room as an enemy was a strange sensation. I tried to push aside the guilt and fear, focusing on the task. But the knowledge that the Mossad document was just a wall away, hidden in Popescu's safe, was nagging in my mind.

There was a photocopier in Popescu's office, a potential solution to my dilemma. I should've had the courage to take it and replace the document with a photocopy, but the risk was too significant.

The connecting door opened, and Popescu appeared in the doorframe as if he'd read my mind.

"Comrade Ana, I must leave the office for about an hour. When you're done, turn off the projector and exit through the door leading to the hallway. We will meet again, as scheduled, tomorrow morning at nine o'clock."

I couldn't believe my luck. My body was tense, waiting, every muscle coiled like a spring. I approached the window to see if Popescu was leaving the building. After a few minutes, his car moved forward in my field of vision, and the entrance door closed after the vehicle passed through. I felt reassured; Popescu had left the site. A wave of relief washed over me, but I knew I couldn't let my guard down yet.

Using several metal staples found on the desk, I picked up the lock of the connecting door, opened it, and entered Popescu's office. I walked around the desk and slid the wooden panel that hid the safe. The safe was now locked.

I snooped around in my handbag, pulled out a powder magazine and spread a thin film of white powder on the safe's numbers. The powder marked the most commonly used numbers. A smile of satisfaction settled on my lips. The simplicity of the safe demonstrated Popescu's confident arrogance in the fear he instilled in his subordinates.

After a few quick combinations, the safe opened with a click. I carefully replaced the Mossad document with a meticulously crafted photocopy, ensuring every detail was perfect. I then photographed the contents of all the envelopes inside the safe, erasing all traces of powder and fingerprints.

With the safe closed, I returned to the other office, my heart pounding with the thrill of the successful operation. It had been so easy that I wanted to pinch myself to convince myself that I had not dreamed the whole thing.

At that moment, a thought crossed me: what if Popescu had set a trap for me to test my devotion? I closed my eyes and recalled the conversation with Popescu; nothing seemed wrong.

I shook my head, giving up looking for answers to the questions invading my mind. There will be no more risk if I leave the building without incident. When Popescu realizes that a copy has replaced the Mossad document, he won't be sure who stole it.

I went to the garage, started the engine and approached the exit. The doors opened, and my throat dried as I entered the traffic flow. My instincts had not deceived me; the coast was clear.

Relieved, I looked for a restaurant. All the emotions had made me hungry.

The sky darkened, and black clouds appeared. I barely

had time to park the car when the clouds exploded, and lightning tore up the wet sky.

This summer was particularly gloomy, and I'd never seen so much rain at this time of year.

I exited the car and scanned the parking lot for anyone following me. People were running in all directions to find shelter from the rain.

During the meal, I couldn't help but notice that no one seemed to pay me any attention, and I felt relieved that nobody was watching me.

When I arrived home, the rain had stopped. I took a shower and prepared tea for myself. Then, I dialed George's number. He answered the third ring.

"George, it's Ana. Can we meet?"

"I'd love to. I can be at your place in half an hour. Is that alright with you?"

"Sounds good."

I turned on the CD player and tried to relax. Thirty-seven minutes later, the doorbell rang, and George stood in the doorway, a large bouquet in his hands. As usual, his eyes lingered on my face without hiding his feelings for me.

I signaled him to follow me as I crossed the corridor to the living room. Despite feeling slightly bothered by his gaze, George's expression changed when I sat down, revealed the Mossad document, and detailed my daring mission. The only sign of his inner turmoil was the slight twitch of his mouth, a testament to the gravity of the situation.

"Ana, I understand your thirst for revenge, but you took an enormous risk by opening Popescu's safe. His secretary could have caught you red-handed. She's used to delivering urgent messages to his desk when he leaves work unexpectedly early," George cautioned.

"In some situations, you have to make choices, George. You take a chance when it comes. In this situation, there were almost no risks."

"It was still hazardous! It takes time to open a safe!"

He was taken aback, his surprise evident in his widened eyes and slightly open mouth. I looked at him, surprised, and then I burst out laughing.

"George, I might be wrong, but I don't recall the last time you cracked open a safe," I teased, a playful glint in my eyes.

"What do you mean?"

"Did you see the safe in Popescu's office?"

"Yeah, I saw it several times, so what?"

"The model is so old that I didn't expect to find it in the head of the Securitate's office. It shows that he is aware of the fear he instills in his subordinates. This time, he will pay for his arrogance. You could have opened it a long time ago. Especially since your office is just a few meters from his."

"It's easy for you to speak like this; opening a safe, it's one of your specialties."

Seeing how embarrassed George was, I changed the subject.

"Here's the camera. I'll give you time to study the other documents I find in the safe while I make some fresh coffee."

I went into the kitchen and started the coffee machine. Through the door crack, I observed George's expression while he was studying the documents on my camera.

While the coffee was brewing, I went to the bedroom and spread out the clothes I intended to bring to Bonn. With automatic gestures, I stuffed everything in my travel bag.

I returned to the kitchen, poured two cups of coffee and joined George, who was still focused on documents. Finally, George raised his head, and our eyes crossed. I saw victory shining in his eyes.

"Congratulations, Ana! You did a great job! These documents will help us enormously. But I'm afraid that Popescu will realize that a copy has replaced the original Mossad document and that you are the guilty party."

"Unless he has to show it to someone and realize it's not the original, we can rest easy. Hopefully, it won't be for a few days, and then it won't be clear who the culprit is. Especially since he trusts me."

"Hopefully.

"How are you going to get this document into KGB hands?"

"This must be done by one of our contacts outside the country. As I explained before, nothing must link us to this information."

"I'm off to Bonn tomorrow morning, so why don't I do

it myself? I will be there for a separate mission but can also assist in this operation."

"I didn't dare to ask. But you can do it."

"And how do I do that?"

"The day after you arrive in Bonn, you will contact this number. Please provide the password *Herr Schmidt*. The answer must be: *Herr Schmidt is on vacation*. You will play a crucial role in this operation by establishing a secure meeting point for the transfer. And I trust you will carry it out successfully."

"I hope so."

"Thank you for your cooperation. I must now leave to notify our contact of your arrival."

He wished me good luck and left the apartment.

I returned to the bedroom and got under the sheets. It didn't take me long to fall into a dreamless sleep.

The following day, at five minutes to nine, I was seated in an uncomfortable chair in Popescu's office's waiting room.

Popescu's door opened as I was about to ask for another cup of coffee, and he signaled me in. For the next fifty-five minutes, he explained what he expected me to do.

"Saturday night is the embassy's annual reception," he explained. "Ambassadors, businessmen, and representatives of the tourist offices comprise the list of guests. After a few drinks, people become more confident and friendlier, and their level of attention decreases. That's why we send agents who work as servers at this party yearly."

"You mean you send them to collect information," I

said.

"Yes. At each reception, we collect a lot of information about the people present, Statements that may be useful to us later in our negotiations with them. So, your presence won't be a surprise to our embassy employees. Nobody other than you, and I must know why you are there."

"What are you expecting of me?"

"Keep your eyes peeled. Our mole can use this evening to establish contact with our enemies. We have to find the rotten fruit. In the small world of espionage, some secret agents use their skills for money. Significant sums of money create big temptations; our agents are no exception.

"I'll do my best."

"Please return with the name of the person selling our secrets to the highest bidder."

I was amazed at the passion with which Popescu spoke. People like him would stop at nothing to protect themselves and their benefits. It was with such impetuousness that people like him had removed the will of his people.

"What you're asking me to do is difficult to define," I replied. "I'm used to particular missions."

"We're getting to that. You will be present as a waitress between seven and nine in the evening. At nine o'clock, a trusted agent will take your place. I want you to go to the annex where the embassy vault room is. Make sure nobody sees you. I want you to hide in the safe room and see if anyone tries to steal documents."

"What makes you believe somebody will try to still document that specific night?"

"Because it is a special night. The mole will take advantage of the opportunity, with almost everyone participating at the reception. If time permits, search the rooms of the people on this list and bring me any information that may seem incriminating to you."

"Wouldn't that be better if someone working at the Embassy would do that? It will look less suspicious."

"As long as I don't know who the mole is, I don't trust anybody."

"What if someone sees me in the vault room and triggers the alarm?"

"Make sure you disappear before they recognize you. Otherwise, they'll know I sent you to spy on them."

"And if they catch me?"

"They don't stand a chance. None of them come close to your caliber. But, if it ever happens, I'll take care of things."

Popescu continued to speak for about ten minutes, and then he pulled the passport I was supposed to travel with out of his drawer.

"My secretary will give you an envelope containing the plane ticket and the money you'll need. Our car is waiting for you in the garage to drive you to the airport."

I understood that the meeting was finally over. I took my passport and left the office. The secretary gave me the envelope containing the money for my expenses and the plane ticket. I had just enough time to stop by my apartment to pick up my travel bag before heading to the airport to board the flight to Bonn.

CHAPTER 6

Ryan woke up at six in the morning, completely rested. He put on his bathing suit, wrapped a large towel around himself that he found in the bathroom closet, and went out into the garden. The dawn was fresh but pleasant, and the rising sun promised a nice day. He quickly crossed the distance between the house and the inviting pool and jumped into the water, which made him shiver.

He swam a few laps with powerful and precise movements. When he felt his muscles exploding, he stepped out of the pool and laid on the chaise longue. He was at peace, enjoying the sun's warmth on his bare skin.

His mind drifted to the reason that had brought him to Germany. Besides the occasional fortuitous weeks at the ranch, he rarely saw Matt, his brother. Every time he read an article about a terrorist attack, his stomach became anxious for his brother's safety.

He had never mentioned this, knowing it would be a waste of time. Matt will be one of the fighters as long as the Cold War, a period of political tension and military rivalry between the Western and Eastern Bloc exists. And the Cold War will never cease because human nature will not change; men will always retain the need to destroy, abuse, and corrupt. Some have to die so others can live.

As if on cue, approaching footsteps broke the tranquility of the serene garden, jolting Ryan back to reality. Matt, leaning on one leg, looked at him, smiling.

"I didn't hear a car! How did you enter?" asked Ryan, astonished.

"Ah! It comes with the job, cowboy! I did get in by car, but you were in the dream world. It's the effect of the garden. I, too, feel calm moments here."

Ryan realized that he had fallen asleep.

"To what do I owe this morning pleasure?"

"I brought you the clothes you'll be wearing tonight. They'll be identical to the ones I will wear. This will save us time, and we can make the switch quickly. I'd also like to give you more information about the people you will meet tonight at the Romanian embassy. I know you're pretty smart, but I want to ensure you get the right answers if the conversation takes a dangerous direction. If a situation like this arises, you'll let Gertrude take over."

"What if someone doubts me, and I get followed outside?"

"It is a thought that occurred to me! Bravo, you're learning fast, cowboy! You're starting to think like a professional!"

"Thanks to you, I'm beginning to gain experience," said Ryan.

With a hint of amusement, Matt rolled his eyes at his brother's comment, a typical reaction to Ryan's eagerness to learn and his occasional naivety. But despite the teasing, Matt was proud of how far Ryan had come.

"You're still an amateur and need a helping hand."

"All right, boss! But I'll have trouble concentrating on an empty stomach. What about a coffee and a cheese omelet?"

"I would gladly have another cup of coffee, but I have already eaten breakfast," replied Matt.

"You can make mine while I take a shower. You've always been better than me at the art of cooking."

Without waiting for his brother's answer, Ryan walks towards the house. Matt followed him with a laugh.

The morning unfolded in a delightful symphony of chirping birds, warm sunlight, and the aroma of freshly brewed coffee. The two brothers shared amusing stories and anecdotes, their laughter ringing out in the serene and relaxing garden, a testament to their strong bond. As noon approached, they savored a delectable meal accompanied by local beers.

After clearing the table, they worked efficiently for the next few hours, meticulously checking every plan detail. Their engagement in the task was palpable, keeping them focused and on track.

As his meeting with Gertrude neared, Ryan left the house, his mind buzzing with anticipation. He was dressed sharply in his anthracite suit, white shirt, and silver-gray tie. Starting the car, he rolled down the windows and shifted into drive.

The BMW's powerful engine responded quickly to his commands, and he focused on memorizing the path he would take again a few hours later.

The area was a picturesque blend of hills and valleys, a sight to behold. With a firm grip on the wheel, Ryan smoothly pressed the throttle, the car responding to his touch.

He arrived at the rendezvous point at five minutes to seven. He turned off the engine and settled in comfortably to wait.

At precisely seven o'clock, an official black Mercedes parked next to his car, and through the open window, he recognized Gertrude. He got out of the car and sat next to her.

As the Mercedes approached the Romanian Embassy, Ryan could not help but compliment Gertrude on her dress. Even though he didn't feel attracted to her, he had to admit that Matt was right: she was physically desirable with her confident look and detached way of looking at people with half-closed eyelids. She would have no trouble drawing attention to herself if he compromised himself.

The Mercedes arrived before a grey-stone building and stopped at the surrounding fence. A copper plate indicated the Romanian Embassy. A guard came out of the gate, recognized Gertrude and said respectfully: "Welcome, madam."

He didn't bother to verify her identity and pressed the button to open the door. After crossing an alley lined with a well-kept lawn, Ryan and Gertrude arrived at a parking area. Several official cars had already arrived.

Gertrude got out of the car and signaled Ryan to follow her. She seemed familiar with the place. Inside the embassy, there was a dark freshness. They walked down a hallway and, following the directions of an embassy employee, walked towards a room that Ryan identified as a conference room.

A long table stood in the center, covered with a starch-white linen tablecloth surmounted by food trays. Two improvised bars occupied the opposite corners of the front door. On both sides of the room, tables lined up where people could sit to eat. The room was filled with guests gathered in small groups, just like any business dinner.

A short woman in her 60s dressed in a gray suit came to meet them, a kind smile on her lips. Thanks to the information Matt provided him with, Ryan recognized the wife of the Romanian ambassador.

"Good evening! Thank you for coming."

She shook their hands and invited them to have something to drink. Then she excused herself and greeted a couple who had just entered the room. Ryan followed Gertrude to the bar. As he passed by, he took a discrete look around.

Some faces turned as he passed, but he pretended not to see them. He sat next to Gertrude, who was flirting with the young bartender and ordered drinks.

While savoring a sip of whiskey, he noticed a young woman walking in his direction. As she drew nearer, Ryan could discern more details: her body was as graceful as her movements, and her ash-brown hair was gathered at the back of her neck, accentuating the elegance of her profile. She advanced, seemingly oblivious to the hubbub around her and the curious gazes of men. Ryan found himself unable to look away, a sense of intrigue building within him. The young woman glanced at him briefly, and he felt like a seasoned observer was assessing him. It was a penetrating gaze, unflinching, without boundaries. Unintentionally, he continued to stare at her. At that moment, it felt like all his attention was suspended in that gaze of almost unbearable intensity. He felt a strange pull towards this woman, a connection he couldn't quite explain.

"Wake up, cowboy! I was under the impression that you despised women!" whispered Gertrude in her ear.

"Jealous?"

"You flatter yourself, my dear! I'd be insulted if you compared me to a waitress. If you like them brainless, I'm sure you'll find plenty. But not tonight. Don't forget the stakes."

"As if it were possible!"
"My dear Gertrude! You look lovely, as usual! "sounded a voice nearby.

A fat man who was sweating profusely approached

them. Ryan searched his memory and realized he had no idea who this man was. As if she had guessed his uneasiness, Gertrude hurried to make the introductions.

"Matt, I'd like you to meet Jean Papineau from the House of France. John has a magnificent cellar where I had the chance to do wine tasting. He claims our California wine will never match the French wines."

Ryan had to recognize Gertrude's skill. Not only had she taught him a great deal about Jean Papineau in a few words, but she had also diverted the discussion to a subject that required no concentration on his part.

For about twenty minutes, Jean Papineau passionately threw himself into a speech about the incomparable range of wines and spirits known worldwide. Ryan, a great wine lover, thought Papineau would make a good guide through the vineyards of France.

Like any proud American, he began to explain the qualities of California wines while his eyes discreetly sought out the young woman who had fascinated him with her presence.

He saw her walking through the room with a soft step, a tray full of glasses in her hand. He noticed her white cotton blouse stretched on her bust, her muscles' outline, and her neck's delicacy, leaving no room for deception amidst this artificial beauty. She had the flexibility of a feline and emanated a natural energy and independence. With her plump lips and deep blue eyes, she looked like a cartoon heroine. As if she had felt his gaze, the woman turned slowly and watched him for a second. Ryan experienced the same odd sense of intimacy towards her. Then, just as suddenly, she looked away.

Unsettled by this young woman's effect on him, Ryan tried to focus on the discussion with Jean Papineau.

"You're quite an expert for a wine lover, I'm impressed," said Papineau. "I would be honored if you would accompany Gertrude next time. I will soon receive a Cadet Sheep of great flavor and a Cabernet Sauvignon, which stands out for its richness with its authentic and powerful taste."

Without giving him time to respond, Gertrude intervened.

"What would you say if we had something to eat? The buffet will be empty soon, and I must eat a hearty meal."

She stared Ryan in the eye, and he understood she was trying to tell him something, but what? He matched her gaze, trying to read her eyes. Imperceptibly, she drew his attention to someone who was approaching. Ryan recognized the Russian ambassador immediately.

His brother warned him that the Russian was a KGB agent: *Be on your guard, he had said. He will undoubtedly try to approach you. Avoid him, and if you don't have a choice, don't get involved in discussions that might allow him to uncover your identity. He's very witty and knowledgeable. Let Gertrude take care of him. He has a weakness for beautiful women.*

Ryan exchanged a meaningful look with Gertrude as he walked towards the buffet. He looked at his watch: seven thirty-three. He had another hour and a half before Matt replaced him. He has to find a way to avoid the Russian.

He continued to chat politely with Jean Papineau but felt a sense of trepidation, the feeling of being on a much more slippery slope than he would have thought.

The buffet was packed with food, and he filled his plate without thinking about what he wanted. Jean Papineau began a story about French cuisine. Ryan pretended to pay close attention to everything he was saying, and uneasiness developed quietly in his mind. The Russian ambassador was only two meters away when he addressed Jean Papineau.

"It's so refreshing to talk about something other than politics. You saved me from some very boring conversations."

To be sure that Jean Papineau would bite, he pointed out the Russian ambassador who had approached Gertrude. He found it difficult not to laugh when he saw the Frenchman's delight in being on the same page.

"Ah! The Russians, my dear Matt! Those are some characters! They screw people twice: by forcing their loyalty and exploiting them without restraint."

"You seem to be reluctant towards them!"

"I am. And it would be best if you were too. Be careful and keep your distance from them."

Ryan expected a different reaction from the French. Not knowing what to say to such judgement towards the Russian, he smiled. He glanced at Gertrude, who seemed focused on the conversation with the Russian Ambassador. Hopefully, she'll keep him away.

"It's crazy how hot it is here," commented Jean Papineau. "I need a refreshment. Let's go sit at the bar."

Ryan stood up to follow the French and stayed idle there momentarily. All he could see was the young woman walking in his direction. He noticed her smooth, tanned skin, which he had an unfathomable desire to touch.

"You're very emotional, cowboy, purred Gertrude's contemptuous voice. We have to be careful!"

Ryan hadn't noticed Gertrude approaching him. He stared at her for a moment without answering, wondering what was so offensive to Gertrude. Was it because he found another woman more attractive than her or because she did not find him worthy of replacing his brother? In both cases, her behavior irritated him.

"Spare me your sarcasm, Gertrude!"

She paced furiously from left to right.

"You'll compromise your brother's safety! I don't understand how you two can be so different from each other!"

She shook her head and walked away towards the bar.

Her words had shocked Ryan, and he felt shame mixed with resentment. He had behaved like an idiot, and he blamed himself.

He swallowed the liquid that remained in his glass with a single sip. Over his glass, he saw the young woman responsible for his behavior. Leaning against the door frame, she watched him through the crowd of guests. As their eyes crossed, she drew her lips into a vague smile, opened the door suddenly and walked out of the room.

Despite his efforts, Ryan sensed a deleterious thought clouding his mind. His will, usually so infallible, melted like snow in the sun. It wasn't comforting. He was attracted to that woman like a moth to the light without knowing anything about her. He swallowed his saliva and turned abruptly towards the bar. He needed another drink.

Glass in hand and cheeks flushed, Jean Papineau beckoned him over.

"Matt, do you know my longtime friend Johann Schwaben, the best journalist in Bonn?" he asked Ryan.

A man in his fifties with a pimpled face and bloodshot eyes nodded.

"It's good to see you again, Matt! I didn't expect to meet you here," said the journalist, addressing Ryan.

Ryan's brain began to run at a hundred miles an hour. This face was not familiar to him. Undoubtedly, his brother had not deemed it necessary to tell him about Schwaben. But Ryan has enough experience with reporters; he'll manage.

"And why is that?" he asked Johann Schwaben.

"You're not usually interested in this kind of reception! Is there something different tonight?"

"You're exaggerating! It's just a courtesy."

Suddenly, they were surrounded by other guests who seemed very interested in what they were saying. Ryan recognized the face of the Russian ambassador among them. The Russian addressed the journalist with a radiant smile that erased his features' harshness.

"I must admit, my dear Johann, that Matt is right. It was courtesy that brought us here tonight."

"How long have you and Matt been playing on the

same team?" the journalist asked, looking surprised.

"We don't play, Johann; we make alliances against suspicious journalists," answered the Russian.

Seeing Johann Schwaben's astonished expression, the Russian ambassador let a booming laugh. Others around them shared his hilarity.

"I would like to point out, however, that there are no permanent alliances, only permanent interests," added the Russian.

Then he asked a waiter to bring him a glass of vodka and water, a subtle signal that he was ready to engage in a serious conversation.

When the vodka arrived, he raised his glass. The others imitated him. With his sparkling eyes and bushy eyebrows, the Russian looked like a buffoon, but Ryan knew better. He thought the Russian played the fool to lure his opponent into feeling a deceptive sense of security.

The conversation drifted over the floods in Cologne. Soon, everyone spoke simultaneously, giving their opinion on climate change. Ryan spent the next hour shaking hands and exchanging courtesies. Followed by Gertrude, present at his side like his own shadow, he found with relief that he had no difficulty in impersonating his brother.

At ten minutes to nine, Gertrude whispered in his ear: "It's time."

Ryan looked at his watch. Within ten minutes, he was to meet his brother.

He looked around. It will be difficult for him to retreat with everybody's eyes on him. He finished his drink and apologized for having to leave urgently, then went straight to the bathroom, checking the hallway leading towards the exit. Except for a young couple who had just given the key to their car to the valet, no one was there.

Without wasting time, he walked down the hallway, out into the garden, and to the gate. The guard asked him if he should send the valet to pick up the car. He told the guard that he needed to make an urgent call but would be back.

The next moment, he found himself in the deserted alley where the bright light of the neon signs made his skin look like an oyster shell.

He took a breath of fresh air and crossed the street to the place where he was to meet his brother. For a brief moment, he thought it was funny that he was looking for the dark corners of the street in order not to be seen.

I am acting like a spy, he thought as a strangled laugh crept up his throat.

When he heard the sudden steps behind him, he snapped out of it and back to reality. A group of young people from nearby houses passed by him and climbed the steps of a nearby residence. A maid dressed in a white apron appeared in the door frame, and the young people disappeared into the house.

The silence returned to the deserted street. He reached the meeting point with his brother and looked at his watch: two seconds before the agreed time. He hid in the shadows and summarized the information he should pass on to his brother.

Minutes went by, and he began to worry. Where was Matt? He was at the meeting point set up by his brother. He followed the clear and precise instructions he's brother had given him.

He could no longer stand still and began to walk. What if something happened to his brother?

He stopped, petrified, feeling a sense of panic, which he immediately repressed; if anything had happened to his twin brother, he would have felt it.

He looked at his watch again. At that moment, his brother's voice, seemingly from nowhere, startled him. He had sprung out of the shadows without making any noise.

"You're very punctual, cowboy!"

"Damn it!" exclaimed Ryan. "You scared me. How the hell did you do that?"

"Ah! I told you before. It's part of the job, cowboy.

"Well! You're doing a good job!"

"I know. Now tell me about your evening. I must replace you quickly, or our "friends" will ask questions."

Hidden in the shadow of the street, Ryan tried to summarize the evening's most critical conversations.

"What do I have to do now?" he asked his brother when he finished.

"Someone's waiting for you around the corner in a red Opel," said Matt. "He's a colleague and an excellent friend; he'll drive you to the BMW. You have to reach his car without being seen. Good night, cowboy and ... thank you."

Ryan watched his brother walk away and for the

umpteenth time, the childhood memories, while they were inseparable, resurfaced in his memory. He realized how much he loved his brother and how much he missed him. But he could do nothing about it; no reason to hope. Everyone had to follow their destiny.

He circumnavigated the embassy building from the left, carefully staying as far as possible and in the dark. The night was silent, broken only by the distant sound of a passing car. He crossed paths with two young women, arm in arm. Trying not to be noticed, he hid behind the bushes surrounding the embassy's walls.

As he bided his time for the two women to depart, a sudden movement near the wall caught his attention. He froze, his senses heightened, trying to discern the identity of the mysterious figure in the darkness.

"A guard? Someone who followed him? Who was it?"

He crouched as low as he could behind a tree in the embassy garden. He wondered what he had to do: hide or leave the scene and go to the car waiting for him on the corner.

He didn't have time to decide; the sound of a fabric grazing a rough surface attracted his attention. Someone else was hiding in the garden. He stuck to the tree trunk. He couldn't move now. The evening had been a success; he could not risk revealing himself and ruining everything.

A man emerged from the shadows and approached the embassy without a sound. Another followed him. Then, he saw a dark shadow, someone slipping along the building wall with the same caution as a cat in the dark. A woman.

The moment she had almost set foot on the ground, she was attacked by the two men who approached her cautiously, their steps heavy with confidence.

Ryan could see the stark contrast between the woman's seemingly delicate figure and the two men's imposing presence. She didn't stand a chance. Yet, as the confrontation unfolded, it became increasingly evident that appearances were deceiving. The woman's true strength emerged with each exchange, shattering preconceived notions of weakness. Despite being outnumbered and physically overpowered, she held her ground with a resilience that belied her outward appearance.

Her movements were calculated, precise, and imbued with a quiet determination that spoke volumes. As the men underestimated her, she seized every opportunity to retaliate, striking back with a ferocity that took them by surprise. She struck back when her opponent prepared to give her the final blow. There were choked noises in the garden's silence, flesh striking flesh.

"Damn it, thought Ryan. Where the hell are the guards? What kind of embassy doesn't have guards at its annual reception?"

He moved slowly, unsure of exactly what to do. He couldn't leave his hiding spot now for fear of being seen.

His gaze returned to the embassy wall. The woman in the shadow remained motionless, glued to the wall, as the two men approached with their arms stretched out, their fingers curled, ready to grab hold of her. One of them pulled something out of his pocket. Despite the darkness,

Ryan recognized the shape of a gun with a silencer. He stopped breathing, fascinated by what he was witnessing.

Fast as lightning, the woman struck her opponent's hand, who held the pistol. Ryan heard the crack of a

bone, and the gun flew through the air and fell with a thud on the garden floor. The man tried to fight back but received another blow to the loins and collapsed.

Still on the move, the women quickly picked up the rope and disappeared into the dark.

Ryan bent his head back and took a deep breath. He could not suppress an outburst of admiration for the woman who had acted in a flash.

He slowly straightened himself up and began to stretch out the muscles of his legs. It was the perfect time to leave the garden and get to the car waiting for him. His conscience told him he should do something for the two men lying on the ground, while reason urged him to leave as soon as possible.

He heard a slight noise, and he raised an ear. As he turned around, he saw the two men who had managed to get up, crossing the space between the wall and the corner of the building and disappearing in the dark.

Ryan walked to where the silencer had landed and tapped the ground with both hands but found nothing. Precious seconds passed as he feverishly searched for the weapon he had seen fall.

Be content with what you are asked to do, warned his brother. *Only take the initiative if your life is at stake. The logic of professionals is very different from yours.*

Lost in his thoughts, he ran across the garden and entered the street. A few moments later, he spotted the red Opel waiting for him. The man seated inside opened the door violently and signaled him to come in.

"You are late," he said in a critical voice.

Ryan didn't have time to answer him. He heard a voice, and the man pulled a receiver out of the inside pocket of his jacket while he started the car with the other hand. A few blocks away, the man shook Ryan's hand, opened the car door, and Ryan found himself in the street where he had left the BMW.

He sat at the wheel and relaxed against the seat. Many questions were bubbling, and he wondered if he would ever have the answers. Every time he infiltrated his brother's world, he came out of it unsettled.

The screams of an ambulance siren that passed his car interrupted his thoughts. He started the car and was preparing to leave the scene when he heard the guttural whirring of a heavy-duty motorcycle popping up at full speed.

He watched the bike veer quickly, barely avoiding a car approaching it on the opposite side of the road, and then stopped in the middle of the street.

The driver pulled out a gun with a silencer and, with his arm stretched out, waited without moving. Ryan heard a loud screeching of brakes, and immediately after, a vehicle hit the bike head-on. The air smelled like burnt rubber and spilled gasoline.

Even though he was thrown into the air before landing

on the asphalt, the motorcycle driver rose and fired three bullets into the car's windshield. Tires screamed, and the vehicle skidded dangerously, almost slamming into a tree. Then, it regained control and, burning the red light, disappeared into a side street. As for the motorcycle driver, he had mysteriously disappeared.

Citizens had gone out into the street, drawn by the noise and the police siren that sounded nearby. Ryan drove cautiously and turned to the first street on the right. He should move away before the police arrive. He did not know the town well and had to be careful to find his way back. He wondered if what he saw on the street had anything to do with the events he witnessed in the embassy garden.

CHAPTER 7

Under the eerie glow of the full moon against the backdrop of the ink-black sky, Ryan found himself at a crossroads, both literally and metaphorically. He deliberated on which street to take to reach the main road, his thoughts momentarily distracted from the task.

With a sigh, he decided to pause and consult the road map he had tucked away before departing Matt's House. Focusing intently, he lowered the map onto his knees, immersing himself in its intricate details, when suddenly, the tranquility of the night shattered. A cacophony of screeching tires and the sickening crunch of metal on metal erupted from his right.

Startled, Ryan raised his gaze only to find himself confronted by an unexpected sight. A woman, her figure illuminated by the harsh glow of headlights, stood defiantly in front of his car, a firearm levelled directly at him.

His heart raced with disbelief as recognition flickered across his mind; she was the waitress who had captivated him at the Romanian embassy reception.

Before he could process the situation fully, a man, evidently injured, staggered into view, poised to strike the woman. Reacting swiftly, she deftly evaded his attack, leveraging her body weight to deliver a powerful counterstrike that sent him crashing through a nearby car's windshield, shards of glass scattering in his wake. Then, she opened Ryan's car door and sank into the passenger seat.

As the chaos unfolded before him, Ryan's instincts screamed at him to flee, but he fought to maintain his composure. Yet, before he could act, a gunshot shattered the tension, the bullet tearing through the woman's shoulder, painting the windshield crimson with blood. Panic surged through Ryan as he spied the shadowy figure of another assailant lurking nearby, armed and dangerous.

In a split-second decision, the woman retaliated, her aim unwavering as she neutralized the threat with lethal precision. Ryan recoiled in shock, grappling with the grim reality unfolding before him.

"God, you killed him!" he exclaimed, his voice laced with disbelief.

"He wanted to kill me," came the woman's terse reply, devoid of remorse.

Before Ryan could utter another word, a pallor swept over the woman's features, her grip on the gun faltering, and she slumped against the seat, unconscious.

Fear gripped Ryan's heart as he realized the gravity of the situation. With urgency coursing through his veins, he knew he had to act swiftly. Ignoring the tumult raging within him, he resolved to save the woman's life. Starting the car, he steered towards the nearest hospital, his only sanctuary in this nightmarish ordeal. Suddenly, he felt the coldness of a gun on his neck.

"What are you doing?" asked the woman, who had regained consciousness.

"I'm bringing you to the nearest hospital!" said Ryan. "You need a doctor!"

She studied his face to see if he was telling the truth.

"I don't need a doctor," she replied. "Keep driving. I'll point you in the right direction. And don't do anything stupid."

Ryan watched her from the corner of his eye; with a knife, she pulled out of her jacket, tore the base of her t-shirt and wrapped it around the wound where the bullet had penetrated her flesh.

Her generous lips were spread, revealing very white teeth. Her long lashes drew shadows on her high cheekbones. The veins on her neck were swollen, but no sound was coming out of her mouth while she was pushing the tissue into the bloody wound.

Ryan felt an outburst of tenderness towards this stranger who continued to fascinate him despite the circumstances. Following the women's orders, he directed the car towards the city's exit and turned to reach the highway. Despite the late hour, many vehicles were moving at a crazy speed.

Ryan was desperately looking for a way out of this situation. If somebody witnessed what happened and gave the police a description of the BMW, Matt would be in big trouble.

Now he understood what Matt meant by being a professional. People like this woman. They acquired deadly skills, and they don't play by any rules. Having been trained to take the fight to the enemy, they were deeply committed to their job. He was sure that, physically, he was more robust than the woman sitting next to him, but he would have been unable to act in the same way as she had. He had grown up with specific values that prevented him from taking the life of another human being.

"Look out!" she spat, her eyes fixed on the rearview mirror.

Before Ryan understood her reaction, a gray Mercedes hit his flank. A noise of metal rubbing against metal resonated through the night. The car that chased them accelerated and reached his window's level.

"Accelerate!" shouted the woman.

Ryan did it, pushing the car to the limits of its power. The woman had pulled her gun out the window, and he heard the whistling of the bullets in rapid succession. The Mercedes swerved dangerously and hit the next car head-on. Ryan entered a tight turn, followed by the screams of the tires.

"Get off the highway," ordered the woman.

Ryan rushed to the first exit lane and narrowly avoided

a bus full of tourists. He felt his temples beating, ready to burst. A parking lot appeared on the bright sign.

"Enter the parking lot," the women demanded.

Ryan pressed the throttle more gently and moved slowly into the parking lot.

"You are free to go now," said the woman.

Without saying anything else, she got out of the car.

"Hey! Be careful!" shouted Ryan as he pulled his head out the window.

The woman turned her face towards him, but her gaze slipped towards the car that entered the parking lot. Following the direction of her gaze, Ryan recognized the Mercedes that had been stalking them on the highway. The woman quickly returned to Ryan's car and opened the door on the driver's side.

"Hurry! Go to the passenger side," she demanded.

"I thought I was free to go!" said Ryan mockingly.

"The people who chased us are professional killers. I'm afraid if I leave you here, you're in imminent danger."

"Don't worry about me."

"I always believed that the American agents were very professional! You must be an exception!" she concluded.

Ryan immediately understood that she had mistaken him for his brother. He was confident that Matt's reactions would have significantly differed from his in such circumstances.

"Contrary to what you think, I can defend myself," he said, frustrated.

"I'm not convinced. You're acting like a beginner."

"Who the hell are those people?"

"Like I said, they are professional killers. It's a category of people you can't face."

"I assume you're in the same category as them."

"Stop talking! If you care about your life, do as I say!"

She kept staring at the review mirror. As soon as the Mercedes parked at a nearby parking spot, the woman pushed the BMW's engine to its maximum.

The car leaped forward, crossed the parking lot and got on the ramp to the highway. Ryan looked back. The Mercedes had left its spot, and despite the BMW's crazy speed, it was closing in on them. They were only a few dozen meters from the highway. A gigantic eighteen-wheeler was riding before them, swinging on its shocks like a heavyweight boxer in an arena. He was completely blocking the off-ramp to the highway.

A look in the review mirror confirmed to Ryan that the Mercedes was gaining ground. A bullet whistled through the rear windshield, leaving behind a black hole. Ryan looked at the sculpted face of the woman bent over the steering wheel.

"Brace yourself," she exclaimed.

She focused on the truck before them and turned on the ramp's grass. At its driving speed, the car skidded dangerously towards the concrete partition. A cloud of dust rose in the air, and the truck suddenly stopped in the middle of the road in a terrible screech of brakes.

Ryan sensed the inflated engine responding nervously to the woman's demands, and the car doubled the eighteen wheels to the right and sank into the flow of vehicles rolling down the highway.

Suddenly, the woman crushed the accelerator pedal and began to slalom between the cars. She accelerated and continued her mind-boggling behavior as in a video game. Looking in the review mirror, Ryan noticed that the Mercedes was no longer following them.

The city's lights became rarer, but they still advanced at a crazy speed on the highway. Ryan glanced at the woman, wondering what insanity could have pushed such a powerful woman into such a horrible world of professional assassins.

They took an exit lane, and soon, the road narrowed, and a sweet scent of flowers touched Ryan's nostrils. They were in the middle of the countryside, and at this time of night, cars were scarce. In the distance, Ryan heard dogs barking. A vehicle crossed them, and the BMW started swinging from one side of the street to the other.

"Have you gone mad? You want to get us killed?" asked Ryan, not understanding why she was driving so recklessly.

The woman did not answer, and the car suddenly stopped on the side of the road. Ryan turned on the light inside the car and looked at her with astonishment. The woman's head was limp on the side of the seat, and her face looked ashen. As he touched her, Ryan felt the lukewarm blood spilling over his hand and flowing into the leather seat. Her pulse was feeble, and her skin was burning.

Ironically, things went wrong during every mission he carried out for his brother. This time, he caused it. He looked at the deserted road as the woman passed out.

His mind was working fast. He couldn't go back to the city; the killers who chased them could still be on the road, and they'd recognize his car. He had to find a doctor as soon as possible.

He took the woman in his arms and stretched her out as comfortably as possible in the back seat. She did not react, but he noted with relief that her pulse was stronger. He started the car and advanced at a speed that allowed him to read the signs on the side of the road. After a few minutes that felt like hours, a village appeared in the light of the headlights.

A police car passed them at high speed, projecting pools of colored lights on the trees along the road. Ryan felt a cold sweat on his back. In other circumstances, the police would have been the best solution, but in the current circumstances, it would only complicate things further.

A sign hung by two chains at the top of a pole showed what he desperately sought: a hospital. Ryan slowed down and entered a gravel driveway that led to a parking lot lit by headlights. He exited the car and ran up the few stairs in front of the building. The door seemed locked, and all the windows were in the dark.

Oh, Lord! Don't let her die, he prayed.

Powerless, he knocked against the hospital door, but only the sound of his fist against the wood answered him. On returning to the car, he saw a window lit within ten meters of the hospital door. He went up the house steps, persuaded that it must belong to a hospital staff member.

Perhaps even a doctor, he thought with encouragement.

After three knocks, the door opened, and a woman in a nightgown appeared on the threshold. Ryan asked her if she spoke English. Seeing that she looked at him dazedly, he forced himself to find the words in German.

"Meine frau is krank. I need a doctor."

"The hospital is closed! Come back tomorrow morning," answered the woman.

She was about to close the door when Ryan pushed his right leg into the opening and stopped her. The woman looked at him with fear and began to cry. Ryan tried to calm her down, but he understood that he was only making things worse. He stepped back, trying again to explain the reason for his night visit, but the door closed with the final slamming of the pulled lock.

Desperate, Ryan looked at the closed door feverishly, trying to find a solution. The sweat of panic was dripping on his forehead. He didn't have time to run around the cities to find an open hospital. He had to see someone in that village who could help him.

He opened the car's back door and listened to the woman's pulse. She hardly opened her eyes at the sound of the door before closing them immediately. Ryan suddenly felt overwhelmed by a feeling of confidence. *She is strong; she'll get through this*, he told himself.

He returned to the main road and began to drive slowly. His eyes clung to a small metal panel stuck to the entrance of a red brick house. It took him a long time to absorb what he saw. It was a vet's house, with light behind the windows. This time, he will try to do it differently.

He parked the car along the sidewalk, took the woman in his arms and rang the doorbell. After a long wait, the door opened, and a man in a white shirt, wearing a pair of glasses, appeared in the doorframe. Ryan tried to explain the situation to him by showing the wounded woman in his arms, and immediately, the veterinarian signaled him in. They crossed a corridor, and the vet opened a door on the left.

Ryan looked around. Except for many shelves with medicine on them, the room contained only a large table in its center with a Labrador lying down, a band-aid around its head. The Labrador wasn't moving, and Ryan assumed the vet had given the dog an anesthetic.

"Excuse me, sir," said the vet in English. "I need to clear the table."

"Ah! exclaimed Ryan, surprised. You speak English!"

"Little. Just passable," answered the vet.

He lifted the Labrador and took him out of the room. Ryan felt the warmth of the woman he was carrying in his arms. The vet returned with a mattress, which he stretched out on the table and covered with a white, immaculate cloth.

"Set your wife on the table, sir," said the vet.

Ryan put the woman on the table. He knew that a series of questions were coming up.

"Now help me get her clothes off. There's a lot of blood. What happened?"

"We're tourists in your country," improvised Ryan. "We were on the road to Bonn when we saw two cars driving at high speed in the middle of the road, hitting each other, in a scrap metal noise. I slowed down and tried to park on the side of the road to avoid a collision. At our height, the passengers in both cars started shooting at each other. A bullet hit my wife."

"Why didn't you call the police right away?"

"It was my first intention. But because I speak German poorly, I was afraid that my wife would die before I could explain the situation to the police. I took the first exit, hoping to get help."

"I can contact the police and explain the situation to them."

"I intend to contact my embassy in the morning. Right now, I want to make sure my wife is safe."

"I understand."

While speaking, the vet removed the woman's black jacket, and a heavy object fell soundly under the table. Ryan bent over and saw the knife she had torn her t-shirt with to cover her wound. He froze for a second and then picked up the knife and slipped it discreetly into the inside pocket of his jacket. He expected a comment from the veterinarian, but this one didn't seem to notice because his attention was fixed on the woman's wound.

"Hum! It's a nasty wound," he concluded.

He cleaned the blood with a yellowish solution. The woman began to stir, and the vet rushed to anesthetize her with a shot.

"Your wife is not only beautiful and strong, she's also fortunate. The bullet could have killed her if it hadn't been deflected by something."

The knife in her pocket taught Ryan.

"She will recover in a short time," continued the vet. "The only problem is she's lost too much blood. She needs a lot of rest. From what I can see, no vital organs were affected. A doctor's opinion is still necessary. I'll call the local ambulance to take you to a hospital in Bonn. They perform better than our little hospital, which is closed at this hour."

As if I don't know, thought Ryan, recalling the episode with the woman who had closed the door on him.

The vet approached a cabinet glued to the wall, opened a drawer and took out a sterilization pouch. He grabbed a gauze pad and wrapped it around the woman's shoulder. Soon, he'll be done, and he will call the ambulance.

It was time for Ryan to decide what to do. He could follow the ambulance in his car into town or take a different direction and return to his brother's. Even though the police will investigate and the vet will say that he dealt with an American, the risk of being found remains low. They'll look for a tourist and never consider checking out an embassy employee.

The only person who could inform the police about him was the woman. But something indicated to him that it wasn't in her best interest to mention anything about the highway chase or his presence. She seemed like a skilled person to get out of an unwanted situation. He looked at her lying on the vet's table, and a shiver ran through him. He couldn't decide what to do.

"Can I use your bathroom?" he asked the vet. He needed a few minutes alone to decide what to do.

The vet showed him the bathroom. Ryan closed the door and looked in the mirror. There were spots of dried blood all over his face, and his eyes were a bit worn.

He washed the blood on his face and hands as a feeling of helplessness gripped his mind. He closed his eyes. When he opened them, his mind was made up; he'd leave the house before the ambulance arrived. And he'll take the women with him. He has to take advantage of a moment when the veterinarian is not paying attention, take the woman in his arms and go out to the car.

The opportunity presented itself sooner than he'd hoped.

"Your wife's clots are ruined," said the veterinarian. "I'll get a gown from my wife's wardrobe," stated the vet.

Ryan prepared to take off his jacket to cover the woman's naked body and leave when the door opened, and the veterinarian appeared smiling, an extra-large sweater in his hand.

"I know it's not the right size, but it'll do the trick in the meantime," he said. "The good news is your wife is out of danger, in my opinion. The bad news is that you'll have to manage on your own to get her to a hospital in Bonn."

"What do you mean?" asked Ryan.

"I called the Emergency. There was a complication with a delivery, and they had to send the patient into town with the only ambulance we have in the village. Drive slowly and remember: your wife needs to rest."

With relief, Ryan took a deep breath, pulled out some bills, and put them on the chair.

"No, no, no! exclaimed the vet. You don't have to do this!"

Ryan wasn't listening to him anymore. He dressed the woman in the extra-large sweater, took her in his arms and walked towards the door.

"I'll open the car door," said the vet.

"You've already done a lot for us; I don't know how to thank you," replied Ryan.

He went to the car, laid her down delicately in the backseat, and backed up to the street to ensure the vet couldn't see the license plate. His mind was running at full speed, and he decided that the best thing to do would be to return to Bonn, not take the main roads to avoid the people who had followed them. But where to go once in Bonn? He knew he had embarked on a situation that was none of his business, a problem that could get his brother into serious trouble. He should have gotten rid of that woman the first chance he got.

He turned and looked at her beautiful sculpted face, so innocent in her sleep. The calculating being, with an unshakeable composure, had disappeared entirely.

The minutes passed, and he wasn't making any decisions. An inner voice told him he was looking for reasons to stay as long as possible with this woman who continued to fascinate him.

I'm acting like an idiot, he thought. He looked around and realized he had no idea where he was, except that the city should be close. He had been out of the vet's house for about 30 minutes. Being still under the effect of anesthesia, the woman slept deeply.

The fuel gauge was very low, and at this late hour, only the gas stations on the highway were open, but he could not risk returning to the road. He decided to find a quiet place to park and wait for the women to wake up. The effect of the anesthesia should wear off soon, and she could give him an address where she would be safe.

A tanker passed him on his left. In the light of the headlights, Ryan saw the structure of a motel. He drove toward the motel and parked in the darkest corner of the parking lot. If he could find a spare room, they could stay the night.

He crossed the parking lot and entered the reception area, hearing the chime sound behind him. The receptionist looked up from the magazine he was reading and handed him a key attached to a numbered metal plate.

The room was small but comfortable. A smell of cleaning products brushed his nostrils. He took the glass ashtray on the table and entered the hallway. A bearded man entered the opposite room and greeted him as he passed.

Ryan took a determined step into the hallway and approached the service exit. The hallway was empty. He positioned the ashtray in the door's opening so it remained ajar and approached the car. The woman was in the same position he had left her. Is it possible that the vet was mistaken in thinking she was out of danger and that she was dying?

He bent over and took her in his arms. The woman let out a grunt of pain, but her eyes remained closed. Ryan approached the exit door of the motel, glancing around him. He was walking down the hallway when a door opened, and a young couple went out and kissed. Ryan panicked, but it was too late to back off. He continued towards the room he'd rented, trying as best he could to cover with his large hands the dried blood stains on the woman's pants. It was a waste of time; the couple didn't even turn around.

With relief, he arrived in the room, laid the woman on the bed, removed her clothes, and entered the bathroom. For a few minutes, he concentrated on washing the blood-stained clothes, wondering for the umpteenth time what dirty business he had gotten himself into.

He returned to the room and, with the help of a damp towel, began to rub the body of the woman lying on the bed. He couldn't help but admire the perfection of her forms. He thought the most prominent fashion houses would compete for a body like hers.

He covered her with the blanket and looked at her face sculpted by the shade from the lamp behind her, wondering who this woman was who had shaken his tidy, rational world in such a short period.

As if she had felt his gaze set on her, she opened her eyes, but her gaze passed over Ryan, and she mumbled a few words in a language Ryan didn't recognize. He put his hand between hers and felt her cold skin and body tremble.

He wrapped her with the blanket. A feeling of guilt was growing in him; he should have taken her to a doctor.

He laid his hand on her chest, which rose at the rhythm of her breathing, and suddenly, a shiver came from the depths of his being. He didn't know if it was a premonition but knew he wouldn't be the same man after that night. He did not understand what role this woman would play in his life, but it was enough to look at her to find himself in the grip of uncontrollable emotions.

She continued to shiver as the blanket was not enough to warm her. Ryan lay next to her and took her into his arms, trying to convey the warmth of his body. He tasted the sweetness of her skin and the scent of citrus and wildflowers that emanated from her. Being in such proximity made her irresistible. Her diaphragm rose rapidly, and the pain of her wounds twisted her body. Ryan's heart shook. He would do anything to erase the pain that this woman was feeling.

Gradually, her breath became more profound, more regular. She was drifting into sleep. Ryan lay beside her for a long time, listening to her regular breathing. He wanted to keep her forever and protect her from all evil. But was he able to defend her? She seemed to be one of those strong ones who chose their fate.

He walked lightly on the floor to not wake her, approached the window, and pulled the curtains. The night was so dark that he had trouble seeing any further than two meters away. His gaze swung towards the door. He couldn't wait any longer; he had to call his brother.

Upon entering the motel, he noticed a telephone booth in the lobby. He closed the window, got dressed, and took one last look at the woman who was fast asleep.

At the front desk, the receptionist was replaced by another.

Ryan approached the phone booth, followed by the receptionist prying eyes. He put in some coins, not understanding the instructions well, but the telephone seemed out of order. Thinking he needed to insert more, he put in more coins, but no sound came from the handset. He pushed on the metal number pad to get the change, but the box wouldn't open.

He exited the booth and stared at the receptionist, who had not stopped watching him. His mocking look told him he knew the phone was faulty.

Ryan was furious. He approached the reception, ready to question him, when an indescribable scream tore the silence. It was a woman's scream. A door slammed shut, followed by a car noise from the parking lot.

A shiver ran through Ryan's body. He immediately thought of the woman he had left asleep in the room.

"I don't understand why people don't drink at home!" said the receptionist, not worried about what might have caused that scream.

Without answering him, Ryan walked over to his room. His heart began to beat fast. He was afraid to open the door, but at the same time, he could not wait to see if his intuition was not the fruit of his imagination.

When he finally opened the door, he felt a surge of

emotion at the sight of the empty bed. A tornado seemed to have passed through the room.

He slumped in the chair and put his neck on the fabric headrest, trying to regain his senses. He shouldn't be surprised that the killers who chased them never gave up, and they were just waiting for the best opportunity to grab the women. And now she was in their hands. He tried vainly to push away such thoughts; he couldn't think of anything but the fate of the woman he believed he could protect.

CHAPTER 8

I opened my eyes, made heavy by the anesthetic, and looked around. Two men of impressive build were watching me. Their muscles were visibly stretching out their clothes. They looked ready for action. I knew who they were: Securitate agents trained to kidnap and make people disappear. Professional killers.

I tried to get up, but my muscles wouldn't listen. Due to the effort I had made, I began to shake, and an almost animal howling came out of my throat.

One of the agents approached me, and he grabbed a fistful of my hair so hard I could hear my scalp begin to pop. Then he struck me across the face. The blow fell like a heavyweight, and the following pain took my breath away. Then he placed a piece of duct tape over my mouth and pushed me inside the trunk of a car. I understood they had left the motel parking lot from the following noise.

After a while, I lost track of how long they had been driving. I was about to faint. Quickly, the shadow gave way to darkness.

When I came to, the pain I felt was unbearable. I moved my arms and legs to see if they were still obedient. My nerves were still working, but my uncomfortable position was pushing on my diaphragm, leaving me feeling strangled and unable to breathe.

The hunt was over. Now they'll break me. And then they'll take me to a safe place and kill me. I tried to move, but my arms and back hurt terribly, and my movements slowed down.

How long had they been driving? Was it still night, or was it morning?

At the cost of extreme effort, I succeeded in changing my position. My face touched something that smelled of leather. I started patting in the dark to find the object I had felt. Those were my shoes. I continued to pat around and found some wet clothes. A glimmer of hope crept into my thoughts.

In other circumstances, opening the trunk and rolling onto the asphalt would have taken only a few seconds. Under the current circumstances, I wondered whether or not I would be able to get dressed.

My eyes began to get used to the darkness, and I slowly started putting on the clothes. It was not easy to move in the confined space, and with each movement, waves of pain were flowing through my body so violently that I had to stop several times.

I put on all my clothes and reached for my shoes. In the back of my mind, a mechanism began to turn like a clock. I could not give up living before finding a way to avenge my family and shed light on what was happening in my country. I have to try to open the trunk and get out, at the risk of crashing into the asphalt. At this point, it was better to have a little hope than no hope.

I tried to find a favorable position to open the trunk, but the car stopped. I heard footsteps approaching, and the trunk opened. The sun blinded me for a moment. The next moment, the face of one of the agents appeared in my vision, a wicked grin on his face.

"Bitch!" he exclaimed. "You thought you could get away with it, but you're wrong. Soon, you will discover my methods of torture. Whores like you, who work for the Americans, are shit. I'll skin your beautiful face. Your mother won't recognize you."

"Thanks to scum like you, I don't have a mother," I replied.

A sadistic smile appeared on the agent's face.

"If your mother is not around anymore, I will gladly look at your pretty-skinned face."

"I don't think you'll be looking at anything from now on," I replied.

Suddenly, I jumped, my right arm recoiled like a spring, and I stuck my thumbs in the agent's eyes. He growled in pain and covered his face with his hands. Two trickles of blood dripped down on his chin.

I heard quick steps, and two men approached the car. They looked with astonishment at the agent, who was writhing in pain.

"You bitch! said one of them. What did you do to him? You've blinded him!!!"

"This is what he deserves," I answered.

"What they say about you is true; you're out of control!" exclaimed the man.

"She must pay for this," said the other man. "An attack dog that gets out of its leash must be put down."

"Shut up and take her inside. The orders are unequivocal; they will come for her tonight, and they want her alive."

Unable to stand, I slid down the side of the car and curled up, wrapped my arms around my knees and placed my head on my forearms. The effort had exhausted me and opened my wounds.

I heard more steps come closer and listened to the voice of someone who used to be in control.

"Idiots! I warned you she was extremely dangerous! Bring her into the house."

I felt strong hands grabbing me and forcing me to walk toward the old house at the end of the parking lot. After crossing a dark corridor, they threw me into a room without windows, even darker than the corridor.

I noticed a slight smell of sweat and had to wait a while for my eyes to get used to the darkness. The room's furniture included a bed, a chair, and a desk. I dropped on the bed and fell into a heavy sleep.

Several hours later, I was awake by the sound of

footsteps resounding on the worn wood of the corridor. I opened my eyes, my senses alert. I stood flush against the wall and then moved cautiously towards the door. Somebody opened the door, and the intense light of the lightbulb flooded the room.

I looked with astonishment at the person standing at the door's opening. It was a woman who looked like a caricature of a sex symbol. Her robe barely covered her time-warped curves, and she had too much makeup on her face. Her eyes were empty of any emotion. A smell of sweat and a fragrance of cheap perfume emanated from her body.

I was getting ready to say something when the woman signaled me not to make any noise.

"Quiet, dear, or we'll both be in trouble."

"Who are you?" I asked.

"Everyone here calls me Grandma."

"Where am I?"

"You're in a brothel, girl. I heard they brought a new girl who doesn't like obeying. I came to warn you. Here, you have to be submissive if you want to live. You shouldn't expect a secretarial job. They lied to you. You'll be tarnished by every single person who pays for your body."

She paused for a moment and looked at me with pity. Then she starts talking again, whispering.

I wouldn't upset them again if I were you, my girl. They will break you, and you will end up in the garden, buried next to those who have not accepted their fate."

I was aware of human trafficking and the immense profit that it brought, but I had trouble accepting that the

Securitate lends itself to this humiliating activity.

This woman thought I was the last acquisition for the brothel, and she came to warn me of the atrocities that awaited me. She was a nice person, a victim of corruption and violence.

"I must go now, said the woman, before these bastards realize that I am here."

"I would like to wash myself, if possible," I asked her.

I was also starving, but mostly, I needed to clean up the wound and the blood that had started flowing again. "If you promise not to make any noise, I'll let you use my bathroom. Come on, follow me."

I followed her along the dark corridor, memorizing every detail. Ten minutes later, I was enjoying the pleasure of feeling the water flowing over my stiff body.

The bathroom door opened, and Grandma handed me a towel.

"Hurry up; you must return to your room before we'll both be in trouble," she explained.

Her eyes lingered on my body, and her eyes filled with rage at the site of my wounds.

"My God! What did those bastards do to you? You need a doctor! This time, I'll tell them what I think of how they treat girls!"

"If you want to stay out of trouble, don't say anything," I insisted. "I'm not who you think I am."

"What do you mean?"

"It's better if you don't know anything about me. It's all my fault. I took advantage of your kindness."

"What do you mean? Who are you?"

"Like I said, I'm not who you think I am; don't mention that you talked to me. Tomorrow I won't be here anymore. I heard the agents say that they would transfer me tonight. Don't mention that you talked to me."

Grandma looked at me with uncertainty and perplexity. Then, suddenly, as if she had made up her mind, she turned away, walked out of the bathroom and returned with a cardboard box in her hands.

A few moments later, I had a new bandage and a box of antibiotics in my pocket.

I sneaked back to my room. The air was hot, and no noise could enter from the outside. I walked across the room, lay on the bed and waited motionless.

I finally realized the true horror of my situation. My only chance was to try and escape as quickly as possible. At that very moment, I heard footsteps in the hallway. The door opened, and Grandma moved towards the bed with a plate in one hand and a glass in the other.

"That's all I found, she said, pointing at the plate and glass."

"You're taking a huge risk coming back here."

"After all I've been through, nothing scares me anymore. Now I'm going to bed. After you eat, hide the plate and the glass under your bed. I'll pick it up in the morning."

"Thanks, Grandma!"

I approached to kiss her, and without her noticing, I removed one of the hair clips that held her hair. I could have neutralized her quickly and taken the key, but I could not hurt her.

"Good luck!" Grandma wished her as she left the room.

I forced myself to eat everything on the plate and slide it under the bed. I felt much better. It was the perfect time to try to escape.

I approached the door and stood still for a few moments, with my ear glued to it. Picking the lock took me only a few seconds, but when the door opened, I was panting as if I had just climbed up twenty floors. I was not in shape to try to escape, but I didn't know if I would have another chance.

After a second of hesitation, I went out into the dark corridor and advanced towards the exit.

After a few steps, I stopped and listened. Something was bothering me. The house was too quiet. I approached the exit door. I could hear muffled voices. I couldn't distinguish the words, but I distinguished two different voices.

I gazed towards the farthest window from the exit door and approached it on the tip of my toes.

I looked outside. There was no movement, just darkness. I grazed the frame with my fingertips to check for an alarm system. Not detecting any, I opened the window.

The shrill sound of an alarm system penetrated the silence of the night, and lights lit up through the trees. My teeth clenched so as not to cry out in the pain my wound made me feel, I hopped through the window.

The moment I hit the ground, I felt the presence of someone. A man stood two meters from me, a gun pointed at my chest. I was trapped. I recognized one of the Securitate agents I had crossed paths with during my assignments.

Two other agents approached from the shadow, exchanging information quietly. Although physically separated, they moved in unison, proving they were seasoned professionals. Their impassive faces showed no emotion.

They seized me and stuck a needle into my left arm. I tried hard to fight, but quickly, my body became heavier and heavier. An indifference crept into me; my knees bent, and I collapsed.

CHAPTER 9

For a while, Ryan stood frozen, his mind a whirlwind of self-reproach. A storm of unease had seized him, rendering him powerless. It was a bitter realization that he was helpless. The abductors of the woman he had tried to shield were armed and perilous. Pursuing them could lead to his demise.

Informing the authorities was out of the question. It would only drag his brother and himself into a vortex of trouble. Now, the wisest course of action was to hasten back to his brother's abode and allow him to take the necessary steps.

Before shutting the door, he cast a final glance at the room, and the vision of the wounded woman materialized in his thoughts as if she were still present. He blinked, but her face had etched itself into his mind, becoming an indelible part of his consciousness. Her memory was a constant torment, a reminder of the shattered reality he could never reclaim.

He left the motel and looked at the map before starting his car. Forty minutes later, he arrived at Matt's house.

Seeing that the house was utterly dark, he sighed in relief. He had time to recover before talking to his brother.

He spent a long time in the shower, adjusting the temperature to the highest bearable limit to stretch out his sore muscles. After two minutes under the icy stream, he exited the shower and draped a bathrobe over himself.

The house was quiet, but the smell of coffee tickled his nose. He walked to the kitchen and looked astonished at his brother.

"To what do we owe this morning pleasure?" he asked, not knowing where to begin.

"Where the hell have you been?" asked Matt with a sense of relief on his face.

"Bring the coffee," said Ryan. "I need it."

They moved into the living room, each with a cup of coffee.

Ryan told his brother everything that had happened since they separated without leaving out any details.

Matt remained motionless during his narration, absorbing his words.

When Ryan finished talking, the first light of the morning was coming through the window. A long silence ensued, interrupted only by the ticking of the clock. Eventually, Matt began to speak.

"This will be your last assignment. After tonight's events, the agency will understand the risk of using civilians."

"I'm sorry, Matt."

"Imagine if something terrible had happened to you," added Matt. "And not just that, imagine how the German authorities would have reacted. Acting like that on their territory without informing them could damage our collaboration."

"I thought the same thing," Ryan interrupted.

"You thought too late! A professional would have acted differently from the beginning. Do you realize the danger you faced? The agents of Eastern European countries are determined, intelligent and resourceful people. They move quickly and discreetly and stop at nothing to achieve their goal. They would have eliminated you without hesitation if you had found yourself in their way."

"You speak as if you have great admiration for them!"

"Not at all! But that's the reality."

"How do you know it's the Eastern country's agents? According to the woman's accent, she could have been of German origin. I even thought, at one point, that she was part of your mission. Her English had no accent."

"I've lived in this shadow world long enough to recognize their origins. Besides, you told me the woman was a waitress at the Romanian embassy reception."

"I wonder why she was working as a waitress? "

"Because after a few drinks, people become more confident, and their level of attention decreases. They release essential information without realizing that it is highly analyzed and dissected by the person serving them a drink. The Romanian secret police, the Securitate, uses brilliant agents that can filter this information. From what you told me, that woman must have been a rogue agent. Their stubbornness to get her back despite the risk of exposing themselves to German security reveals how important she is."

"What could happen to her?"

"If it's what I think it is, the Securitate will neutralize her. But not until she talks. Few people resist torture."

"What if she resists?"

"Do you think the spy service can't afford to clean their own house? She's probably already dead as we speak."

"Maybe it's not what you think…"

"That's not the point! The problem is, I now have to report your mess to the agency. In detail."

Ryan stared at him in silence, not knowing what to say.

"At the same time," continued Matt, "it will serve as a lesson to Langley. "

"What do you mean?"

"To participate in an operation like this is to advance on unsteady ground. Amateurs are quickly spotted and rejected. You could have died."

A minute of silence had passed, then another. Finally, Matt got up from his chair and walked towards the exit door.

"I'm glad you're alive, cowboy. You have to forget everything that happened," he said before closing the door.

Ryan closed his eyes. He thought of the woman he held

in his arms for a moment. Her head was nestled against his shoulder, and she was breathing softly in his neck, teetering on the edge of consciousness.

He remained for a long time without moving, trying to banish his emotions and focus on reality.

Matt was right; he had to forget everything that had happened that night, including the woman who had awakened in him that crazy desire.

CHAPTER 10

I awoke, tortured by a horrible headache. A continuous purring resounded in my ears. After a few moments, my eyes regained their focus. I realized I was in an airplane. I was seated in the back row, wedged between the two stern-faced agents who had captured me in Germany. My handcuffed hands were hidden from view by a blanket.

I observed the dark sky through the porthole. How did I get here? The memory of the needle the Securitate agents had stuck in my left arm when I tried to escape returned. They drugged me, and the rest mustn't have been easy. A note from the Romanian embassy explaining that the patient must be urgently transferred to her country, a wheelchair, and customs clearance became a formality. Soon, I will pay for not being loyal to the Securitate.

I closed my eyes before the agents found out I was

awake. I knew the amount of drug administered was calculated to keep the person unconscious until they arrived at their destination. Ignoring the pain that pierced my worn-out body, I concentrated on my breathing until I got a deep and regular rhythm.

A question kept running through my mind: how could I have been so naive to believe that I wouldn't be considered a suspect when Popescu had discovered that someone had replaced the original Mossad document with a copy? I should've gotten rid of the document when I arrived in Germany.

What is happening to me? I recapitulated the events of the last few days in my head to understand the reason for this change. The only explanation I found was that since I had discovered my true identity, emotions impossible to explain had surfaced and disturbed my determination.

My unwavering coldness had melted like snow in the sun during the embassy reception. Slowly, I remembered everything that happened from that evening until now.

From the moment the American with sandy hair and deep blue eyes entered the room, I succumbed to his charm. From how he looked at me, I thought he was a lady's man, but my observation did not prevent me from feeling an exciting sensation every time our eyes crossed.

Amid emotions that I had never felt before in the presence of a man, I left the reception to carry out Popescu's order: ensure that the mole who stole the Mossad document doesn't try to take advantage of the fact that embassy employees are busy with the reception and steal another document from the vault room. And if I find out who the mole is, I intend to tell him he's in danger. Popescu would never know the truth

At that time of the evening, I had returned to my room to change my clothes without knowing what was in store for me. I had put on a black suit, put a hood in a pocket in case I had to hide my face, and hung a rope around my waist. If one of the guards decided to enter the vault room while I was there and set off the alarm, I could run out of the window without being recognized.

Why didn't my instincts, usually so sharpened, tell me that someone had entered my room while I was at the reception and had rummaged among my things? I would then have seen that I no longer possessed the Mossad document. Could it have been because of the emotions that I had felt all night?

And when I got to the vault room, I hadn't sensed the presence of the two agents there either. I pulled out the flashlight, and, at that moment, the dimly lit room was flooded with beaming light. Two agents with silencers were standing by the door. One of them had looked at me with a mocking smile, and his words, spoken pitilessly, still resonated in my head.

"Are you looking for another document like this one, Comrade Petrescu?" he had said, showing me the Mossad document.

I had felt a cold sensation running through my veins. The Mossad document was now my death sentence.

"You are under arrest for treason, comrade Petrescu,"

the agent had stated.

Feeling like time had stopped, I tried to let his words sink in. These agents, my colleagues, had ganged up against me.

I had taken a deep breath and somersaulted on the floor towards them. When I got up, the palm of my right hand violently struck the base of one of the opponents' noses. The blow had been so decisive that the cartilage of his nose had cracked, and he had collapsed on the floor.

The silencer he held in his hand had struck the floor, making a metallic sound. A hail of bullets had whistled near my ear. The other agent had opened fire, but I had been faster than him. Still crouched down, I had taken refuge behind the massive desk in the middle of the room.

While moving, I recovered the silencer that had fallen on the floor. When I raised my head, I saw the opponent's shadow moving towards the desk. I had pointed the silencer and had fired. I had seen the agent's head thrown back, blood gushing from his forehead. Without missing a beat, I approached the window, and with the help of the rope, I let myself slide along the wall. Two other agents were waiting for me in the garden. I should have known that Popescu had made sure I wouldn't escape.

Stuck in the maze of my memory, I heard the flight attendant announce their arrival at Otopeni airport. I closed my eyes and pretended to be under the influence of the drugs they had administered to me. I had to avoid them injecting another dose at all costs.

We had been on the airstrip for a while now, but the

two agents did not move to stand up. Exhausted both physically and mentally, I thought that from this point on, every minute brought me closer to the moment when my colleagues would carry out my execution. Through my barely open eyelids, I saw a movement.

Several security guards armed with guns were walking towards my seat.

I felt a needle piercing my arm; I tried pulling away, but I was held down and forced to stay motionless. A few seconds later, I felt a warmth in my stomach, radiating towards my fingertips and relieving my sore body.

I woke up sitting on a metal chair in a concrete room. The straps used to buckle straitjackets held my wrists and ankles to the metal armrests.

On a cart, I saw several steel tools used for torture. Other tools were hanging on the walls, giving no doubt about their use. Usually, they will start the interrogation with the drug administration, but in my case, Popescu wanted to make me suffer.

I tried to move but stopped when I heard the sound of a door opening, and Popescu's voice echoed behind me.

"There's no use in trying. You can't free yourself."

He circled the chair and stared at me like a reptile trying to hypnotize prey.

"For many years, I trusted your devotion," he stated." But I was wrong about you. You're just a snake that I unquestioningly protected. You better start talking right now. Otherwise, when I'm done with you, you'll be nothing more than a corpse that I'll have to dispose of."

I tried to ignore Popescu's words and the sight of the instruments of torture.

I had been trained to endure the traditional methods of torture, but I knew all too well the methods of the Securitate and the damage that they could inflict on a human body. The hatred I could see in Popescu's relentless eyes confirmed that I would not leave this room alive.

"So, you refuse to answer me?" continued Popescu. "I promise you it won't be for long. I always get what I want."

He nodded, and I heard the door open again.

There had to be a window where people from the outside could see what was happening inside. I was right.

A man with a butcher's apron tied around his waist walked in. On his apron, many bloodstains showed that this wasn't his first experience today.

While waiting for Popescu's order, he approached the cart, put on latex gloves, chose a tool and swirled it between his fingers. I tried to escape my mind by staring at a point on the wall. I hoped that my already exhausted body would not resist torture for long and that I would find peace in death.

Popescu signaled the man to begin. I noticed the sinister smile on the man's face as he shoved the end of a steel tool into my flesh. The pain was so intense that I could barely breathe.

I used my last ounce of energy to circulate air through my lungs. The room was filled with the smell of blood mixed with sweat.

"Tell me what I want to know, Ana, and I let you die,"

said Popescu. "Otherwise, I'm going to keep you alive until every fibre in your body is nothing but unbearable pain. You will want to die, but before you do, I promise you'll tell me what I want to know."

That's when I heard the door opening, and someone told Popescu he had an emergency call.

Popescu stood up from his chair, annoyed. He preferred to be uninterrupted. After a few minutes, he came back and addressed the man who was torturing me.

"I have to live," he stated. "Stop torturing her. We'll continue when I get back."

"I can continue without you, Comrade! You know I'm the best at this. When you get back, you'll find a pitiful cripple ready to talk."

"I said no!" replied Popescu. "This one's got a lot thicker skin than you think. Besides, I wouldn't miss out on her agony for anything. She'll pay for every penny I've invested in her training."

No, don't leave, I begged him in my mind. *Finish what you started.*

My mind and body were prepared to endure the agony that would result in my death. I didn't want to wait.

After he left, a dead silence settled in the room. I tried to shift my position, but my body no longer obeyed me. My throat was on fire, and a damp mist surrounded my brain. I felt it engulfed me, sweep me up, swirl me around and lure me into a bottomless black hole.

I tried to struggle, but I was unable to move. The darkness continued to surround me, and my movements became slower and slower. With my chest on fire, I tried in vain to hold on to something, to stop the panic that was overwhelming me.

Suddenly, the darkness turned into a cascade of cold water that poured over my shoulders, refreshing my sore body and giving me the strength to move my hands and feet. Slowly, I arose. Words floated and resounded in the air, but I couldn't understand their meaning.

"Ana, wake up! Ana!"

There was an urgency in the voice that pushed me to open my eyes. A blurry face appeared in front of me. Someone was leaning over me to take a closer look.

My vision became more apparent, and I recognized George's face. I closed my eyes, convinced that I was delirious. George couldn't be there; I was in a torture chamber, and I wouldn't be able to leave until they broke down my body and mind. This room would be my tomb.

Someone tipped my head back, and I felt a cold liquid splashing down my throat, then heard words spoken by a voice I recognized as George's.

"Ana, wake up; we don't have much time."

My heart started pounding in my chest. George's voice was authentic. He was here; he had come to save me. I opened my eyes and looked around.

"Ana, it's me, George. Wake up! We only have a little time. We have to get out of here as soon as possible."

"George! What are you doing here?"

"Ana, please, focus. I don't have time to explain now; we must leave this place immediately."

Using George's arms as support, I managed to stand up, and we moved slowly towards the door. George listened through the door, opened it, and waved me forward. There was a long hallway in front of us.

Trying to ignore my pain, I focused on my walking. One foot in front of the other, one at a time, don't stop. You can do it.

After a few steps, my movements became automatic. We padded through the hallway and stopped in front of a mahogany door. George approached the door and knocked three times. The door opened, and a man with a bald head appeared, signaling us to follow him.

The smell of grass reached my nose. In the light from the streetlamps, I saw a poorly maintained garden surrounded by a concrete wall.

A guard popped up from behind a corner of the house, a gun strapped around his shoulder. George quickly pushed me towards the wall. With a nod, he pointed out a small door with a sign above it saying *Authorized personnel only*, making me understand that we would get out that way on his signal.

The guard continued his walk without changing his rhythm. I felt that I could not stay in this position for long. Pain coursed through my body, and all my muscles began to tremble uncontrollably. My vision blurred, my knees gave out, and I fell along the wall. My last strength had abandoned me. My survival instinct was running out.

When I recovered my senses, the guard was at their height. Despite exhaustion, I saw someone approaching the guard from behind, moving in complete silence. He threw rapid succession punches, and the guard collapsed.

I felt held by strong hands. George carried me in his arms to the other side of the concrete wall. I heard the sound of an engine and the vibration of a fast-moving car. The car stopped, and George carried me into the back seat.

Nearby was a shooting, followed by a powerful burst of glass. A bullet hit the rear windshield of our car, and the impact shattered it.

The tires spun wildly, and the driver muscled his way over to the far-right lane, slamming the gas pedal to the floor. The man sitting in the passenger seat opened the window, and a few seconds later, I heard the bursts of a machine gun. Then the gusts stopped, and the car continued on its path.

I fell into a lethargy of body and soul. I should have been happy that I was free, but I felt empty of all feelings.

After what seemed like an eternity, the car began to decelerate, the driver seemingly in search of something, an elusive address or a hidden road sign. The distinct sound of the tires on the rough, unpaved road hinted at our location in the countryside.

After a few hundred meters, I felt the car make a sharp turn and reach a standstill, and George took her in his arms.

A white house with peeled paint revealed itself in the light of feeble perceptions. A woman with a chubby face and brown hair opened the door for us.

George followed the women into the house and gently

laid me on a bed. He was saying something to me, but I was too exhausted, my body aching from the journey, to understand. I closed my eyes, and for the first time in a long time, I felt at peace.

As soon as I fell asleep, I began to have nightmares. I was moving blindly through a labyrinth of darkness, sweat dripping down my face and my heart beating fast. I heard voices but didn't know where they were coming from. It was cold and dark, and I was so tired that I couldn't move anymore. I let myself fall onto the hard ground and closed my eyes.

After what seemed like an eternity, I heard footsteps getting closer. A beautiful man with sandy hair and deep blue eyes knelt beside me and embraced me. I felt the heat emanating from his body, and with my final strength, I opened my eyes. A woman's shape appeared in my vision, and I felt a hand holding mine.

"Take it easy, child! Stop moving, you'll hurt yourself!"

I stared at the woman who spoke to me, and reality overtook my senseless dream.

"Where am I?" I asked the woman.

"You're in my house. My name is Lina, and I'm George's aunt."

I looked around. Judging by the decoration, the room certainly belonged to a teenager, a boy.

"You are very weak," said Lina. "You've been tortured without pity. You need rest. This will help you sleep," she said as she raised a cup of tea to my mouth.

I drank the hot liquid and fell back to sleep. Several

days went by before I was able to get out of bed.

At first, my physical needs took over: eating and sleeping. A doctor had come a few times to examine me, and I had watched him change the bandages on my slimming body.

While people cared about my physical well-being, the feeling of drifting without a rudder took hold of my mind. Two weeks later, I finally managed to get up and walk around the house.

Lina suggested that we eat together in the kitchen. Their conversation was minimal as if each respected the other's silence. One night, watching Lina bustle around the stove, I couldn't help but ask.

"Lina, why are you doing this?"

"You mean, why did I welcome you into my home?"

"Yeah. I want to make sure that you made your decision knowing the potential consequences."

"I do, but that will not stop me from helping you."

"Have you thought about your family? The room I live in seems to belong to your grandson. If things went wrong, I would never forgive myself for being the reason that would deprive him of his grandmother."

Lina's eyelids blinked several times quickly.

"This isn't my grandson's room. It was my only son's room."

"It was? Ana asked. You mean he doesn't live here anymore?"

"He's dead. He was only 18 years old when he died."

"Was he sick?"

"No. Securitate agents killed him."

"But ... why?"

"For the same reason that they killed so many young men."

"You want to tell me what happened?"

For a moment, Lina remained silent, lost in her thoughts.

"A few years ago," she began, "my son started coming home late some weekdays. I thought he was dating, that he met a girl. Until the night he came home with a head injury. It was not because he was in love that he was coming home late but rather because he had joined an anti-communist group."

"Who had wounded him?"

"That night, the young people who were part of the group had a meeting, and someone had betrayed them. The Securitate agents had arrived unexpectedly and ambushed them. He had managed to escape only with a head injury, but he could not hide here in the house; that would be the first place the agents would look for him. He had to hide somewhere else."

"They find him before he had the time to hide?"

"No. He kissed us goodbye and took the path to the forest. Four days later, the police rang our doorbell. They brought back his inanimate body. They told us that all enemies of the Communist Party would end up like our son. I'll never forget that day. His body was icy and marked by the blows he had suffered."

"I'm so sorry to hear that. Didn't they accuse the family

of conspiracy?"

"We barely had time to bury our son when they came back to interrogate my husband. He survived only a few months following the torture they put him through. I don't know how I survived."

I was stunned long after Lina had finished speaking. I now understood why she took the risk of welcoming me into her home. She had nothing to lose.

I was struck by a sudden realization, a painful truth I had avoided for far too long. How could I have been so blind, so oblivious to the suffering of others? The weight of my ignorance bore down on me, and I felt a deep sense of shame.

I looked at the raindrops falling on the window, their rhythmic pattern contrasting the chaos outside. Lightning and thunder were crossing the pitch-black sky, illuminating the room in brief, eerie flashes.

A few days earlier, the sky still looked bright blue, a promise of endless summer, on top of the lush greenery. The same landscape was colorless today, and the rain was hitting the house horizontally as if trying to escape the storm. Summer had given way to autumn, and with it, a sense of foreboding had settled over the house.

I looked back at Lina. She appeared frail and vulnerable. Tears were running down her pale and wrinkled cheeks, and a great sorrow was visible in her eyes.

I resisted the desire to take her in my arms and comfort her, knowing perfectly well that nothing and no one could dispel the pain she was feeling.

A terrible rage was building up inside me, a feeling. that had been familiar for some time now. How many innocent and powerless people have gotten lost in this maze of manipulation and lies, consumed by hatred and pain?

CHAPTER 11

Several weeks passed, during which I recovered my physiological and physical strength. My wounds were beginning to heal, and the fatalism that had overwhelmed me gave way to old habits. My training and my survival instinct were pushing me.

I resumed my running routine, crossing the forest to the surrounding hills. I increased the pace and distance daily while decreasing the rest time. Lousy weather and falling temperatures in the area reduced the risk of being seen by passers-by.

Wearing clothes bought by Lina and my hair covered with a cotton scarf, I looked like a peasant. Instinctively, I memorized the narrow and winding roads of the surrounding area.

Lina's house was located near the resort town of

Herculane, which is rich in thermal springs and mountain landscapes. The city's history goes back to the second century. A forest stretched out behind the house, and little traffic disturbed the tranquility of the place except for the bus, which passed twice a day.

Two months after arriving at Lina's, I felt my best today. I walked into the house through the back door and went straight to the bathroom. I looked in the mirror, touching the scars on my skin with her fingertips. For the rest of my life, my scars will force me to remember those moments of torment.

The warm water relaxed my muscles, and during these few minutes, I enjoyed the pleasure of well-being. As I was drying herself, I got wind of a conversation. A visitor?

I put on my bathrobe and headed for the living room. Snippets of the conversation escaped through the open door. I sighed in relief when I recognized George's voice and hurried into the living room. A big smile set on George's face as soon as he saw me.

"Ana! I'm so happy to see you! You look great! I expected you to make some progress, but you look better than ever," he said as he hugged me.

"I'm thrilled you came, George. I was beginning to think you'd forgotten me here."

"I imagine you have a lot to talk about," intervened Lina. "I'll make some coffee."

"Thank you, Auntie! I don't know about Ana, but I need a cup of coffee," said George

A gust struck against the windows, and the rain began

to fall again with such force that it caused a short power outage.

"I don't know how to thank you, George," I said.

"For what?"

"You risked your life for me!"

"I'm sure you would have done the same for me."

"How'd you find me?"

"As I told you, through the Organization, we had connections everywhere. When our contact in Bonn informed us that you had missed the appointment when you were supposed to give him the Mossad's document, we immediately thought that something had not worked out as planned. A few days later, another contact informed us that you were being held captive in Bucharest in a building we call The Cemetery. We find out that you are badly wounded and drugged.

At first, we thought we had no chance of getting you out, and even if we try, you'll be dead by the time we get there. No one came out of that torture building alive. Popescu takes the death row inmates there. Only a tiny group of people knows what is happening inside that building. The prisoners are being watched by a limited number of assassins trained at the highest level, ruthless agents who feel no compassion for the horrors to which the prisoners are subjected.

We were watching the building, hoping for a miracle. When we saw Popescu leave the building, we knew this was the miracle we were waiting for. You know the rest."

"Popescu must be mad!"

"You're right. He hates losing. The day after you disappeared, you've been convicted and sentenced to death for treason whiteout a trial. Your picture's been distributed everywhere. I don't need to tell you how many people are looking for you. You won't be safe anywhere."

"You mean I have to live in hiding and endanger innocent lives! I can't accept that!"

"I expected that reaction from you. That's why I arranged for you to leave the country."

I looked at him, surprised.

"No, that's out of the question! I'm not going anywhere before avenging my family. I have to admit that Popescu does not lack ingenuity, and he thinks I'm completely stuck and that it's only a matter of time before he catches me, but he forgets that I know how he thinks. I will beat him at his own game!"

"You're crazy! You can't fight the Securitate on your own! You need to leave the country while I can still help you!"

I remained silent for a moment. I had never considered this situation.

"What makes you think I want to leave the country?"

"Because you have no choice! Here, they will hunt you like an animal. Even outside the country, your life will be in danger."

Deep down, I knew George was right. I would not be safe anywhere if I was considered the enemy. There was a strong collaboration between international terrorism and the Securitate. Millions of dollars have been deposited in the terrorists' accounts to find and kill the Romanians who had managed to desert and who had important information against the system. Still, the danger was less imminent than inside the country, and that would give me time to make an intelligent plan.

"How long until I have to leave the country?"

"The final date has not yet been established. I didn't know in what physical condition I would find you in."

"I'm ready.

"I can see that, but I need a little more time. I'll have to check with our contact again."

"How long will I have to stay abroad?"

"Not very long. Anyway, you won't be on vacation. Members of the Organization who are active outside the country will need your skills."

"Really? Doing what?"

"Due to the Securitate's orders, no Romanian family living abroad is safe. In addition, hundreds of Romanian children disappear without a trace in the atrocious world of human trafficking. It's time for you to join those who want to change an unjust world. We must try."

"What about the revolution."

"We're almost ready. Every person in this country is ready to fight for freedom."

"I hope you're right. You're very far from a victory. People are sad and afraid. And they are not armed. If the army doesn't take your side, we'll lose."

An ironic smile appeared on George's face.

"You're a desperately sad woman, Ana! I understand

you have no reason not to be; you have suffered far too much. I think you need to get out of this house before you fall into a depression."

Ana envied him for his simple way of seeing things. There was no point in talking. But he was right about one thing: she had to leave this house before she lost her mind."

"How will I cross the border?"

"You'll have to swim across the river Nera, where it joins the Danube. The hardest part will be getting to the crossing point. According to my contact, it takes three days to walk through the mountains."

"That much! According to my geography knowledge, the distance isn't that great!"

"No. But you have to be very careful not to be seen. The people who live in the small villages scattered in these mountains are mostly shepherds. It would be best if you always found out which path they'll take to feed their animals. You have to avoid them at all costs. They know each other, and the Securitate pays them well to denounce every stranger they meet in the mountains.

In that region, it is as challenging to get to the border as it is to cross it. At the crossing point, the river Nera separates in two arms before emptying into the Danube, which makes the downdraft very strong. It can push those who aren't good swimmers into the deep waters of the Danube."

"I'm surprised these shepherds would denounce their fellow citizens!"

"They're sentenced to death for treason if the Securitate

finds out otherwise."

"How come your contact knows the area so well?"

"He was born there and grew up in those mountains."

"Why not choose a place closer, more accessible? I can cross a border without anyone's help."

"I'm not ignoring your extraordinary talents. But it would help if you recognized how the Securitate works when they want to eliminate someone, especially when the head of the Securitate has a special interest in that person. The borders must be overrun with soldiers."

"I think you're exaggerating! Popescu has more important things to orchestrate than to catch me!"

"You're wrong! His job is to make this Securitate machine work perfectly. That's why he recruited the best people. You were part of his elite club. He had the highest regard for your professional talents. He'll never forgive you. He'll do anything to get his revenge."

A gust shook the windows. The silence settled, each one lost in his thoughts.

I thought all those years I had devoted all my being to the Securitate were reduced to nothing. I felt no bitterness, just a vast emptiness, even though circumstances seemed to justify the right direction.

"You look... distraught," said George. "Is something wrong?"

"I'm all right. Before I leave the country, I will need a few items and clothes."

"I've already packed a few things for you."

He got up and left the room to return a few seconds

later with a backpack he dropped in front of me.

"If you need anything else, I'll bring it to you next time."

I opened the bag and pulled out the objects that were piled up in it: two pairs of soft black leather boots, two pairs of black trousers, two pullovers with turtlenecks of the same color, two pairs of socks, a folded black hood, a tiny flashlight, a gun with a silencer, ammunition, a hunting knife, a tranquillizer dart thruster, a small metal box that contained several steel rods to open locks, a pair of binoculars and a compass. At the bottom was a black vest designed to accommodate all the necessary arsenal, including firearms.

Astonished, I assembled the material. George had brought almost everything I needed in anticipation of the many obstacles I would face. I smiled a little and shook my head in disbelief.

"If you want to know, it wasn't me who prepared the bag," said George defiantly. "It was Alex Florescu."

"Alex Florescu!!!"

"Yes. Alex is working with us. He's a double agent. Thanks to him, Mossad obtained the information on arms trafficking. He'll be one of your contacts abroad."

"Lord!" I exhaled. "I would never have thought that of him!"

"I must leave you soon," said George. "In this pouch, you have Austrian shillings, German marks, and the address in Frankfurt where you will be staying when you arrive. Destroy the paper after you memorize the address."

"Does the house belong to the Organization?"

"No. The house belongs to Andrei Munteanu and his wife, Elena. They and their son are members of the Organization. You will receive further instructions from their son, Paul. I'll return with the last things you need and the exact border crossing date as soon as possible. In the meantime, you have to be careful not to be seen. As I told you, your picture was posted everywhere, even in small villages."

"I'm still thinking about those shepherds. I find it hard to believe they can denounce their fellow citizens!"

"There is an explanation. Some have adapted to survive by any means; only the result counts. They fear for themselves and their families. They know the consequences they have to face if they are doing otherwise. And even if some people don't report you, regardless of the punishment they will receive, you have to take precautions and always be on your guard. To think otherwise isn't realistic.

"I understand."

"I hope so. I have to go now."

He hugged me and walked to the door but stopped like he was too indecisive to live. I wondered if he'd forgotten something. As I was about to ask him the question, George turned around. He looked troubled, and the words came out with difficulty.

"Ana, I just want you to know that you hold a big place in my heart…"

Then he left the house, and two minutes later, I heard his car driving away from the house.

CHAPTER 12

The days that followed were gloomy. An opaque fog shrouded the house, and you couldn't see further than twenty meters away. Dressed as a countrywoman, I continued running on the roads near the house, trying to focus on my physical fitness.

A week had passed without any news from George. My wounds were completely healed, and my body had regained all its strength.

Today, I stayed outside longer than usual. Dusk had fallen when I went down the steep hill that led to Lina's house. The fog was stagnating on the roads, and as I passed a strip of trees, I noticed a countryman walking directly toward me. It was too late to hide. Our eyes met, and I saw his disbelief.

George's words came to mind; *your photo has been*

distributed to police stations nationwide and posted for the entire population in every town and village. I don't need to tell you how many people are looking for you. You won't be safe anywhere.

The countryman seemed nailed in place and looked at me without saying anything.

He recognized me, I thought. My instinct took over. I leaped forward and was preparing to hit the man's body when I saw the fear in his eyes. His face was frozen, and his whole body started shaking. I came to a standstill, realizing that I was ready to hurt an innocent stranger to save my skin.

I put my hand on the man's shoulder quickly and affectionately.

"You scared me," I said, trying to explain my first reaction.

"You scared me too!" answered the old man. "I didn't expect to see anyone in this bad weather!"

He was perfectly cordial while he observed me with suspicion.

"I'm used to training no matter how bad the weather is," I told him. "I intend to register to participate in the Olympics."

"But... you're not from around here; I don't know you. Are you visiting someone?"

My brain rapidly calculated my chances of getting out of that encounter without risking Lina's life. All it took was a single word spoken by this countryman to the Securitate to impose the most severe sanctions on Lina. I had to draw the man's attention in another direction.

"I live in the town of Herculane," I said. "This was my first time going in this direction, and I got lost in the forest."

"You must have a lot of ambition; the city of Herculane is very far from here," answered the countryman with an apprehensive look."

"Yeah, the city's far away, so I must go now. Stay safe."

Without giving him a chance to reply, I disappeared through the trees, going in the opposite direction of Lina's house. I knew the area's layout, and the fog was on my side.

All of my spy instincts screamed danger. I couldn't wait for George's return. If this countryman decided to denounce me, the area would be swarming with Securitate agents in an instant. I had to leave Lina's house as soon as that night, the threat of capture hanging over me like a dark cloud.

I stopped for a moment to check directions. Ten minutes later, I rushed to the rear of Lina's house and peered through a kitchen window, standing slightly back so as not to be seen from the inside. Lina was in the kitchen cooking.

Pulling back from the window, I approached the door and listened briefly. Everything was quiet, and there was no danger. At least, not for now. But I can't take chances. I must leave as soon as possible, but before I have to bring Lina up to speed.

I opened the door and headed towards the kitchen. The kitchen was warm and comfortable, and appealing smells reached my nose. That's when I realized she was starving.

At that moment, Lina looked up and let out an exclamation.

"Oh, My God, Ana! You're soaking wet! You need to take a hot shower before you get sick!"

My eyes filled with tears. Lina's presence was like a ray of sunshine in this muddy, dark world. During my few weeks here, Lina treated me like her own child. Unfortunately, I had no choice but to leave, my heart heavy with the weight of my decision.

I took the shower before telling Lina I had to leave. The warm water touched my body like a caress, but I could not relax. I was on high alert, and thoughts were rushing through my head. I couldn't predict the countryman's reaction. The only solution was to prepare for the worst.

I got dressed and returned to the kitchen, where Lina was waiting for me with the supper. In a few words, I explained to her the unexpected encounter in the forest and the need to leave the house as soon as possible.

Lina tried to convince me to stay until George found another hiding place for me. She had no idea that I was preparing myself to cross the border, and I had no intention of telling her. It was safer for her not to know.

"Where will you go in the middle of the night?" Lina worried.

"Don't worry about me. I have friends in the town of Herculane," I improvised. "I'll manage."

I kissed Lina tenderly and left the kitchen. Time seemed to have stopped while I took one last look at the room.

Despite the adrenaline flooding my body, I didn't move for a few seconds. Then, the feeling of having nowhere to call home faded, and reality settled, cold and implacable.

I glanced out through the window. The rain had ceased, but every moment longer I waited, I was endangering Lina's life. I swiftly put on the leather boots and the black vest, checked the weapon clip, and secured the bag to my back, my movements a blur of urgency.

After a brief hesitation, I crossed the yard entirely in the dark. The air was cold and damp. I looked around to make sure nothing moved. Then I unzipped my backpack, pulled out the black hood and put it over my head.

At night, my completely black attire will make me almost invisible. I went to the left, toward the town of Herculane. I needed a map of the area and food until I reached the border. I walked along the road with my ears open. The only noise I could hear was that of my footsteps despite the thick rubber boots.

Soon, my movements became automatic, and the anguish began to dissipate. I thought maybe I was safe. Perhaps the countryman didn't recognize me.

Off in the distance, there was a low growl of thunder. I had been walking for a long time without slowing down. I stopped to catch my breath, and then I saw the first lights of the city. Continuing at this current pace, I could be in the town in about twenty minutes. Suddenly, out of nowhere, engine noises resounded in the silence of the night.

I crouch, peering through the fog in the darkness, my eyes perceiving beams of headlights between the trees. I bent forward with my body close to the ground, looking at the beams of the headlights almost at my height.

Four SUVs roared toward the village. Only the Securitate had such strong cars; the hunt had started. Fear gripped me, my heart racing. I had to move quickly because they would soon be everywhere.

I went in long treads along the trees. The reflexes acquired during my long years of training took control. I pulled out my weapon, equipped with a silencer, and put it in my belt. I had to get off the road. I entered the woods, my feet sinking into a carpet of pine needles and tree leaves that had dropped in the early fall. My feet were constantly slipping, and my muscles began to tire.

The sound of an engine on the road indicated they were not far away. The four SUVs had probably separated to cover the route between the town and the village.

I felt my legs shaking from forcing myself to walk on the slippery ground, but that was the least of my worries. I would only stop once I reached the town of Herculane. Suddenly, I heard a whistle, and a projectile struck the tree before me. I looked at the white mark left by the lead. The bullet had missed by a few inches.

Instinctively, I resumed my course at an irregular speed by changing direction frequently. It was the only way to escape the gunfire. Two more bullets had just gone into the wood. The silent shooting continued, and deadly projectiles continued to sink into the trees around her.

I threw myself to the ground behind a tree. There were at least two shooters, considering the time interval of the shots. I looked around without making a move. The darkness of the night surrounded me, and the silence had set in.

I thought the shots were too accurate. They are indeed equipped with scopes. The fact that they were using snipers proved that the Securitate did not want to attract the attention of citizens who lived nearby. Guns without silencers would have made a hell of a noise in the silence of the night.

The rain had started again and turned into a violent rainstorm, hammering the leaves of the trees. Luck was on my side. The rain would help cover the noises I would make as I moved. I kept going full speed for quite some time, telling myself I would make it.

I heard a noise on my right, and I stood still. About ten meters in front of me, I saw a shadow, a dark mass barely visible. With my left hand, I opened my bag and pulled out the night vision goggles. There were two of them. One of them had a radio transmitter in his right hand.

I knew they're calling for backup by radio. The one thing I had going for me was that the storm had erased my tracks. There was no way they'd be able to track me. They'd have to send men in every single direction. I knew what I had to do.

I gauged the distance, hoping the backup would arrive late. Minutes passed, and I felt my muscles rebelling because of my uncomfortable position, but I remained focused on both agents.

Eventually, one of them began to drift away. Slowly, I

pulled out the weapon, pointed in the direction of the agent left and fired. I heard a dull whistle, and the unconscious body slipped quietly to the ground.

Moving quickly, I lifted the agent's body, pressed it against the tree trunk, and then positioned his weapon as if it were aiming. At first glance, the trick was likely to work. I hoped to be far enough when they found out the truth.

Stay calm, I repeated in my mind. *Almost there.*

But as I said those last two words to myself, I knew it was a lie. I wasn't almost there. I was far from it.

I knew I had to leave this forest immediately and get back on the road. The other agents would arrive by car and rush towards the forest. If I could get to the road before them, I'd have a chance to escape.

I moved slowly, silently, peering into the darkness through the rain. I began to run when I considered that I was far from the second sniper. The forest was becoming less dense. I was close. Now I had to wait for the SUV's. I lay on her stomach against the ground.

The wait was short. Shaded lights appeared among the trees, followed by engine noise. They were all coming at the same time. I was lucky again. The road would be evident if they all looked for me in the forest. My entire strategy depended on the darkness.

I heard a car door slammed. They were close.

I didn't know if the agents had been ordered to fire at close range, no matter how loud their weapons would sound. Weapons with overpowering eyeglasses have a reduced field of view, and, in the current situation, they need to move around in the forest.

I calculated the position of the SUV that had stopped furthest towards the city, considering the noise's reverberation in nature. I run in that direction, parallel to the road.

Now, the whole team was after me. It was about getting out of their vision zone before it was too late. The earth was slippery and wet under my boots. Concentrating on clearing my mind, I stepped in an imaginary straight line like a robot.

Remain in control of yourself under any circumstances. Repeated so many times during my training by the Securitate, those words resounded under my skull. A slight shiver ran through my spine, and the image of my former Superior popped into my head for a few seconds.

A loud explosion rang out somewhere in the forest. I stopped running and stuck to a tree trunk. I had her answer; as long as it justified its deployment, the intrusion of violence in this haven of peace was the Securitate's last concern. Another shot sounded even further than the first. With relief, I moved smoothly between the trees towards the city.

As I neared the city, a wire fence blocked my path. I desperately sought a breach but gave up after a few seconds. I couldn't risk getting over the fence and exposing myself to sight. I had no choice but to get back on the road.

For several moments, I stood and listened. There was silence. But I knew it was only a short intermission. Popescu's men would follow in my footsteps, regroup and hunt me down.

My eyes searched in the night, discerning contours and shapes. The road was close by. I advanced almost in slow motion, my heart beating in my temples. I spotted the outline of an SUV on the road and froze on the spot. An automatic weapon snapped, and the ground shook under my feet. A bullet brushed my head so close that I felt the projectile's breath on my face. The shooter knew precisely where I was.

I fell to the ground, wondering how they found me so fast.

I waited for a long time without moving. No sound reached my ears, no sign of pursuit. The moment I changed position slightly, the automatic weapon snapped again, the burning powder licking my temple.

Following the noise of the bullets, I fired in the direction of the shooter. I heard a groan and the sound of a weapon clattering to the ground.

I lay on the damp ground without moving. I waited for any return fire, and when none came, I began to move again, rolling behind a tree. Nothing happened. I would have wanted to wait a few more minutes to verify that there was no other shooter who had located me, but I feared that by extending the wait, I would give the other pursuers a chance to get closer. The sound of the automatic weapon had undoubtedly caught their attention.

I stood up and shook myself to revive my circulation. Hidden by the trees, I moved towards the SUV the agents left on the road while watching for shapes and noises. The

SUV was now a few meters away. Around me, silence and stillness.

I started having a bad feeling, and my instincts were on high alert. Something wasn't right. I stood still, trying to think, and realized that a second chance was not an option. I should act now.

I ran towards the SUV and threw myself into it. The keys were in the ignition. Once again, my instincts rebelled against the easy way out. Perhaps they had left the car with the intention that I would try to get to it. But there was no other choice. Like it or not, their vehicle was my best option.

Undoubtedly, all my possible escape routes were covered by roadblocks at strategic points. But, my ability to adjust to the facts on the ground made me an exceptional operative. No matter what happened, I would adapt and overcome.

Taking a deep breath, I pulled the handbrake and made contact. The sound of the engine tore through the night. I had been driving for a few minutes when I heard the sound of an engine nearby. I accelerated suddenly, then pulled the foot off the pedal and let the vehicle run free. The speed change and the other vehicle's acceleration resumption confirmed that the agents were getting close.

I was sure now that the agents chasing me had left the keys in the ignition with intent, hoping I would fall for it. And I did.

I was approaching a turn. I pressed the brake pedal slowly and stopped the car in the middle of the turn with the hand brake, the engine still running. Afterwards, I exited the SUV and ran until I reached the forest.

Once there, I waited, motionless, hoping my plan would work. The vehicle chasing the SUV I was supposed to be in approached the turn. Its speed was so high that the driver could not avoid the collision with the SUV. There was a single scream when the two vehicles entered a fatal crash. The explosion was brief but blinding, and a warm smoke filled the air.

A thick mist of burning metal debris floated through the air and slowly descended to the ground. The SUV I had abandoned in the middle of the road was destined to be my coffin. Now, it was the coffin of the pursuer. No one would survive such an impact.

I started waking as an icy calm settled over me. The other pursuers will soon be on my tail. It wouldn't take them long to realize I wasn't among the dead. I didn't have time to finish my thought when I heard the sound of a vehicle getting very close, and the blinding headlights forced me to speed up my pace. Here, I became too easy a target. The ground was flat and devoid of any vegetation.

The engine noise intensified. According to the brightness of the headlights, I had a few seconds left before they would spot me. Completely soaked and covered by the mud that had clung to my clothes, I felt like a hunted animal. My eyes sparkled with fury.

I waited in the middle of the road for the vehicle to set in my sight. One second was enough for me to adjust my shot and plant deadly bullets in the passengers. The car swerved to the left and crashed into a tree.

An unusual silence ensued. I approached the vehicle. Inside, no one escaped my accurate shots. When looking at their inanimate bodies, I did not feel any remorse. I had reached the point of no return.

As a precaution, I fired two bullets into the gas tank and left. Streams of rain fell upon me. A few minutes later, I was reaching the city of Herculane.

CHAPTER 13

I moved quickly and carefully, protected by the darkness of the night. The rain had stopped abruptly, and a cold wind had begun to sweep the city. Water dripped from my mud-stained clothes, and I looked like a fugitive with my backpack on.

I tiptoed through gardens for about half an hour, avoiding the city lights as much as possible. I was looking for a safe place to change. Then, I had to get a map of the area. I needed to figure out the right direction to the border before returning to the forest. I also needed to find a grocery store. I can't make it without food,

I continued to move forward, my eyes peering around. Most of the houses were in the dark. A light suddenly turned on to my left at the end of the garden I was passing through. A door had just opened, and a man and a woman came out having a loud argument.

I came to a standstill. I could not hear what they said, but their anger was apparent. The woman swivelled around and walked away from the house. The man followed her and tried to kiss her. She protested aggressively, pushed him away and began to run. The man started running after her, and they both disappeared around the corner.

Creeping from one tree to another, I approached the house, not losing sight of the couple walking away in the street. They had relationship problems, and I had to take advantage of that before they made up.

In their hasty departure, they had left all the lights on in the house. It was an unexpected opportunity I should take advantage of. I could look for clothes to change into and not use the ones I had in my bag. It would be a long way to the border, and I'd undoubtedly need them later.

Ensuring the coast was clear, I removed my leather boots to avoid leaving traces. Swiftly, I entered the house. With only two wardrobes to search, I quickly found a navy blue sportswear, a pair of socks, and a red cap. The house phone rang as I changed, but it didn't alter my focus.

I looked out the window. The street was silent and deserted. I stepped away from the window and entered the bathroom. After cleaning my boots, I removed any trace that might have given away my presence in the house. Before the young woman noticed her missing clothes, I would be far from the city.

Back outside, I observed the deserted city. For now, the only signs of life came from the lit windows of the house I had just left. To find what I needed, I had to go downtown, where usually there are food and convenience stores. I would have preferred a secluded and quiet area, but I risked wasting too much time not knowing the city.

I steadfastly navigated the alleys that led to the city center. At this late hour, the streets were deserted, and the few souls I crossed paths with paid no heed to my purpose.

A bookshop window materialized in my line of sight, its glass reflecting the dim streetlights. In the center of the window, a region map was displayed, its intricate details beckoning to me.

I circled the building, my footsteps echoing in the deserted alley, until I reached a dead end. A weathered wooden door, the entrance to the bookstore, stood before me.

I scanned around with my eyes and approached the door. The lock was as old as the building. The wood all around was covered in rust dripping from the metal, proof that this door had not been open for a long time. The lock was easy to pick, but the sound it would make when opened would be awful.

Returning to the corner, I cast a cautious glance in both directions. No one would expect a robbery at a bookstore, but I couldn't discount the possibility of late-returning neighbors. The street was eerily quiet, and I proceeded with utmost caution, fully aware of the potential risks.

Reassured, I returned to the dead end and pulled out the metal pins designed to pick the locks. I chose a steel rod, pushed the curved back into the keyhole and turned it slowly to feel the vibrations of the metal.

Blocked by the rust accumulated over time, the lock did not want to give way easily. I pulled out a second rod and inserted it into the keyhole, trying to release the opening mechanism. As I held my breath, I pulled the door firmly towards me. After several tests, I heard a screech of rubbing metal, and the door opened.

With a sigh of relief, I stepped inside, careful not to disturb anything in my path. The tension of the lock-picking was finally behind me, and I could now focus on finding a map identical to the one exposed on the window.

The rays of light from the window pointed me in the right direction. I found several maps of the area stacked on the cash register counter. I sat behind a row of books, hidden from possible night passers-by, pulled out my tiny flashlight and unfolded the map.

I focused on the path's topographical details, leading me to the border. George was right; I would have to walk for three days inside the country, crossing many checkpoints. Even if someone knew the locations of the checkpoints, there was still the danger of running into a shepherd at any time, who would report the presence of unknown people in the area. In addition, climbing mountains for three days requires excellent physical fitness.

I once again concentrated on the open map in front of me. Things were getting complicated. The town of Herculane was about an hour's drive from where I should get into the woods and head for the border. On foot, I will constantly expose myself to gunfire from my pursuers.

I looked at the time: twenty-two thirty. Time was running out. I slipped the map inside my vest and walked out of the building. Heavy clouds were blocking the moon's light. I sneaked up to the edge of the building and inspected the street, which was quiet, except for a few passers-by who were in a hurry and two cars that were driving down the road. Everything seemed normal, and yet, something was bothering me. Something wasn't in balance, as my trainer used to say.

Suddenly, a car's headlights came out of a nearby garage and swept across the street. Surprised, I squatted along the wall of the building. I had just seen what I couldn't see before: an SUV was parked in the dark across the street. It was a powerful car that only members of the Securitate could possess in a country where the vehicle was considered the most incredible luxury. From behind the wheel, a strong man was watching the street.

The proximity of my pursuers was shocking. Had I begun to lose my clear-sightedness? Yet, I never allowed myself to underestimate the capabilities or determination of my enemies. I have to decide what my next move should be.

Do what you must do. To survive, you must win. If you fail, you're dead. This mindset was drilled into my head during my training. Everything is about the state of mind and how you perceive the situation.

I relaxed my muscles. I knew the methods of my pursuers, the coldness with which they could implant a bullet into human flesh. But I will not be trounced. Their proximity was only a slight advantage.

The slamming of the SUV door grabbed my attention. The man sitting behind the steering wheel climbed out of the car. He took a long, slow glance around his immediate area before he looped around the back of the building and began to climb the emergency staircase.

He was carrying a bag used to accommodate a long-range rifle. He's a sniper, I thought. They're positioning snipers across the city, waiting to spot me. I need to move fast before he settles on the roof. I returned to the dead end, climbed over the fence and jumped the short distance to the house next door.

I did the same for the next two houses, and a few minutes later, I made my way to the edge of the building where the sniper was. The SUV was only a few meters away. I felt the tobacco smoke reaching my nose. The sniper wasn't alone; there was someone else in the car he left.

I approached the service stairs of the building and began to climb up. When I was only a few meters away from the roof, I slowed down my pace and, inch by inch, I reached the edge of the roof.

I took a quick look over the roof. The terracotta tiles that covered it were not favoring me. I was in danger of exposing myself, the first step I took. But I had the advantage that the sniper wasn't expecting company. Plus, he had to be focused on loading his rifle.

I tried to distinguish a shadow among the roof ledges, but it was too dark. I grabbed my weapon, squinted my eyes, and found a more comfortable position until the sniper revealed himself.

It wasn't long. Cleared by the clouds, the moon's silvery reflection lit up the roof, allowing me to spot the sniper positioned against the chimney. I raised her weapon, aimed at the sniper's head and fired. The sniper's head rolled back, and he stood still, spread out on his back. He was still holding the gun.

Slowly, always on the alert, I went down the back stairs of the building. I reached the ground and prepared to approach the Securitate's SUV when I saw the other agent a few meters before me. He had gotten out of the car and looked at me with dismay. But his dismay lasted only a second. The next second, he drew his weapon and prepared to fire.

Like a predator attacking her prey, I dived forward, my forearm sinking into the carotid artery of the man. With a sudden movement, I cracked my opponent's neck with such force that he died instantly.

I let the lifeless body slide onto the ground. I searched him and removed his pistol, the sharp knife like a razor and the small revolver inserted in a holster attached to his ankle. In one of his pockets, I found the keys to the SUV.

I glanced around the area, wondering where the other Securitate's SUV was. I counted four when I left the village. I had destroyed two of them, but there must be one left. Certainly, Popescu had been informed, and he will send more agents after me. I had to flee before they arrived.

I reached the SUV and slipped behind the wheel. The headlights suddenly pierced the darkness of the street, and

I felt the mighty engine roar under the hood. Every second that passed brought me a little more relief.

The road was deserted. Too deserted. As if the traffic had suddenly stopped. Deserted roads always made me nervous. I'd been ambushed several times before, and the scene had always looked the same. People who are hunted have a highly developed prey drive. They could sense the presence of those chasing them long before they could see them.

They must have blocked the road somewhere. I should have known better. They will never let me out alive. I slowed down and began to analyze the road carefully when, suddenly, the sound of an engine approaching at full speed whistled in my ears. The driver had to have his foot on the floor.

The man who sought to control my destiny had given exact orders. This scumbag, willing to do anything to get what he wanted, was very determined. But I was no less. I grabbed my gun from my vest and held it between my knees. An acute sound reached my eardrums: a train. I must have been close to a train station. Another way to escape popped into my head.

Don't be too confident, my mind shouted.

A few moments later, I was frustrated when I saw the passengers leaving the station. Calmly, they headed towards a bus, from which smoke escaped through the engine's two rear grilles. I had to slow down, or I was going to run over an innocent person.

My hesitation gave the car following me the time to

get closer. The driver accelerated again, swung the wheel to pass me, and the two SUVs were now parallel. Several blasts followed one another, bullets smashed through the windows, and I saw the two dark circles of the guns pointed at her.

I grabbed my gun and pulled the trigger twice; two of my pursuers were dead. Still alive, the driver pressed on the accelerator and arrived at the height of the bus parked in front of the station. A second SUV arrived in a whirlwind and parked in front of the station with a loud screeching of brakes. Several shots followed, and I had to make the car drift left to right to avoid being shot.

The crowd was hysterical. Panic-stricken, men and women were screaming and running in all directions. Others threw themselves to the ground, covered their heads with their hands, or climbed the few steps of the train station to rush into the building.

I aimed at the back window of the SUV and fired. A hail of bullets was the answer. I lost control of the vehicle, slid off the road, and crashed the car's hood into a bush. I slipped across the seat in the direction opposite the road and let myself roll on the grass. I crawled, hoping to escape among the bushes lining the railroad tracks.

It was very dark, and the pursuers were shooting blindly into the bushes. I needed to find a diversion to escape; otherwise, they would capture me.

I lay flat against the ground and remained motionless. Several shadows broke away from the crowd and rushed to the bushes. I noticed the weapons in their hands. I grabbed my pistol and pointed it toward the shadow closest to the crowd. The shot emitted a muffled bang, and the shadow collapsed with a groan.

I moved as I pulled the trigger and passed on the other side of the track. People ran around without clear direction, not understanding what was happening or where the danger was coming from.

Taking advantage of the agitation, I ran like I had never run before, feeling the veins in my neck swell up.

A gust of wind from the mountains refreshed my face and sweaty body. The sound of bullets and panicking people began to fade in the distance.

Arriving at the forest's edge, I hid among the trees, pushing through the branches aggressively, gasping for air. I could no longer see or hear anything but the wind blowing through the leaves.

I felt like I was back in childhood, moving forward without thinking, relying solely on my instincts. The wind had chased the clouds away, and the moon intermittently illuminated the forest. My muscles began to tire, but I kept the same rhythm. If I slowed down, I would miss my only chance of escape.

Suddenly, I felt a whiff of anguish and heard branches crackling under the weight of heavy soles. I crept behind the trunk of a tree, holding my breath. According to the sound, my pursuer should soon pass close to the tree I hid behind. I crouched to the ground and listened intently to the sound of footsteps. The pursuer was alone.

I quickly analyzed the situation; I had to eliminate

him quietly. Otherwise, the others would be on his heels quickly.

The pursuer was approaching. He was now a few meters away from me. He carried an automatic weapon in his hands. As if he sensed something was off, he slowed down and looked around suspiciously.

I had no more doubts. Popescu had sent his best men, extremely skillful criminal brutes who could sense their prey like hunting dogs. I followed his movements, my body tense like a bow.

The call of a night bird, followed by the sound of it flying by, attracted the attention of my pursuer.

I leaped, my left hand covering his mouth while my right hand twisted his neck in a precise and quick gesture. He was dead before he hit the ground.

With an unfazed face, I laid the inanimate body in a thick bush. Then I grabbed his gun and continued on my way. I had to get as far away as possible before they brought the dogs.

I took out the map and, in the light of the flashlight, studied the best paths to follow. If my calculations were correct, I was close to a stream that ran through the forest. I used this chance to delay my pursuers as much as possible. Dogs would lose track of me in the water.

I advanced as fast as the moon's light allowed me, almost tripping over roots, my body and face whipped by the branches hidden in the dark. I had not travelled more than a kilometer before I heard the sound of the water running down the creek. My resourcefulness was my best weapon.

I walked the remaining few meters as fast as the slippery ground allowed me to and let myself slide into the stream. The water was cold, and my body began to shake. The rain had increased the stream's volume, and I had difficulty moving forward.

My feet grew numb after more than half an hour of walking in the cold water.

Soon, my whole body shook with fatigue. An inner voice crept into my brain and chased away all thought. I was exhausted, but I couldn't afford to stop.

You can do this. Extreme physical effort combined with high risk is what you're trained to be good at despite it pushing you beyond your limits, I told myself.

I concentrated on entering a state of forced serenity. The world no longer existed. My only focus was walking through the creek's water, one step before the other. I had to keep the dogs from finding my trail too fast and buy some time.

The following moments were a whirlwind of light and shadow, but I refused to let my pace falter. At the end of the road, danger loomed, but I clung to the flickering hope.

In some places, the stream was more profound, and the water reached my knees, while in others, the depth did not exceed my ankles.

Moving forward became increasingly excruciating, and every stride caused a painful ringing in my head. I looked at her watch; it was seventeen minutes past two in the morning. I came out of the water and looked around.

I couldn't see any places to take shelter.

I continued walking along the stream. My eyes reflected the cold glow of the moonlight through the clouds.

The forest had become denser, and the ground-level darkness was impenetrable. Even with night vision goggles, moving forward was difficult. But I decided to push myself forward.

I heard the sound of a torrent in the distance. According to the map, the creek was supposed to transition into a waterfall not far from where I was. I could not risk continuing in this darkness and falling into a ravine. I stopped and leaned against the trunk of a tree. For the moment, I was out of danger. My pursuers had yet to see the direction I had taken, and until they didn't have a team with dogs, they would not venture so far into the forest. Besides, it was too dark to follow her path.

Resourceful and determined, I stripped off my sweat-soaked clothes, plunging into the creek to cleanse my weary body. With careful movements, I washed away the day's hardships. When I felt clean enough, I donned fresh clothes and set out to find a dry place to rest.

The wind had stopped blowing, and faint stars shone in the sky. I rolled into a ball on a carpet of leaves, using my backpack as a pillow, and quickly fell asleep. No nightmare came to disturb my deep sleep. The birds chirping and fluttering among the trees began to wake me from stillness. I straightened myself and stretched my joints and my stiff neck.

The tall trees blocked the first signs of light but did not

wholly mask them. I slowly got up and walked towards the stream, moving so discreetly that my approach did not disturb the birds. I splashed water on my face and looked around. There was no time to waste.

I put my backpack over my shoulders and quickly moved away from where I had spent the night. Staying close to the stream so that the sound of my movement did not carry too far, I slipped with ease and suppleness between the bushes.

The world around me buzzed with a thousand sounds: water, insects, birds, and all the invisible little creatures. It was a world where everything was alive, lush, and green.

The stream suddenly turned west, and the water fell loudly. A draft of humid air came up from the waterfall that went out, rumbling from a small gorge in the heights and running into the creek. A landscape of large blocks of stone and abrupt hills replaced the forest.

An hour later, I found myself on top of a ridge and turned my gaze to the blue mist of the mountains, which stretched as far as the eye could see, with their peaks rising above the wooden masses. It was going to be a hot day, and the first rays of the sun were already heating my sore body. Continuing through the rocks, I entered a deep ravine leading into a dark canyon.

Out of instinct, I entered a narrow passage intersecting the canyon wall. I occasionally stopped all other movements to focus on my sense of hearing. Once sure there was no other sound than the one of the forest, I continued my journey, choosing the challenging path through the rocks where my tracks would be more difficult to detect.

After progressing a few hundred meters, the passage made a sharp turn and came to a dead end. In front of me, an insurmountable wall of rocks stopped me in my tracks. I had little choice: climb the high rock masses or return to look for a more accessible path.

After analyzing the situation and the risks involved, I decided to climb the rock mass, an option unlikely to be used by my pursuers. I began climbing the rocky mass, bending to avoid sliding on the rounded surface. The way grew steeper, and I could feel my heart hammering in my chest. One mistake would send me plummeting off the path, down into the passage.

When it seemed the way couldn't get steeper, I arrived at the top of the rocks and let myself fall forward.

I was alert but relaxed when I sensed someone's presence. I stood up and took a slow glance around the area. I may have seen something move in my field of vision. It was only visible briefly, disappearing the next, but I wanted to avoid taking any chances of being spotted. Another movement in the tall grass and a sheep followed by another appeared before my eyes. A few moments later, I could hear an irritated voice nearby, addressing a person I couldn't see.

"Costel, where are you hidden?"

"Here, Dad," answered another voice, followed by the appearance of a young boy playing with a dog. He threw a stick at him, and the dog caught it in his mouth.

"You must move the sheep. Otherwise, they will fall

into the ravine," the father said in a tone of reproach mixed with affection.

I jumped when I saw the dog. But before the animal had time to get close to where I was, the boy threw a second stick, resourcefully distracting the dog away from me. Then, he let out various high-pitched screams while running to keep the sheep away from the ravine. The dog remained glued by his side.

I sighed with relief. I remained motionless, waiting for the shepherds to leave. The only path left for me was a steep, rocky slope. I have to take advantage of all the shadows to avoid being seen by the shepherds. Without wasting any time, I pushed towards the rocky slope, my determination unwavering. I eventually developed a rhythm. Kilometer after kilometer fell away behind me. But the border was a long way off.

It was a long and challenging road, forcing me to climb almost vertically the mountain that rose as far as the eye could see above me. The sun's rays burned my skin, and my body was soaked in sweat. Contrasting with the rough rock of the slope, a luminous greenery awaited me at the top of the mountain. I discerned the light reflecting off a stream and rushed towards it. Kneeling at the shore, I satisfied my thirst with the fresh and pure water of the mountain. Drops of water splashed on my face, and frightened fish swarmed at my approach.

I turned my ear to detect any suspicious noise that might indicate danger, but I only noticed the rustle of the creek itself.

I looked for a place to get the best view of the path to follow. Under my feet, the ground was hard and compact. With the map in one hand and the binoculars in the other, I traced an imaginary path that I should follow, marked by the peaks of the mountains to cross. My plan was simple: stay out of sight and as far away from civilization as possible.

CHAPTER 14

George stood in front of the big map hanging on the wall of his office. His eyes ran along the road that Ana was travelling, the road to freedom.

This morning, he had received confirmation that the men chasing her had received an order to return immediately to Bucharest following a series of riots and protests across the country against the re-election of the regime and its president, Nicolae Ceausescu.

The elections were scheduled for 26 November, and every effort must be made to ensure his re-election. The tension was palpable, as Securitate's role was to use varied and effective strategies to suppress dissidents.

Popescu had no choice. For the time being, he had to forget his vengeance and concentrate on ensuring the security and the re-election of a regime that had made him rich and powerful.

He needed all his men sent on smaller missions, including those sent to capture Ana. George, feeling a wave of relief, sat at his desk. From then on, he could focus on the Organization and its members, setting up the next move they have to make to achieve its goal, fully aware of the weight of their decision.

CHAPTER 15

Bathed in the dimming light of the evening, I moved forward with determination in my steps, sweeping the forest with my eyes. I had not stopped walking all day, fearing to hear the search dogs barking at every moment. But the forest remained silent and deserted, and I had covered almost half the way to the border. Soon, the darkness would follow the dusk, and I have to find a place to spend the night. A refuge from which I could observe the surroundings and leave easily and quickly without being seen would be perfect.

I searched through my memories and remembered the caves I used to play in as a child. If there were mountains, there were caves.

An indigo veil reflecting off the sunset covered the forest, forcing me to slow down. I took out my binoculars and studied the terrain to determine the direction to take. Suddenly, two eyes staring at me through the foliage of a shrub appeared in my field of vision. They were so close that a shiver struck me. The next second, they were gone, and I heard quick footsteps. Somebody spotted me. Instinctively, I leaped toward the direction I saw the person watching me. The chase dragged on. The person I was chasing slipped among the trees with the agility of an animal.

I began running as fast as the dim light that preceded the sunset allowed me to focus on one thing: moving as quickly as possible and catching up to this person. The wind brought the sound of a large stone failing, and the steps stopped.

I moved slowly in the direction I had heard the stone falling. I had barely walked a few meters and saw a small shadow before me: a gypsy boy. Like a spider, the boy was trying to climb the steep pile of rocks. Alerted by my footsteps, he backed into the rocky wall and looked at me anxiously. He was cornered.

At first, I didn't know whether to laugh or feel guilty for scaring the boy. I moved one step closer to him when I saw the ground crack. A strip of land collapsed, and the boy remained suspended above the void, his hands trying to hold on to the rough surface. I threw herself forward without wasting a second, grabbed him by the shoulders and set him on the ground.

"Please, don't hurt me, said the boy as he subtly tried to take a few steps away."

His tiny body had begun to tremble, and he looked at me with his eyes wide open and a terrified expression.

"I'm sorry I scared you! I have no intention of hurting you," I tried to reassure him."

I didn't understand why he was so afraid. I remembered gypsy children being braver than this one.

"What's your name?" I asked in a gentle voice.

"Purdel," answered the boy, his eyes studying me.

"You know, Purdel, when I was your age, I knew a few gypsy children. They taught me how to follow traces of wild animals in the forest. They were my friends."

"Then why did you come after me?"

"Because I thought you were someone else."

"But...you are not from here! There are only shepherds who live in this region."

I remained motionless for a while, absorbing his words. As it set behind the horizon, the sun gave way to a calm wind that made me shiver. But was it the wind or Purdel's words that gave me the chill?

"Where are the others?" I asked.

"Not too far. We were on the road when one of our wagons broke. The men went to the nearest village to repair it. The women and children stayed to prepare a shelter for the night."

As Purdel spoke, the wind changed direction, and I smelled of grilled meat. I didn't feel hungry, but my body needed food to continue on my way. There was no point in hiding now that Purdel had seen me. I would have time to invent a story to justify my presence here. According to my calculations, I had estimated I would cross the border the following evening, but I needed to refuel to keep up with the pace of my journey.

"Purdel, take me to your shelter."

He looked at me with panicked eyes.

"Purdel, didn't you hear what I said?"

"I'll only take you there if you promise you won't hurt them."

"I have no intention of hurting them! Why do you think that?"

"Because you have a gun. And you don't look like a hunter."

I was amazed at Purdel's insight. I had to do things differently with him.

"I could have hurt you, and I didn't," I said. "I haven't eaten since last night and am very hungry. Do you want to let me starve to death?"

With a sigh that meant "I have no choice," Purdel beckoned me to follow him.

With quiet steps, I followed Purdel under the cold moonlight. Nothing disturbed our quiet walk in the forest. At times, the moon hid behind the low, full clouds, but its white light was still enough for us to move forward.

After ten minutes of walking, we arrived in front of a small cliff no taller than four meters. At the foot of the cliff, the ground was flat, completely hidden from view by bushes and shrubs. It was the place the gypsies had chosen for their shelter.

I heard angry growls, and dogs ran towards us with

their fangs uncovered. As they approached, their growls turned into aggressive barking. I knew that gypsy dogs were violent animals, able to attack wild animals and human beings.

With my right hand, I pulled out the tranquillizing dart thruster from my backpack and positioned it toward the animals coming closer.

While preparing to shoot, I heard Purdel speaking to the dogs in the Gypsy language. I wasn't surprised to see them running and hopping happily. The familiar voice had reassured them and calmed them down. I put the tranquillizer dart back in my backpack and looked at Purdel, gently pushing back the dogs surrounding him and licking his fingers.

I moved cautiously behind Purdel. About twenty meters in front, I saw six gypsy tents around a massive fire. The Gypsies were sitting on the ground, eating. A song about the sea and distant lands rose in the silence of the night.

A Gypsy woman got up and began swinging her upper body to the rapid rhythm of the melody. The other Gypsies joined her by clapping their hands.

I felt the presence of someone close to me. A shadow distanced itself from behind a tree and moved in my direction. I remained motionless momentarily, looking at the shadow getting closer; my fingers closed around the knife handle I had instinctively pulled out of my pocket.

"Grandma!" The voice of Purdel echoed. "What are you doing here?"

I hid the knife under my jacket and did not move. I knew that it was now too late to leave. In the diffused light emanating from the fire, I looked at the deep, wrinkled face of the old Gypsy who had approached quietly. She signaled Purdel to get closer to her.

"Go and join the others," she told him. "You will not say a word about her presence here, she continued, pointing at me. If they ask where I am, tell them I was tired and went to bed."

"I didn't want to bring her here, Grandma," Purdel tried to explain to her in a panicked voice. "She promised me she wouldn't hurt us; she was just hungry."

"Do as I say," insisted the old Gypsy.

Reassured by his grandmother's words, Purdel walked away towards the fire.

The old Gypsy signaled me to follow her. "I'd better go," I said.

"It won't change much now," said the Gypsy. "I know who you are. I saw your photo posted in the village. I know the Securitate wants you. Don't be afraid; the Securitate members are not our friends."

She started to walk towards the tents, and I followed her. Instead of walking directly into the clearing, where the other people were, the Gypsy made a detour and stopped in front of the sixth tent.

After glancing around to ensure nobody was looking in their direction, she slipped inside the tent and motioned me to follow.

The Gypsy walked away and returned a few seconds

later with a burning candle in her hand. After inviting me to sit on the only chair in sight, she disappeared into a corner of the tent, separated from the rest by a hanging goat skin.

I felt the smell of vegetables and lamb meat heating up. Then, the Gypsy laid a bowl of food on a small table, placed the table in front of me, and sat on a small mattress on the floor. Without saying a word, I began to eat under the Gypsy's curious gaze. I realized how hungry I was and did not stop until I had finished all the bowl's contents.

The Gypsy took the empty bowl to the kitchen and returned with a glass of water.

I didn't know what to do: should I leave or try to explain the situation to the Gypsy? The torrent of emotions released throughout the day had drained her.

"Don't torture yourself, child," said the Gypsy. "You can tell me your story. You'll feel better afterwards.

She had spoken softly, and her velvety eyes had a soothing effect on me. Apart from the buzzing insects and the crackling fire, the tent remained silent.

I closed my eyes and opened the door to her memories. I started explaining everything like it was in a dream, recounting everything I remembered about my life. When I had finished, the light of the candle fluttered before it went out, and I heard the stifled voice of the Gypsy.

"A real horror, your story!" she concluded.

A complete silence settled.

"I'll get another candle," said the Gypsy.

She rose and disappeared out of sight. Sitting in the

darkness, I basked in the calming silence. Like waking up after a deep sleep, I had a strange feeling and couldn't understand what had pushed me to reveal my entire life to the Gypsy. It was almost like she had hypnotized me.

I heard muffled steps, and the Gypsy returned with another candle. Impulsively, I got up from my chair. It was time for me to leave.

"I don't know how to thank you," I began, "but I must go now. Me being here can cause you a lot of trouble."

"Sit down, my child, said the Gypsy. I won't let you go in the middle of the night. Your sorrow is now mine. I thought I'd never see you again."

"But... what do you mean? You don't know me!"

"I knew your family," answered the Gypsy without a preamble. "I was there when your family was slaughtered. Your grandfather had hired our musicians to play at the harvest festival. I saw a man take you in his arms and save your life. Many of us had seen it. But we never talked about it.

Your grandfather was very good to us. He was a very generous man. He purchased our horses and had us sing at the various festivals held in the village. After the night of the massacre, we set off for sunnier countries. Over the years, our tribe began to part ways. Today, all that's left of our tribe are the people you saw around the fire and a few men who went to the village."

"What happened?"

"After the regime closed the borders in the communist countries, thanks to their freedom to cross the borders, many gypsies became very rich by making black market. Eager for money, many governments let the gypsies settle in their countries against the will of their people. Only a few, like us, still love the nomadic lifestyle.

"You don't want to live in a house? "

"We could never live lock up in a house. This world is full of so much beauty. We love being surrounded by nature, the heavy and rich scent of forests, the secret shadows of the mountains, the vast flowery plains and the infinite blue sea. Adventure means more to us than stability. We especially love freedom."

The Gypsy went silent, her eyes with an absent look drifting towards a point in her past.

"I, too, love nature," I said. "Sometimes, in my dreams, I cross the prairie on my horse's back. I feel the wind in my hair and take in the smell of wildflowers. I feel happy. And then the smell of flowers is replaced by the smell of blood, the blood shed by my family on the night of the massacre."

"Time is the only real cure for pain, child. Tragedies like the one you experienced are happening all over the world. Give me your hand; I can tell you if you'll find happiness one day."

I extended my hand with a bitter smile, knowing it would never happen. The Gypsy looked at the lines of my hand for a long time, and when she began to speak, her voice was full of tenderness.

"Your pain will never completely go away, but it will be alleviated. You'll learn to live with it. There won't be any big changes shortly, but that will only last for a while. After a very hectic period, you will go far away from these lands to join the man you love. You will have two children and a life full of happiness. But your heart will always be split."

She got up and walked towards the improvised kitchen.

"Now, I'll make you tea to help you sleep. You need rest."

I did not take the Gypsy's prediction seriously. I had no intention of going far away from my country, and there were no men I loved and wanted to join. It was just a Gypsy story.

She returned with a full tea cup, and I drank the contents in a few sips. The liquid warmed my body, and a pleasant sensation spread through my limbs. I stretched out on the mattress and fell asleep right away. I dreamt of lying on a bed in a room I didn't recognize. White lights were flashing in my eyes, and my bruised body was sore. I could hear the squeaking of a door opening, giving way to a tall man with broad shoulders and sandy hair. He approached the bed and took me in his arms, whispering sweet words in my ear. I let myself in the warmth of his body and the strength of his arms and fell into a deep sleep.

CHAPTER 16

Just before dawn, I woke up hearing the sound of footsteps. Instinctively, my hand slipped into my jacket to grab my weapon, but by the rustling of her skirt, I recognized the benevolent Gypsy who had welcomed me. A bit of light penetrated from outside, but the tent was still very dark.

"Good morning, Ana. It's time to go. I'll heat some water for you."

Through my barely open eyelids, I saw the Gypsy crack an egg on the corner of the stove and slide it into the hot grease. The fire crackled and smoked, grilling a piece of meat stuck to the end of a stick.

"You didn't tell me much about my family the other night," I said. "You're the second person I know to have known them alive."

"I can't say I knew them well. The people of the village, including your family, did not mix with the Gypsies. Thanks to our musicians, the people let us set up our tents on the forest's edge close to the village. Once a year, for the harvesting festival, we had the right to participate. People wanted to have fun, and our musicians were the best."

I felt there was something she wasn't telling me, but I didn't insist. The Gypsy handed me a paper bag containing a slice of cheese and bread, which I put in my backpack, thanking her.

A dim light penetrating the tent announced the beginning of the day. I thanked the Gypsy again, took my backpack, and approached the exit. The time on my watch was five-thirty in the morning. For a few seconds, I stood still, listening.

From the exit doorway, the Gypsy signaled everything was in order, and I could go out. I slipped outside and left silently, moving quickly to the edge of the woods. Soon, the noise of my footsteps was covered by the forest noise.

The land was gently sloping down, and the dim light of the early morning still prevailed in the forest as if the sun's rays did not yet have the strength to replace the darkness of the night. Pushing deeper between the trees, I accelerated my step.

For a long time, I heard only the familiar cracks of the branches under my steps. After a few hours, I had to slow down. No path crossed the forest, and I had to move forward by spreading the branches to make my way through, stumbling here and there on rocks. Each slope was a deep ravine that followed tall mountains to climb higher and higher.

I continued relentlessly, stopping to quench my thirst for fresh water flowing in small waterfalls from place to place. Whenever my mind suggested that I stop, if only for a moment to catch my breath, I redoubled my efforts and pressed forward. I tried to convince myself that the agents looking for me would not venture so deep into the forest. And even if they would, there was no way they could track me. My determination was my strongest ally.

Arriving at the top of a mountain devoid of vegetation, I scanned the way toward the border through the binoculars. All I saw were other mountains covered in trees.

It was three forty-seven in the afternoon when I stopped to catch my breath and ate a few bites. The sun was barely visible behind the clouds, and the air was fresh and humid.

I put the rest of the food back in my backpack and walked several kilometers, leaving the tall mountains behind. Now, there were only bare hills left.

If everything went as planned, I should reach the border by dusk. The anticipation of reaching my destination kept me going.

As a precaution, I quickly climbed to the top of the hill and positioned myself behind a rock. For several minutes, I scanned the land with my binoculars. This would be the most challenging part of crossing without being seen. Small villages were scattered all over the hills. I'll have to walk around them.

I removed the map from my backpack and set it on the

ground before me, carefully planning my route.

Using the binoculars, I compared the map with reality, trying to locate where the border was.

Then I took out my compass and fixed it in the direction to follow. Nothing on the map indicated the existence of the villages that I saw through my binoculars. A trap for those who took that route to get to the border. With the help of a small branch, I marked the position of each town by making small holes in the map and estimated the distance between them. I knew it wasn't accurate, but I aimed to target the places where I had to be more careful.

Appeased, I again plunged into the depths of the forest and began to run in the direction indicated on the compass. It was essential to stay consistent and keep the same pace. I quickly realized that it took work. The weakening sunlight and the imposing trees were obstacles in my path, but they couldn't deter my determination.

As I approached the first village, I slowed down my rhythm. My calculations were more precise than I had dared to hope. I strategically moved in the opposite direction to the town, pausing to catch my breath and reorient myself. The clouds, like a tactical ally, almost completely blocked the sunlight.

If I'm lucky, it will rain tonight, I thought.

Except for the forest's whisper, everything was quiet. On the horizon, there was nobody in sight.

I have about an hour left before darkness replaces daylight. By then, I should be close to the border. I have night vision goggles, but I preferred to have an overview with my binoculars. There were still two villages I had to go around, but I wasn't too worried about the people in those villages. At nightfall, they will all return to their homes.

I decided to run the remaining distance. My shoes sank into the soft ground, but I continued making as little noise as possible on the unfamiliar land. I stopped and listened from time to time, but all I could hear was the sound of the forest and my fast heartbeat. The steep slopes slowed me down, robbing me of the time I desperately needed. The light of day will soon be replaced by the darkness of the night. Eventually, the trees became more and more scattered, and my progress dwindled.

Choosing a tall, sturdy tree, I began to climb. The rough bark scraped against my legs as I ascended, the dense foliage providing me with a hidden vantage point.

Peering through the binoculars, I examined every meter of land between me and the border. A few hundred meters away, the forest was replaced by a much sparser one. A rectangular stone building, about ten meters tall, appears in my field of vision. A central column supported a small turret on the roof: the border watchtower. On both sides of the watchtower, the foliage had been completely cleared.

I focused on that area, the dividing line between terror and freedom. Countless people have died here, putting their dream of freedom above their fear of dying. You don't have to be an expert to know that border guards were selected among the most loyal soldiers to the communist regime, soldiers who took pleasure in chasing innocent victims.

On the other side of that area, thick vegetation was contouring the river Nera. The dim light between day and night did not allow me to see beyond the river, but I didn't need to. If I had managed to get to the other side of Nera, I'd have finally completed the objective of crossing the border. That didn't mean I'd be out of danger of being captured.

I didn't move a muscle for a long time, memorizing my surroundings perfectly. The first border guard appeared in my field of vision, a rifle on his shoulder. He strolled and seemed bored. Fifty meters further, his colleague walked by at the same pace. They approached each other, chatted for a few minutes, then turned around and started the same routine.

It all seemed so easy. But if my years as a field agent had taught me anything, things usually got worse before they ever got better.

Through the wind, I could hear a dog's faint barking. I analyzed the surroundings methodically again, trying to see through the darkness, and I started to stroll. There was no indication that Popescu's men were waiting for me at the border. Where were they? Had they gone in the wrong direction, or was the quiet atmosphere at the border just staged?

A drop of rain touched my face, and the sound of thunder shook me. It was an excellent time to get close to the border.

The guards were undoubtedly on their way to the watchtower to get shelter from the rain, and the dogs would follow them. I rushed to my right through the trees, my face and body whacked incessantly by plants and branches. After six hundred meters, I veered to the left and stopped at the forest's edge.

I slipped among the bushes, hunched over and dodging to avoid the clearings as much as possible. The thunder became more frequent, but the rain refused to fall. I reached the edge of the young forest and dropped to my knees. The guards had turned on the spotlight from the watchtower, but the spotlight did not have the strength to reach me. I stood still, waiting.

Suddenly, I saw flashlights approaching, and I fell to the ground. Two border guards pass very close, scanning the surroundings for anything unusual.

Lying on the ground, I didn't move. A whiff of evergreens reached my nose. I stood still for about twenty minutes. A lightning bolt, more potent than the others, lit the sky, and I stealthily saw the two guards running toward the watchtower to shelter themselves from the torrential rain that had just started.

I crawled through the dark until I heard the noise of the Nera River.

I was shivering, and my heart was beating very fast. The dogs could sense my presence, but I needed to catch my breath and regain strength. I also needed to protect the dry clothes I had left.

I slipped my backpack into a plastic bag to protect it from getting wet and fixed it firmly on my back.

Then I stood up and ran to the edge of the river.

Without hesitation, I dived into the water and swam as fast as possible with powerful strokes.

The water was much less agitated than I had imagined. After several strokes, I reached the other edge. I quickly found myself in front of a dense foliage that formed an almost impenetrable wall separating the two courses of the river. Taking out my hunting knife, I made my way through the thick vegetation.

My hands were bleeding profusely but I couldn't stop now. I knew that the pain I was feeling now was nothing compared to what I was going to be feeling in the morning.

I removed my hood and wrapped it around my hand like a glove. With raging force, I continued to use my knife like a machete to break through the branches. Eventually, I made my way through to the other side of the green wall. I was now close to the second course of the river.

The rain continued to fall aggressively. As I moved towards the second course of Nera, I tripped over tree roots and stopped to free my feet embedded underneath. For a moment, I felt like an animal in captivity. All I could hear was the sound of the falling rain and the groaning of the river.

I felt the rage building inside me but ignored it. It was freezing, and I had difficulty keeping my body from shaking. I walked towards the second course of the river and threw myself into the water. I suddenly remembered George's warning: *At this point, the Nera River splits in two before emptying into the Danube, strengthening the downdraft. Be careful.*

He was right. It was a nightmare. The water current was powerful; mud and floating dead threes prevented me from moving forward, and a hard object hit my head.

For a second, I felt that I was losing consciousness. My body became heavier and heavier and wavered from left to right, caught in the whirlwind of the current. In an instant, the water sucked me down into it, and I started kicking and stroking for the surface.

I hit another object with my shoulder, and, in an ultimate survival effort, I clung to it. It was a tree trunk. I knew that if I lost hold, I'd sleep back down and drown.

I had utterly lost track of time while trying to stay on the water's surface. My main concern was to get to shore before my arms and shoulders weakened, something much easier said than done.

Summoning one last burst of strength, I pinned myself against the tree trunk by pushing it toward the stream. Perfectly concentrated, I progressed slowly, using the water current to my advantage. After several tens of meters of drifting, I felt the water current slow down. I was close to shore. Shortly, I felt the ground under my feet. I had made it.

I crawled forward, looking for a place to rest. The rain had stopped as abruptly as it had begun. I rolled on my back and stared at the black sky. A false silence reigned over the border, hiding the proximity of guards ready to shoot the fugitives.

For a moment, I let my thoughts wander about my country, which I had just left, about the people who were locked up inside like in a prison cell. I now understood better the desperation of those who were humiliated and stripped of all rights, then killed at the various country's borders. They took their chances because they had nothing to lose except their unhappy lives.

If you want to survive, you must always remain in control. Feelings are for the weak.

Who said that? It was definitely one of the Securitate members who had to assure my loyalty through intense brainwashing. I didn't want to remember; it wouldn't help right now.

The cold night pierced my body, and I stretched to get my blood circulating. Except for my hands, which I had seriously scraped in the branches, my body responded like a charm. I wanted to change my wet clothes to dry ones; my boots were in poor condition, but I had no choice but to keep them. I still have a pair of boots, a sweater, and a pair of pants, but I also have two more borders to cross.

I walked through the thorny vegetation and reached a country road. There was no sign of life on the horizon, only the wind that had stubbornly pushed the clouds.

After half an hour of walking, I saw large haystacks across the field. They were an excellent place to sleep. I removed part of the hay and slipped inside, masking myself as comfortably as possible.

I felt a soothing warmth and fell asleep right away. However, my sleep was restless, and the slightest sound forced me to open my eyelids briefly.

After a few hours, I emerged from hiding, stretched

out my legs, and looked at my watch. It was half past three in the morning. The air temperature had risen, and the moon had appeared in the sky.

I hurried back to the country road, ready to jump through the greenery at the first sudden sound.

As I turned a corner, I saw the outline of a village. I enter the dark alleys as silently as possible.

Uncovered light bulbs shone weakly over the doors. Only a few stray dogs felt my presence, and their barking could awaken the villagers. The proximity of the border would be the only explanation for my presence, and the police would be on my heels in no time.

I knew that Yugoslavia received one carload of salt for every person arrested and handed over to the Romanian authorities. I couldn't take any chances tonight. I was still too far from my goal and close to my enemies to risk being spotted.

What might have worked in another part of the country was out of the question in this region so close to the border, where the cops were so corrupt it was often impossible to distinguish them from the enemies across the border. Still, the most challenging part was over. She needed to get moving.

Less than twenty meters away, I spotted a moped in the shadow of a hangar. The moped was precisely what I needed to move faster. I heard the engine of a car amplified in the silence. People were beginning to hurry to their place of work, and it would be easier for me to hide in the traffic.

I grabbed the moped's handlebar and returned to the

main street.

The first gleams of the day began to descend from the sky. Large buildings gradually replaced the quiet countryside, and soon, I found myself in the center of a big city. Up ahead was a sign for the Central Station. I applied the turn signal and took the direction of the parking lot. I found a space near the entrance and parked.

People were walking up and down the sidewalks, and there was plenty of car and bus traffic. I was worried that my soiled clothes would attract attention, so I had to get change. In the train stations of big cities, so many people were walking around that it was easy to go unnoticed.

Once inside the train station, I headed straight for the bathroom. In the oval mirror, I noticed my face covered in scratches and irritated eyes.

Women of all ages walked in and out of the bathroom, looking at me with apparent disregard.

I would have given anything for a hot shower and a bed. But those modest luxuries were still days away. I threw the soiled clothes into the trash and left the bathroom. I needed a car.

A crowd of city dwellers had flooded the area, moving in all directions. I headed towards the parking lot, watching every car that passed by.

After half an hour of observation, I saw a man in uniform, an employee of the station, who had parked his car in a private parking space. That's precisely what I was waiting for. He will realize his car was missing at the end of his shift, giving me a lot of time. The man entered the station three minutes later, and I followed him.

I examined the crowd, encouraged by the size of the queues stretching out in front of the registers, and began to walk as fast as possible without really running. Pretending to trip over the floor slabs, I bumped into the man and stole his car keys. I would be close to the Austrian border in a few hours if everything went as planned.

As the car gained speed, I started looking for the exit to the freeway. I drove carefully, following the flow of vehicles.

The sun reflected through the car windows, and I felt a buzzing in my head and pulsations in my temples. A weakness took hold of my legs, and I had to force myself to keep my eyes open. I had not eaten since the day before, and my body was beginning to react.

I stopped the car in the parking lot of the first restaurant on the highway. Inside, there was a smell of tobacco and grilled meat.

The entire restaurant clientele consisted of a few couples and truck drivers. I wasn't likely to be recognized at this distance from the border. In addition, foreign currency was in high demand in Eastern countries, and thanks to George, I was sure the waiters wouldn't look at my dirty clothes when I showed them the German bills.

I was right. Within fifteen minutes, a large plate with meat, fries, salad, and a basket full of fresh bread appeared on my table. Such a heavy meal would make me lazy, but I needed it to regain my strength.

Having cleared my plate, I ordered a coffee, then another. As I left the parking lot, a wave of relief washed over me. I rolled down the window, allowing the chilly air to soothe my face. I made a deliberate choice to drive slowly for the next two hours, contentedly following the line of cars.

It was half past two in the afternoon, and the fuel gauge indicated minimal kilometers left before the gas ran out. The train station employee would finish his shift around four o'clock and notify the police of the car's disappearance. Before long, I would have no choice but to abandon it.

There was a slowdown in the line of cars, and I felt frustrated because I was wasting time. Honks sounded, and a car passed on the service road at full speed. A few meters further, the car drifted and hit the back-right door of a Skoda. The Skoda propelled and, in turn, crashed into another vehicle, blocking the passenger door.

Men rushed out of their cars, trying to help, and I felt that every second seemed to pass excruciatingly slowly.

The police arrived, and I was quick to devise a plan. Spotting a narrow gap between the two cars, I skillfully maneuvered my way through, exceeding the speed limit, and then seamlessly merged with the vehicles on the opposite side of the road. I exited the highway at the first intersection and smoothly transitioned into a residential area.

After about forty minutes, the engine began to struggle. The tank was empty. Undeterred, I left the car halfway down a slope and started walking, blending in with the surroundings. The late afternoon sun, a fiery ball on the horizon, reminded me of the time ticking away.

It was now four o'clock. It would get dark around seven o'clock. I needed to go unnoticed for the next three hours, so I planned to take hidden routes and make all kinds of detours until I approached the border between Yugoslavia and Austria.

At this time, the car I had stolen was undoubtedly the subject of a BOLO, and if they found it, they would quickly surround the area. Caution became essential for every distance I covered.

I went toward the highway and took refuge in the tall grass that lined its sides. The flow of cars was constant. I walked parallel to the road at a distance, allowing me to follow the edge of the light from the headlights.

The shadows of the cars stretched from one side of the highway to the other, making me indiscernible in the dim light of the evening.

After a few kilometers of walking, the road curved, obscuring my perspective. I slowed down and decided to climb the adjacent hill. Once at the top, I lay on my stomach and checked the area through my night-vision goggles.

Less than five hundred meters below, the traffic flow was slowing down. I saw the Austrian flag flapping in the wind at the customs. A black-and-white barrier was supposed to regulate the flow of vehicles. A short building with underpasses on either side of the road added a physical obstacle to a legal obstacle. Strong lights illuminated both sides of the road.

I tightened her boot's laces. The night was very still,

almost too still. Above, the crescent moon was bright, and there was virtually no breeze. There was a specific silence at the borders, where death lurked around like a hungry predator.

From now on, I have to calculate every move. I put on my night vision goggles and strolled towards customs. Cars and trucks filled the road. Soldiers armed with guns and accompanied by dogs were walking in pairs from one vehicle to another. They leaned to the windows to check documents and ask questions. After that, they directed the cars to the customs booths.

For more than an hour, I studied the woody and sloped land which separated me from the Austrian territory. The trend for people who wanted to cross a border illegally was to get as far as possible from customs.

I knew that the area near customs happened to have the least surveillance because the people didn't dare get too close. I also learned that electrical wires or photoelectric cells could not be installed in a wooded area like this because of wildlife. Their passage would set off the alarm all day long. The only real problem was the dogs.

Slowly, I moved forward. Customs were now less than two hundred meters away, slightly to the left.

Suddenly, I froze against a tree, relying on complicit darkness. The dogs were getting agitated. Could they feel my presence so far?

I observed them between the branches. A dark brown Volvo advanced towards a customs cabin, and the dogs began to yap towards the car. Guards approached the vehicle and signaled the occupants to get out. A middle-aged man and a woman descended from it.

The woman was carrying a small crate in her right hand. I could not see what kind of animal was in the crate, but I understood why the dogs were agitated.

In disbelief at my luck, I took advantage of the moment and ran towards the border. I would have to cross the border while the dogs' attention was drawn to the animal in that crate.

The closer I got to the dividing line between the two countries, the harder my heart pounded. With my night vision goggles on, I took one last look at the line separating the two countries, wondering if there was anything I couldn't see that would set off the alarm as I passed. Then I started running, and I did not stop until I reached Austrian soil.

I walked silently through the forest's shadows for two hours, following the highway's lights in the distance.

When I finally felt it was safe to stop, it was almost ten o'clock at night. The night was peaceful and perfectly silent.

Now that the danger had passed and the adrenaline had come down, I felt the fatigue weighing on my body. All I wanted to do was close my eyes. I dropped on a pile of dry leaves and fell into a deep sleep.

CHAPTER 17

I awoke with the first rays of the sun, basking in the serene beauty of the early morning. I took in the silence and solitude for a few minutes and then went to the highway. Many young people travel across Europe hitchhiking. I'll do the same.

The first vehicle to stop was a heavy truck going to the town of Gratz. The trucker, a Turk from Istanbul, kept talking about his country and its architectural wonders. His German was rudimentary, but this did not prevent him from constantly talking. I remained silent for most of the trip.

Once in Gratz, I thanked the truck driver and quickly went to the tram stop. About ten minutes later, I stepped out of the back door of the crowded tram in front of the Bahnhof, the city's central station. I entered the station and proceeded to the ticket office without hesitation, avoiding the passengers exiting the white Mercedes taxis.

In an impeccable Austrian, I bought a ticket to Salzburg. With a warm smile and a polite tone, the cashier handed me the ticket and wished me a good trip. Reassured by the cashier's kindness, I smiled and pocketed the ticket.

Anticipation and excitement bubbled within me as I glanced at the departure sign, signaling an hour to prepare for the next leg of my journey. Before the train set off for Salzburg, my stomach rumbled, a gentle reminder that it had been a while since my last meal.

As I walked, I counted the shillings in my pocket, relieved to find enough for a meal. I settled at an empty table, ordered a black coffee and an apple pie, and let out a sigh of relief.

I was seated on a bunk at the train's rear an hour later. The hustle and bustle around me and the steady sound of the metal wheels on the railroad tracks helped me relax.

Arriving in Salzburg, a city I knew and loved, I felt a wave of comfort wash over me.

A unique combination of scenic Alpine landscape and architectural richness has led to Salzburg's reputation as one of the world's most beautiful cities. A mix of Italian and German cultures, Salzburg has managed to preserve an urban fabric of exceptional richness developed between the Middle Ages and the 19th century. A baroque city that has emerged intact from history, Salzburg is intimately linked to many famous artists and musicians, the most famous of whom is Wolfgang Amadeus Mozart.

The day was beautiful, and the city was crowded with tourists.

Near a cathedral of great architectural richness, I tried to bypass the American tourists who crowded around a guide. Suddenly, an overweight woman slipped on the pavement and sprawled out at my feet. Heads turned, and curious eyes set on me and the woman trying to get up without succeeding. I grabbed her and helped her to her feet.

"You'll have to be more careful," I told her.

"Ah! You're American! "she exclaimed.

There was a pang in my heart, a moment of hesitation. I almost answered: *No, I'm not American. But I can speak your language without an accent. I'm a fugitive. Until a few months ago, I didn't even know my identity. I was trained to be anyone, to blend in seamlessly.*

At that moment, even though, as an agent, I learned never to let emotions take control, I realized that I had allowed myself to tap into an emotion I had been trying to hide for so long: my rage.

I walked away quickly, not taking the time to answer the American and knowing I was rude. Half an hour later, I reached the steep mountain slopes surrounding the city. I have to find the way to the German border. A small signpost appeared on my right, indicating the fork with a road up the hills. The Austrians were big fans of hiking through the mountains; they would not be surprised to see me. I could stay on the beaten track for now.

I walked up and down the hillsides for a long time,

listening to the birds chirping and the leaves rustling. At the top, I stopped, not knowing which way to go.

Using my binoculars, I saw the highway in the distance, towards the west. The border with Germany should be pretty close. I'd better go down the road to avoid getting too close to the demarcation line and encountering German guards.

After navigating the rocky mass, I approached the highway without trouble. Crouched by a log, I observed the cars passing from one country to another. The traffic was light. German customs were in a narrow valley between two wooded hills. Everything seemed calm, but sneaking into German territory required a lot of caution.

I considered my situation; anyone else could surrender to the German authorities and apply for asylum. If I did as anyone else and they found out I was a Securitate agent, I would end up in prison for the rest of my life.

The thought of being imprisoned in a foreign country, away from everything and everyone I knew, sent shivers down my spine. There was no evidence that I was no longer working for the Securitate. My only chance was to cross the border illegally and let George's connections settle my situation with the German authorities.

I stood still for a few minutes, assessing the best route and path. There were only so many options. Soundlessly, I moved through the trees as quickly as I could while continuing to scan the surroundings, expecting at any moment to see a hidden soldier's gun pointed at me.

Slowly and then speeding up, I crossed the stretch

of land separating the two countries. Silence took over until I heard the angry barking of a dog in the distance. I got further into German territory with every step and disappeared among the trees.

Suddenly, my foot slipped, and I landed in a pile of dry leaves. Fear gripped me as I managed to grab hold of something and slow down my fall. Below, the hill was steep, leading into a river.

Clinging to branches, I carefully went down to the river. After cleaning myself, I crossed the river and continued my journey. Only when my legs got tired did I stop to check the time. I had been running for almost two hours. I did it.

Dusk was slowly transitioning into a starry night. I didn't want to sleep another night in the forest. I crossed the distance to the highway, trying to get as far away as possible from customs. I had to hitchhike.

An hour passed, but the cars kept driving by without deigning to stop. While following the curves of the motorway, I arrived at a parking lot.

The smell of food reached my nose. There were two restaurants, a gas station and a motel. I was hungry and needed to get rid of my soiled clothes. I still had some money left, but without ID, I couldn't risk renting a room in the motel. I knew some places in Munich where, when people pay cash, no one asks about their identity. But first, I had to find a way to get to Munich. I'll have to find a way to hitch a ride or even steal a car.

The day had turned to night, and the wind was picking up. Lurking in the motel's shadow, I watched the cars that stopped for gas. I was less interested in small cars. I'd have a better chance of getting to Munich with a cargo truck. At that moment, I saw a vehicle carrying the Zoll sign: the German border patrol stopping in the parking lot of one of the restaurants.

Had they spotted me? Focused on the vehicle's rear lights, I prepared to sprint into the forest I had just left. The patrol officer got out of the car and headed towards the restaurant. He didn't seem to be in a hurry or looking for anyone. After all, it could be a coincidence.

A few minutes later, the patrol officer emerged from the restaurant with two cups in his hands. A wave of relief washed over me, and I felt the tension in my muscles ease.

While the patrol vehicle returned to the highway, a truck stopped beside the gas station. The huge refrigeration unit hanging from the cabin sparkled in the streetlights' reflection. The truck had a Munich license plate.

I quickly made a detour to give the impression that I was leaving the restaurant and approached the driver, who was filling the truck's tank.

"Excuse me, sir. Are you going to Munich?"

The driver raised his head.

"Perhaps," he answers, checking me out from head to toe. His weathered face and rough hands told a story of a life spent on the road. "Why?"

I didn't quite trust the way the driver was eyeing me. I'd heard too many stories about women who hitchhiked. I wasn't scared; I could handle myself, but I didn't want any trouble. I paused for a moment before responding.

"I must be in Munich in the morning; otherwise, I risk losing my job. My friends and I had problems with our car. They're getting it fixed tomorrow. It's the green van you see in the motel parking lot."

The driver turned his head in the direction I pointed. I had noticed earlier that an old green van was parked in front of one of the motel windows.

"I'll pay you for the ride," I continued.

I pulled out a banknote of one hundred marks before his face. The driver revealed a big smile, displaying his tobacco-stained teeth.

"Okay. Deal," he said.

He snatched the money from my hand and shoved it into his pocket, his eyes never leaving mine.

I took the passenger seat and waited for the driver to get behind the wheel. Before starting the engine, the driver turned and looked at me.

"You can rest if you have to work tomorrow. Our warehouse is on Ammerstrasse. Do you live far from there?"

"Yeah, but it's okay. The important thing for me is to get to Munich. Then I'll take a taxi home."

The car engine's warmth enveloped my body during the journey. It felt so good to be still, to be off my feet. I could feel the physical and emotional tension slowly dissipating, allowing me to sink into a soothing nap, a much-needed relief after the days of hiding and survival.

I woke up in a loud screech of tires. We had arrived in Munich.

"There is a cab stand across the street," the driver

showed me.

I expressed my heartfelt thanks to the driver once more before stepping out of the truck. Despite the city's usual odors, the air felt invigorating. A surge of joy filled me as I realized I had overcome all obstacles and was finally free after countless days and nights of hiding and survival.

I crossed the street and got into the first taxi. The driver, who spoke with a strong Arabic accent, showed no reaction when I gave him the address of the neighborhood with the worst reputation in the city.

The night was utterly dark as they drove down streets that became narrower and narrower as they approached the destination. Finally, the driver wheeled around a corner, made another left and stopped in front of a hotel wedged between two dilapidated buildings.

I paid for the ride and entered the lobby, which reeked of cigarettes and cheap perfume. With her tired eyes heavily made up, a prostitute looked at me emotionless.

Pretending not to notice, I paid for my room and disappeared into the poorly lit corridor, feeling a growing sense of discomfort in my surroundings.

I was startled when I looked in the mirror. My face and neck were full of scratches, and my gaze was haggard, with exorbitant eyes in a livid face. My hair, usually so shiny and smooth, was dull and filthy.

I removed my clothes and entered the tiny bathroom. In the hope of getting rid of the filth, I let the water run, but it was freezing. Realizing there was no hot water, I shivered in the cold shower.

I turned off the lights a few minutes later and slipped between the surprisingly clean sheets. I quickly fell asleep. And with sleep came the same dream I'd had so many times; I was lying on a bed in a room I didn't recognize. White lights were flashing in my eyes, and my bruised body was sore. The unease in the dream was palpable, making me wonder what it all meant.

I could hear the squeaking of a door opening, giving way to a tall man with broad shoulders and sandy hair. He approached the bed and took me in his arms, whispering sweet words in my ear. I let myself be rocked in the warmth of his body and the strength of his arms and fell into a deep sleep.

When I woke up, it was still dark. I tried to go back to sleep, but my mind was too agitated to doze off.

The dream continued to emerge in my mind. Why did this man that I met so briefly haunt my dreams? Without giving myself time to answer, I threw my legs off the bed, my mind still swirling with confusion, and walked towards the window. It was too early to leave the room, but I could no longer stay in one spot.

I showered, got dressed, and went outside. Behind me, I heard the roar of an engine. I turned around and saw a taxi slowly driving down the street. I was lucky at this time of day and in this neighborhood.

I beckoned him to stop, grabbed the back door handle, and got in. The taxi driver was staring at me.

"Is there a problem?" I asked a little defensively.

"You look like you spent the night on the street," said

the driver in a voice damaged by long years of nicotine. "And even so, you look stunning! It's a shame."

Despite the driver's assumption, I held my head high, a beacon of resilience in the face of his misjudgment. His words could not diminish my self-worth, for I was not about to let his misjudgment define me.

"It's none of your business where I spent the night! My money has the same value as someone who slept in a bed. Central station, please," I asserted, my confidence unwavering.

My firm voice had the expected effect. The driver, taken aback by my assertiveness, remained silent until we reached the central station. I paid the fare, got out of the taxi, and walked down the street, my determination unwavering. I was on a mission to satisfy my body's craving for food.

I stopped in front of an entrance with a giant coffee mug symbol. Inside, the smell of ground coffee and fresh bread filled the air. I sat on a bench. A waitress placed a menu in front of me and served me coffee. With tired eyes, she looked disdainfully at my clothes.

I ate my breakfast with an appetite and ordered another cup of coffee. Its taste did me good and warmed up my body. While drinking my second coffee, I calculated how long I had to wait before the clothing stores opened. I had a plan, and I would execute it with precision.

An hour later, I walked out of a clothing store dressed in jeans, a navy blue turtleneck, and low-heeled boots. My jacket, which I had carefully put in my backpack, was replaced by a thin black windbreaker. I had thrown all my dirty clothes in the plastic bag from the store and disposed of them in the first garbage can.

It took me twenty-five minutes to get to the central station. I still had four hundred kilometers to go before I reached my final destination, but this time, I no longer had to hide. In the next instant, I realized, shocked, that I felt more comfortable in Germany than in her own country.

The corners of my mouth rose to form a bittersweet smile. Soon, it would all be over. The Organization would overthrow the communist regime, and I could return home permanently, a beacon of hope for a better future.

CHAPTER 18

I arrived at the Frankfurt train station at four o'clock. There were crowds of people all over the station's shiny tiled floor. I studied the city map on a panel attached to the exit. Andrei Munteanu and his wife Elena lived on Dortmund Street. To get there, I had to reach across the city center.

I admired the city's beauty on the bus cruising along wide avenues. After mainly being destroyed by the Allies' bombing during the Second World War, on March 22, 1944, a British attack destroyed almost the entire historic center.

Frankfurt is considered a world-class city thanks to its economic power, infrastructure and cultural wealth.

It was a beautiful day. Expensive German cars moved along the smooth asphalt. I decided to get off the bus and mingled with the passers-by. Andrei's house was a few blocks from the stop, so I walked the rest of the way there.

Arriving at the address I was looking for, I climbed the four paved stairs and rang the doorbell. I heard muffled steps, and the door opened to reveal a tall, slim woman, around fifty years old, with gray hair tied up in a low bun. She had a second of hesitation, during which she studied me from head to toe, then asked in a deep voice.

"Can I help you?"

"I'm looking for Andrei or Elena Munteanu," I answered.

"I am Elena Munteanu."

"My name is Ana, Ana Zaikovich."

Elena's face lit up with a massive smile as she looked around. She invited me in and signaled me to follow her.

"We weren't expecting you any time soon!" she said. "Crossing three borders illegally is not easy!"

We walked through a hallway, and Elena stopped before a door.

"This will be your room. It has a small bathroom. You'd like to refresh yourself after such a long and challenging journey. When you're done, come and join me in the kitchen. I was making supper. Andrei will be home soon."

I entered the room. The furniture was straightforward and discreet, and the atmosphere was very warm. I looked at the photos on the walls, each depicting the same person: a boy with big green eyes and brown hair.

Another kid's bedroom, I thought. I hope this one is still alive.

I put my backpack on the floor and walked into the bathroom. Soon after, a cloud of steam filled the bathroom, smelling like a grassy field. I rubbed my sore body for a few minutes. My hair, no longer filthy, shone like silk. The scratches on my face and neck looked like drawings on my skin.

I got dressed and put my backpack on the dresser. Following the delicious smell of food, I walked to the kitchen. Sitting at a wooden table, an average man with a receding hairline rose from his chair.

"Ana, this is my husband, Andrei," said Elena.

"Welcome to our home!" Andrei said with a warm handshake, his eyes reflecting genuine hospitality.

I didn't know what to say at such a sincerely kind welcome. I sat down and leaned back in my seat.

Andrei opened a bottle of wine and filled three glasses. His wife had prepared a zucchini soup, followed by stuffed lamb leg served with glazed onions and butter broccoli. After a delicious caramel custard, Elena made coffee.

While drinking their coffee, the doorbell rang several times, and Andrei left the kitchen. He returned with a tall, athletic man in his thirties with brown hair and a light complexion.

"Ana, this is my son, Paul," Andrei said, his voice hinting proudness.

"I must admit, you are even more beautiful than George's description!" says Paul, his unexpected compliment catching me off guard.

"How well do you know George?" I asked, ignoring

the compliment.

"Very well!

"My son is part of the Organization," added Andrei.

"I thought that those who left a communist country at a young age no longer shared their parents' feelings and concerns for their country of origin and its people!" I exclaimed.

"And you're not mistaken." agreed Paul. "But I was nineteen when we managed to escape. At nineteen, we can't forget the past or erase it from existence. The horrors that my grandparents and my friends have endured will remain etched in me for the rest of my life."

"Are your grandparents still alive?"

"No. My grandfather died in prison while being tortured."

"I'm sorry to hear that. What about your grandmother?"

"My grandmother was a frail woman; she died shortly after. I don't need to explain the pain we felt and the frustration of not being able to do anything. That's when my father approached the Organization."

"Did you approach at the same time?"

"No. The management of the Organization was cautious about selecting new members. I was too young."

"How did you manage to escape the country?"

"It's a long story..."

"If you don't mind, I want to hear it."

Paul paused, losing his gaze somewhere far away when he began speaking.

"I was part of a group that disagreed with the policies

of the Communist Party. We were young and impulsive. We got together after my grandparents' funeral and decided to leave the country."

"Without your families?"

"Yes. Just us. It was during summer vacation. We told our parents we were going camping in the mountains. But we decided to swim across the Danube and flee the country. We chose a place where the forest on the banks of the Danube was denser.

We left the car on a country road and walked into the woods. Slowly at first, then faster, with more confidence, we moved towards the banks of the Danube. The silence that surrounded us so close to the border encouraged us."

"There's always a false sense of security surrounding frontiers. The patrols stay hidden, waiting to surprise those brave enough to try and get through to the other side," I said.

"I know that now. We were a few meters away from the river when my best friend slipped on dry leaves and could not stop his fall. The hill below was steep, and he risked a fatal fall. Desperate, he grasped the earth with his hands and feet and hit a tree trunk.

The impact was so powerful and painful for him that he couldn't stop screaming. He made a considerable effort to get up when suddenly, without us knowing where it came from, bursts of gunfire rang out, and bullets ricocheted off the rocks. One of the bullets drilled a perfect hole between my friend's eyes. His limp body swirled in a horrifying silence, fell off the tree trunk and stopped with a thud on the banks of the Danube. Terrified, we watched his broken body."

"Did the patrols fire without giving you a warning?" I asked.

"As I said, they did."

"What happened next?"

"Two guards popped up between the trees; the smiles on their faces looked evil and satisfied. They moved towards us cautiously, ordering us to surrender. Their guns were still smoking, and their fingers were still on the triggers. A short silence prevailed until we heard sirens closing in.

For a moment, I thought our desire to escape was over. But I was wrong. Grimacing with rage, one of my friends jumped towards the guards. We followed him impulsively. I've seen the ground rise, blown to dust by the bullets. A bullet hit our friend in the throat before coming out the back of his neck.

Without considering the consequences, we killed the two guards, crushing their skulls with their weapons. I will never forget the faces of my friends, void of emotion. Our dream of freedom had been replaced by a reality that had erased all traces of humanity in us."

"Did you swim across the Danube then?"

"The sound of footsteps approaching quickly motivated the rest of us to flee. As more guards came, my friends headed towards the Danube and started swimming towards the other side. Even today, I don't know why I didn't follow them. I was trapped in my body, completely frozen. In my head, I desperately looked for a place to hide.

The guards were close, and that's when I came up with the idea of climbing a tree. Hidden by the branches, I witnessed the massacre that followed. Hit by bullets, my friends kicked and pulled to stay on the turbulent surface of the Danube. But the water eventually seized their bodies, dragging them into complete silence and darkness.

I stayed hidden until nightfall. Finally, I found the courage to come down. I walked back without trying to hide; I was terrified, and my legs trembled. It didn't matter anymore what could have happened to me.

But I was lucky. I found the car in the same place we left it. Back home, I told my father what had happened. From that day on, I've been a different person."

There was a heavy silence in the room. The evening had plunged into nighttime, and memories of all the suffering had taken hold of us, leaving us frustrated but powerless.

Andrei's voice interrupted the silence.

"Since all his friends had died, there was no evidence that Paul had participated in murdering the two guards," he said. "But he was terrified of the memory. I feared for his health. It was during this time that I decided to leave the country.

Rumors about a man named El Dorado were circulating. They claimed he could trick the guards on the Romanian border and take you to any Western European country for a large amount of money. The rumors weren't exaggerated. The hardest part was getting in touch with him."

"I assume you were able to contact him?"

"Yes. After eight months of waiting, we arrived in

Frankfurt. Years passed, but Paul always remembered his friends.

Officially, he's a gym owner. Unofficially, he is working for different organizations that fight against human injustice, such as arms trafficking and human trafficking. Nothing can stop the members of our government when it comes to filling their pockets."

"You don't need to tell me about the atrocities our government has committed," I said. "For many years, I was ignorant. I was doing what I thought I had to do, my duty. Since I learned the truth, I've been trying to forgive myself for my evil. But I realize I won't be able to until these incompetent people, to whom we have entrusted the power, pay for their crimes.

"That moment will come," said Andrei. "For now, try to rest. You've been going through a lot. In the meantime, we have to be very careful. You are illegally on German territory. As long as you are a Romanian citizen, you are still subject to Romania's laws, which means extradition. The Securitate has contacts everywhere. We must act intelligently. I already arranged for you to obtain German citizenship; Paul has close contact with the BKA, the Federal Criminal Police."

I looked at him, perplexed.

"All this is very nice, and I thank you for your efforts, but becoming a German citizen is not the goal of my escape!"

"We know that, but it's the only way. Otherwise, it would be too risky. This country has welcomed us and given us every opportunity to live a better life. Keeping an agent of your caliber in hiding in our own house would be equivalent to betraying the trust we have built over many years."

"But I'm not a Securitate agent anymore!" I insisted.

"Do you have any way to prove that?" asked Paul.

A long silence ensued, during which I realized they were right. I have no right to create problems for this family who had welcomed me with open arms.

"There is a way to prove that you are no longer an agent of the Securitate," Paul said, breaking the silence.

"I guess I have to confess my work at the Securitate?" I asked, knowing the trades of the espionage world.

"Yes," answered Paul. "The BKA is waiting for my call. With your permission, I'll do it in the morning. Does that sound fair to you?"

"Very well," I answered after a short moment of hesitation.

At that moment, Andrei excused himself, left the kitchen for a few minutes, and returned with an envelope in his right hand.

"You have three thousand marks in this envelope," Andrei assured me with a comforting tone. "In a few days, you will move into a small apartment nearby, and this money is for your daily expenses. After obtaining a German passport, you can find a job. We, with our extensive network, will be there to assist you."

"But this wasn't my vision when I agreed to leave the country! "I exclaimed, my voice echoing my frustration.

"According to George, the Organization needs people like me to accelerate the resistance against the communist tyranny in our homeland!"

"You're angry, Ana!" replied Andrei. "And I, of all people, understand your desire to fight the evil that has taken hold of our country. But we must not rush. We need people like you, but we must be careful."

"A large number of agents have left the country, I insisted. "You must have a good team within the Organization."

"I imagine George has informed you that the Organization operates on a shoestring budget. Most members have jobs that barely make ends meet. Agents like you, who join us, often find themselves playing double roles. They sell their services to the highest bidder."

It dawned on me that George had misled me, leading to an unexpected turn in my life. I had envisioned a self-sufficient, robust organization with extensive European networks. But I was deceived, and there was no turning back.

Without commenting, I took the envelope and wished them good night.

"I'll leave you the key to the house on the kitchen counter," Elena added, a gesture that symbolized her trust in me during her absence.

I let out a big sigh. It was past midnight, but I couldn't fall asleep. I stared at the point on the ceiling where the lamppost reflected from the outside. I felt helpless. My life had taken such an unexpected turn that I was unsure what to do.

Being realistic, I knew there was no immediate solution, not in my world. I'll let time decide my fate. I let myself sink into the comfort of the bed and focused on clearing my head so I could sleep.

The next day, I awoke rested but with an acute sense of loneliness and uselessness. I slipped out of bed and went into the bathroom.

After a quick shower, I dressed and went into the kitchen to make myself a coffee. On the kitchen counter, I found the key to the house that Elena had left before she left for work.

The coffee woke me completely, and after a second cup, I left the house. The cold wind was blowing in my face. I began to run at full speed, taking deep breaths. Despite the temperature and distractions around me, I didn't slow down my rhythm.

The bus stations were crowded with people. Overwhelmed by the cold, I decided to get on the bus.

Arriving in the city center, I immediately realized something unusual was happening. An enormous crowd had come down the streets singing the national anthem, and I heard horns from all directions.

Trying to understand what was happening, I approached a window where people were cramming to watch a television screen. I saw vast columns of East German nationals crossing the Berlin Wall on the screen.

"The Wall is open!" announced a journalist sitting on the Wall.

Stunned, I tried to comprehend the extraordinary event that was the opening of the Berlin Wall. The Iron Curtain, a symbol of Europe's division for more than twenty-eight years, was no more. It was more than just a wall; it was a complex military structure. But now, it was a relic of the past.

This event held a personal significance for me, as it symbolized the end of an era of fear and division that had shaped my life.

"Wall of shame" for the West Germans, "death track" for the East Germans and "anti-fascist protective wall" for the Russians; it was the Wall of a vast prison where the leaders locked up citizens who had only one thought: fleeing!

As I watched the West Berliners welcome their counterparts with music and champagne and some citizens begin to chip away at the physical barrier with sledgehammers and chisels, I felt a surge of emotions. The Wall of fear was gone, and with it, a new era was dawning. The overwhelming sense of loneliness and helplessness that had plagued me seemed to dissipate in the face of this historic moment.

I wandered around in the street, letting myself get carried by the frenzy around her. Strangers fell into each other's arms, a happy look on all their faces. Bars were overcrowded, and smiling servers were walking around with heavy trays full of glasses, surrounded by laughter and loud conversations.

Basking in the happiness of that day, I realized that the

end of the Iron Curtain in Europe was inevitable. After the changes in Poland and Hungary, the contagion of freedom spread to Germany, ensuring the end of the Soviet Empire. I found myself slipping into a daydream world in which Europe was united.

I sneaked into the crowd, the emotions coursing through my entire body. People were running around, celebrating the resolution of the ambitious system that was communism. No matter how long I live, I will never forget the day that marked the decline of the communist regime: November 09th, 1989, a few minutes before midnight, the Wall was opened. It was like heaven on earth, a huge day.

I momentarily felt out of place and alone among the crowd swirling around me. Then I realized that I wasn't alone and that there was an emotional bond between me and the millions who were still living under communism terror.

Lightning crossed the sky, and raindrops began to fall on the asphalt. People started running in all directions for shelter. I exited the crowd and rushed to the bus station, feeling the need to share my joy with Andrei and his family. The rain had turned into light mist, and the sky was filled with darker masses of swirling clouds.

The atmosphere on the bus was the same as on the streets. Everyone was smiling at me, and I felt that this city was the friend I needed, holding me close and easing my frustration for the last few weeks.

I went up the stairs of Andrei's house with a light step and was very happy to see Paul in the living room. He was reading the paper.

"Hey, Paul! I'm so glad you're here! I needed to share the news with someone."

I sat on the chair, not understanding why Paul did not share my joy. He looked up from his paper, avoiding my gaze. He didn't seem too happy to see me.

"Paul, are you all right?"

"I've been waiting for you. I'm sorry, Ana, but I must take you to the BKA right now."

His words shocked me, and I almost jumped out of the chair. My nervousness had returned. I leaned over in my seat with one question on my mind: why so quickly? Did they change their minds about her?"

I sunk so deeply into myself that it took several moments before I realized that Paul was talking to me.

"Ana, we have to go."

"I don't understand the hurry!" I said to Paul. "Especially today! I thought the entire German population was celebrating!"

"To tell you the truth, I'm surprised myself."

"Do you know what this is about?"

"Not really. All they told me is that they want to meet you right away."

"Then let's not keep them waiting."

We got into Paul's car. I tried to look calm on the way, but I was very anxious. I could quickly get rid of Paul and flee. But ... to go where?"

As if he could read her mind, Paul touched my wrist.

"I'm sorry, Ana. I can see the stress that this meeting

must be causing you."

As I did not answer, he began to comment on the fall of the Wall. He could no longer hold back the excitement, which would have been contagious under other circumstances.

I stared at the landscape passing through the windshield without seeing it. In a few minutes, my life would change radically. I would know soon enough, and I consoled myself with the knowledge that as bad as things might get, I had lived through much worse, and it only made me stronger.

I tried to think of the essential information the BKA might be interested in and realized that Popescu's determination to catch me was mainly due to the Intelligence I possessed against the Securitate.

The car slowed down, and Paul pulled into a parking lot in front of a state-of-the-art glass and steel building in the business district, right next to wholesale clothing companies, banks and insurance companies.

"We have arrived," said Paul.

"But... this is not the BKA building!" I exclaimed, my confusion growing.

Paul shrugged his shoulders.

"I know, but that's the address they gave me."

"Have you been here before?"

"No, it's the first time."

"Are you absolutely certain it was the BKA who contacted you?" I pressed, my doubts surfacing.

"Without any doubt, my regular contact called me!"

It was unsettling to think that they wanted to meet me

elsewhere than in the BKA building, a place where security could monitor. It raised questions about my safety.

We got out of the car and entered the building. In the vast hall, a flurry of business people hurried in and out of the elevators. A list of the building's companies was displayed on the Wall opposite the front door.

It was very clever of BKA. It's the perfect cover.

I followed Paul, who had taken the elevator's direction. He exited the 7th floor and rang a bell beside an import-export company sign. The door opened instantly, making me think there was a well-hidden security camera. As soon as we entered, a middle-aged man with a large belly stood up and signaled us to follow him.

After leading us through some offices filled with posters and pamphlets about an import-export company, he stopped at one door and signaled us to enter. The door opened and closed quickly, and we were surrounded by complete silence.

This room is completely soundproof, I told myself.

A woman with an austere face, seated behind a desk, lifted her eyes from a document and focused on us.

"Good Morning, Mrs. Klein," said the middle-aged man. "I received an order to bring them here immediately after arrival."

Not knowing what awaited me on the other side of the door, I maintained my composure. In this uncertain situation, keeping calm was my greatest asset. Mrs. Klein reappeared two minutes later, her cynical smile doing little to shake my resolve.

"Please come with me," she said coldly, addressing me. You wait here," she added, looking at Paul.

I followed Mrs. Klein into the office next door. When I entered the room, a man nearly six feet tall and well-built stood up from his chair. He walked around his desk and vigorously shook my hand.

"Fred Solingen," he introduced himself.

I noticed he had not added titles to his name, but I knew better than to ask questions. With a hand gesture, he designated me a seat. His features were refined but austere. Behind his oversized glasses, I noticed bright eyes exuding Intelligence.

"I've heard a lot about you, Ana Zaicovich, AKA Ana Petrescu," he said.

"Can you specify?" I asked, my tone deliberately disinterested. I wasn't easily swayed by flattery or intimidation.

Fred Solingen hesitated momentarily, then pulled a piece of paper from a file on his desk and handed it to me.

I start reading;

October 16, 1986

Agent Ana Petrescu's professional qualities are impressive. Her ability to improvise under adverse conditions is nothing short of mind-blowing. Her loyalty to her superiors is intact. She always accomplishes her missions.

I glanced at the end of the document to see who had written these comments, but the signature of the person who signed it had been erased.

"I could let you read the entire file," interevent Solingen, "but we don't have time. Today is a great day for us and all the countries of the Communist Bloc, including yours. But the Cold War continues. I asked you to come because we need your help."

"My... help!" I exclaimed, my surprise evident in my voice. The unexpected request took me by surprise.

"Yes, we need your help. Of course, you have the right to refuse, but in your current situation, this might create complications. You're a security agent who illegally entered German territory. It may take years before you can prove your good intentions."

For a split second, Fred Solingen had an icy expression, and his gaze was piercing.

I felt my mouth dry out. I quickly understood that the only way out of this office as a free woman was to accept Solingen's proposal, even though my freedom would be derisory.

"I'm listening," I said.

"You're well aware that the Stasi isn't just any secret police force; it's the most pervasive globally. When the RDA was born, it began as a modest division of 4,000 employees, overseeing 21 million people. Now, it boasts 94,000 members and 194,000 non-official staff, serving a population of less than 17,000 million. In addition, there are 6,400 officers and 33,000 unofficial staff in the RFA. Between the USSR and the RDA, there are 15,900 employees. No corner of the world is untouched by such a formidable secret service. But this isn't news to you."

Indeed, I was familiar with these facts and then some. I could have pointed out that, in terms of population ratio, the Romanian secret police were the largest in the Communist Bloc. But I chose silence over an unnecessary debate, a testament to my patience.

For a precise four seconds, silence hung in the air, and our gaze locked in a silent duel. Solingen cleared his throat, breaking the tension.

"We know with certainty that the Russians got rid of all essential documents before the fall of the Berlin Wall. But they will try to keep their collaborators. Especially the most important."

"But there are thousands of collaborators," I replied. Among them are those who had no choice but to collaborate to protect their families."

"I'm referring to a significant fraction of hardened Stasi. Their names are known only to the few highest-ranking officers in the KGB. We understand there's a list with their names. We tried everything we could to get our hands on that list. We're as far along as we were at the beginning of our search."

"I don't understand; how can I help?"

"We know that the fall of the Wall will lead to the reunification of West Germany with the East, and those who were loyal to the Stasi will be free to do the Russian dirty work inside the West too. We need to find that list."

"And you want me to find it!"

"You guessed right."

"But... I have no idea where I could find that list other

than in the KGB safe!"

"You guessed right again!" Solingen confirmed with a cold smile. "We have confirmations from a trusted source that the list is in Moscow. It's in the KGB's safe."

I couldn't believe what I was hearing. The task was impossible, and the consequences were fatal. I leaned back into my chair, my mind reeling in disbelief.

"This is madness! You want me to break into the Moscow KGB vault and steal a collaborators list! It's a death sentence, plain and simple!" I exclaimed, my fear palpable in the air.

There was a moment of silence before Solingen answered.

"Not necessarily."

I froze, the weight of Solingen's words sinking in. The horror of reality set in. For the first time in my life, I wondered what it would be like to have an everyday life where I get up in the morning for a typical day of work. With my knowledge, I could be a history or geography professor, teach languages, or even train athletes.

There are many things I could do. But my fate was established when the Securitate recruited me. In my line of work, everything was black or white. Life or death.

I was no longer an individual but a pawn in a deadly game. I had no choice but to obey, to carry out the mission, or face imprisonment or death. Solingen knew this, and he gave me no choice.

"You know that the probability of me getting out of this alive is almost zero!" I said.

"Well, I don't believe that at all. On the contrary, you have a chance of succeeding. The Russians have a lot on their hands these days. The movements in the Eastern countries are distracting them. It's the perfect opportunity for us."

"But... why me? You have agents who are more than capable of doing the job!"

"Under the circumstances, using one of our agents wouldn't be brilliant. The Wall is down. The Russians are defeated. During this period of celebration, the German authorities wanted to avoid any action that could trigger a conflict with the Russians. This is why the BKA cannot get involved directly and must use intermediaries."

Anxiety creeps up in my stomach.

"You mean you're not part of the BKA?"

Instead of answering, Fred Solingen asked if I wanted something to drink.

"No, thank you," I answered, a knot of unease forming in my stomach as I wondered what I had gotten myself into.

Fred Solingen took a small sip of cold coffee and began to speak.

"To everyone, we're an import-export company. But in reality, we're a BKA branch. We take care of the things they can't get involved in. I know you have a lot of unanswered questions bothering you. Regarding all your questions, I have only one reply: after this mission, you will receive a German passport, allowing you to move freely within our territory.

I wanted to reply that I wasn't interested in having a German passport, but I decided against it.

"Do not forget that the loss of Russian power will lead to the disintegration of the communist system and, thus, to the liberation of your own country," added Solingen. "By accepting this mission, you are indirectly helping your people."

It was immediately clear to me that there was no escape from this web of intrigue.

"Very well," I said. "How will I enter the Soviet Union?"

"We will give you papers confirming that the World Health Organization employs you. You will also have identification with Russian names. You can use them, if necessary, after your arrival."

"This won't be a walk in the park," I acknowledged.

"I know that. But you won't be alone. We already have an excellent team on the ground."

"How do I get in touch with them?"

"They will contact you when you arrive at Moscow airport. The code phrase is: Taxi to the countryside? You will answer: I prefer the City."

"And if my contact won't be there, can I have an address, or can I contact someone?"

"He will be there," replied Solingen

I knew what a one-way meeting meant. Solingen wasn't taking any chances. He made sure that if Russian security services stopped me at the airport, the connection to my contact would be wholly cut off, and I would be on my own.

As if he had read my mind, Solingen added.

"No need to point out that if you fall into the hands of the Russians, you'll be on your own. We never met. As soon as you leave, this office will move to another address."

"Fred Solingen isn't your real name, either."

Solingen smirked a little but didn't answer. I had my answer.

"Do those who will wait for me in Moscow know the true purpose of my mission?"

"Of course not! And they're too well-paid to ask specific questions. Someone working for us for a long time recruited them."

"And you trust this person?"

"Completely. His livelihood depends entirely on his reputation for absolute discretion."

"There's a little problem. How will I justify my absence to Paul's family?"

"We thought of that. In a few minutes, we will advise Paul that your interview is going very well and that we will keep you with us for a few days."

"They will certainly worry!" I replied.

"I think they will be relieved," answered Solingen. "This is the first time they are hosting an agent of your caliber in their home, and they know the consequences very well. The Securitate has a very far reach. They're willing to help, but not to the point of putting their son's life in danger. It all works out for the best."

I remained silent. The conversation with Andrei popped up in my mind:

This country has welcomed us and given us every opportunity to live a better life, he had said. *Hiding an agent of your caliber in our house would be equivalent to betraying the trust we have built over many years.*

I felt a strange loneliness mixed with a dull pain in the pit of my stomach, understanding the inescapable obviousness: I had nowhere to go. Solingen was right. The whole thing worked out perfectly for everyone.

"Is there anything else you want to tell me?"

"No. Our meeting is over," answered Solingen. "My secretary will take you to the apartment where you will stay until you leave for Moscow. Everything you need for your disguise will be there, as well as your travel documents. You'll live tomorrow at noon. Get some rest, and good luck!"

Without looking back, he left the office.

When he left, his secretary called me to follow her. The janitor intercepted us in the lobby.

"An envelope has arrived for you, Mrs. Klein."

Mrs. Klein signed the acknowledgement and politely thanked the man. I followed her, and fifteen minutes later, we arrived on the third floor of a building across the street.

She slipped a key into a prominent polished wooden door and signaled me to enter. Then she put the envelope the janitor had given her on the coffee table in the middle of the living room.

"These are your travel documents," she said in a neutral tone. "If you're hungry, you have everything in the refrigerator. Good night!

And without another word, she left the apartment.

I walked straight towards the bathroom, undressed, and took a warm shower. During these few relaxing minutes, I did not want to think about the dangers I would face the next day. Then, I sat on the comfortable sofa and opened the envelope the secretary had placed on the table.

Within the envelope lay a Norwegian passport bearing the name Marguerite Valdemar and papers asserting her employment with the World Health Organization. The passport, worn and softened by apparent use, was stamped with evidence of numerous European travels. Pages titled "destroy after memorizing" held the life story of Marguerite Valdemar, a woman I was to become. An official invitation to Moscow was also enclosed. The documents, each carrying a piece of my new identity, seemed to whisper secrets I had yet to uncover.

I found myself lost in the sea of documents, my gaze unfocused, my mind wandering. The world was a vast chaos of human creation. Some sought to enforce a rational, logical system rooted in humanitarian rights, decrying wealth as the root of all evil.

Others manipulated global industries to amass wealth and power, arguing that money was a tool to mold the world to their liking.

And then there were those like me, operating in the shadows, their actions incomprehensible to the average person. A force that worked underground, resorting to violence if needed. I reasoned it was a service to all, as most of the world's population allowed themselves to be swayed by promises of a better life.

Shaking my head to dispel the negative thoughts, I reminded myself of the mission that Solingen had requested me to accomplish. Now that I'd accepted, I was committed to fulfilling it.

Leaning forward, I focused my attention on the passport. The picture depicted a woman in her fifties, a perfect candidate for my impersonation. I glanced around the bedroom, my anticipation growing as I prepared to change my appearance for the mission.

I moved towards the window, drawing in a breath of the night air. The city was alive with lights, its inhabitants oblivious to her presence. I watched them, a pang of envy stirring within me. I longed for the simplicity of their lives, free from the shadows I operated in. But for now, I stood on the precipice of a risky gamble, a game of life and death with no other options.

I began to memorize Marguerite Valdemar's biography. Half an hour later, I destroyed the sheets summarizing the biography and got into bed. I felt tired. My body needed to recover strength, and I had to process all the new information.

CHAPTER 19

Groups of Militia in grey coats patrolled the customs area and immigration control at the Moscow airport. In character, as Marguerite Valdemar, I got the suitcase and walked through the crowd upon arrival. A salt and pepper wig covered my hair; black lenses hid my blue eyes. Prosthetics widened my face, and underwear altered my figure sufficiently to make me look completely different. Businessmen and women, especially Russians and some foreigners, walked silently toward customs and immigration control.

"Your ID, Madam?" the official asked harshly.

I handed him my passport and the letter of invitation. The official studied my documents for a long time.

"Open your suitcase," he requested.

As asked, I opened the suitcase and put its contents

on the counter. At any moment, I expected to feel a police officer's heavy hand grabbing my shoulder.

But nothing happened. With an indifferent look, the employee handed me my documents. Relieved, I picked up my suitcase and heeled through the crowd, thankful that virtually everyone was on the move, making it easier to lose myself as I made my way toward the exit.

Large snowflakes swirled lazily through the air before landing on the ground. The door of a taxi parked between two streetlights opened as I passed, and a bearded driver signaled me to come closer.

"Taxi to the countryside?" he asked.

"I prefer the city," I replied, reassured by Solingen's meticulousness.

I sat in the passenger seat, and the taxi started right away. He crossed a large part of the city, and I saw people lined up before food stores and stray dogs roaming the grey streets.

I had a feeling of déja vu. I knew all too well how the country operated. Everything good is coming at a heavy price. The Securitate constantly watches people. In a command economy, the state decides what goods will be produced, in what quantity and by what deadline.

For ordinary people, most of everyday life consisted of searching and waiting for essential material goods, including food. They awoke each morning and retired each evening in a small apartment where, sometimes, more than one family shared two or three small rooms.

Many, but not all, had reliable plumbing and electricity.

It was why so many of these people were so miserable.

One thing was clear to me: the communist system was a modern-day slavery that had lasted too long. This display of poverty and exploitation saddened me and gave me a sense of helplessness. If I had hesitated to accept Solingen's proposal, now I was convinced that my mission was for a good cause.

The taxi slowed down. We were in the suburbs of Moscow, going down a deserted street. It was still early, but the days were getting shorter, and the night started falling. In the darkness, lights shone on each side of the street, illuminating the houses.

The driver parked the taxi in front of one of them and signaled me to follow him. He pushed a small gate, and we descended a gravel path in an alley. I could only hear the wind whistling between the bare branches and our footsteps.

The driver opened the house door. As soon as I stepped in, I heard the voice of a person speaking on the phone. I knew that voice. I stopped abruptly in my tracks. What if the Russians got wind of Solingen's plan and set a trap for me?

Then I saw him; our eyes met, and almost at the same time, an exclamation of surprise escaped both our mouths:

"Ana!"

"Nikolai!"

With a sigh of relief, I relaxed. Our paths crossed several times during my career as a Securitate agent. Russian agents worked with agents from Eastern European countries when it was a common interest. Nikolai was an accomplished agent; I could not have a better contact than him.

We spoke quietly for a while, recounting the events that had led us to this house in the Moscow suburbs. I learned things about Nikolai that I didn't know. During our assignments in the field, we never confided in each other. He told me he had been a double agent for several years. He was married and had a three-year-old son. His family lived in Frankfurt, but he hoped to move to the United States soon.

He had collected a large sum of money, but working as a double agent was becoming more dangerous daily, and he did not want to endanger his family. His wife had no idea what he was doing, thinking he was a businessman who had to travel around the world to ensure his company's success.

"You shouldn't have accepted this mission," I told him. "This time, there's a big possibility we'll be killed. If that happens, your son will grow up without a father."

He looked me straight in the eye before he replied with a convincing voice.

"Trust me, Ana. I have no intention of dying. Success is the only option. Remember, I'm at home here. This is the last time I'll be risking anything. I can settle in the United States with the money they will give me for this assignment.

"Why the United States?"

"If I stay in Europe, I'll be hunted down by the Russians.

As you know, they never forgive those who betray them. Especially those of my caliber. The United States is still a land of opportunity. The only limits are the ones you set for yourself. Besides, I'll be a long way from Russia. My family will be safe."

"I hope you accomplish your dream! Now, I need to know your plan for getting that list."

"Before we start, how well do you speak Russian?"

"My Russian is excellent, but my knowledge of Moscow is purely theoretical. If things go wrong, I don't want to run unthinkingly without precise direction and not knowing whether my path will lead to a dead end. You can help me fill that gap."

"Don't worry, Ana. I got it all planned out. You'll know the city better than a Muscovite quickly."

"How much time do we have?"

"We'll take as long as it takes. I have a small but excellent team waiting for my instructions. They were all selected by Grigoriev, a former colleague and an excellent friend. I trust him. Besides, I have loyal friends and trusted colleagues at every level of the KGB."

"You have no loyalty to your people?"

"In my heart, I'm still a Russian patriot. But I'm not a blind patriot. As long as my country benefits from my actions, I see no harm in making a profit. Idealism is not for me. For a long time, the pain of my people nearly made me lose my mind. Finally, I realized that we are not the ones deciding our fate. It was then that I chose the way of wisdom. We are guinea pigs for a group that ruins nations and rewards those who help it achieve its goal. They are several years ahead of the people who stand in line in front of empty shops and yearn for a better life."

"That's true. But we must remember that the people standing in line in front of the empty shops are starting revolutions. History proves that a revolution can bring about radical changes in the world!"

Nikolai looked at me, surprised.

"Your desire for justice is so strong that it prevents you from seeing clearly! Open your eyes, Ana! It's all manipulation! They let you believe in victory. I know that the number of those who genuinely realize that has increased, but the day of true liberation is still very far away.

I don't think I'll still be on this earth when it comes. What I believe is that the communist system in Europe is over. This means that you and I, as Securitate agents, will be undesirables in our own countries.

"Me, I have no intention of running," I said. "When the communist regime falls, I intend to return to my country."

Nikolai looked at me, unable to hide his surprise.

"It'll be madness! Don't forget that for the people of your country, you're just a Securitate agent!"

"Not anymore, and I'll prove it."

"And how will you do that? You're going to do a press conference?" asked Nikolai mockingly.

I didn't have time to answer. The door opened, and a muscular man with a strong jaw approached Nikolai, whispering something into his ear.

Almost immediately, Nikolai got up from his chair. "I've got to go meet someone," he said. "Your room is down the hall. Get some rest. Starting tomorrow, we'll get to work."

CHAPTER 20

Aweek had passed since my arrival in Moscow, but I could not say that the city had no more secrets for me. With Nikolai, I had walked the streets from morning until late at night, stopping only to eat.

The city's Cartographic information was a state secret. On a variable scale, there were only rudimentary plans that showed little. The KGB headquarters didn't exist on those plans. As a result of the randomly positioned buildings on the streets, even well-informed city dwellers could easily get lost. On most avenues, rows of buildings stretched hundreds of meters and were marked by a single number. It was almost impossible to know which level of a street you had to go to. The plan deficiencies were supposed to be supplemented by a signs system, but we found none.

With my ability to do the orientation and Nikolai's

knowledge, we established several schemes to leave the city in case of an emergency. We also established meeting points if we had no choice but to separate. If we couldn't use the same passports anymore and then exit via an airplane, Nikolai knew several routes that could help us leave the Soviet Union by other means. Through tunnels that the KGB ferociously sought to make them unusable.

We studied the KGB building through powerful binoculars, recording every detail. We concluded that it was impossible to know which day was the best to try to get inside; people came and left too inconsistently.

Once outside the KGB building, I knew our chances of escaping were high. We graduated from the same school and training and had the advantage of knowing the KGB's techniques.

However, if we are trapped inside the KGB building, our chances of survival will be very slim. No human being can stop his brain from spilling information after extreme physical torture, to which are added drugs such as scopolamine or sodium amobarbital. The Russians wouldn't spare us once they got all the information they wanted. And yet, I have to recognize that this mission was a challenge for my skills and courage.

From this building, General Vladimir Kriuchkov, the president of the KGB, carried out his orders with a determination that made them particularly compelling.

Compared to those who believed that the KGB's sphere of action included the same functions and powers exercised in the United States by the CIA, I knew that the KGB was not just an intelligence service operating like its Western competitors. Its tasks were manifold: the liquidation of political opponents and counter-revolutionary organizations within Russia and abroad, border guards, foreign espionage, counter-espionage and the security of the Communist Party, the heads of state and the property of the Soviet state.

Given its powerful influence and multiple functions, the KGB had a large staff and one of the largest international networks of agents capable of infiltrating any environment, whether industrial or military, political or religious, intellectual or humanitarian.

A notable success of the KGB was retrieving foreign intelligence and Western technology from double agents in the Western secret services. They also achieved great success with infiltrating the West German government through the Stasi.

Solingen knew what he was talking about. If Germany united, the Stasi, a vital ally of the KGB, could pass on information to the Russians.

Like the Securitate, the Soviet secret service is responsible for the deaths of thousands of citizens considered to be enemies of the people.

For years, I've been living a lie. Oblivious to the signs, I've been treading a path I thought was right, only to realize it's a dark, treacherous road.

Nikolai was right; even if the Securitate deems me a traitor, the people are unaware of this. To them, I'm still a Securitate agent. I must show them that I'm now on their side. I know the odds are against me, but I'm not one to give up easily.

I closed my eyes, refusing to dwell on the uncertain future. The possibility of my demise in this perilous mission was all too real. But in death, there would be no need for further proof.

"Priviet, Ana," said Nikolai in Russian as he entered the room. "You look rested. So, what do your instincts tell you? Do we have any chance of stealing that list without getting caught?"

"It is simple once we get inside. It depends on the safe model they use. But that doesn't change the fact that that place gives me the creeps."

"Well, you're the expert on opening safes. You're going to have to use all your skills. If the alarm goes off, I don't know if we'll have time to get out. Remember that the danger in this mission is as great on the outside as it is on the inside. You know, as well as I do, we will be dealing with elite assassins. The KGB will not bear defeat on its territory. They won't give up until death takes away our last breath. And I have no intention of dying. Today, we will go over a final recap of the details. Follow me; I have something to show you."

I followed him into the house kitchen. Nikolai pushed a button hidden behind a drawer, and the sound of a mechanical system started. The wall, on which various kitchen utensils were fixed, sank to the left, and we entered a room with an area of about twelve square meters.

I glanced around the room, which contained a veritable

arsenal of weapons, including bulletproof vests, night vision goggles, powerful binoculars, digital cameras, and grenades. Nothing was missing.

I chose a bulletproof vest, a gun with a silencer, ammunition, and several small tools to open locks. It was all I needed. The day after my arrival, Nikolai gave me what I had asked for to open the safe. In a few hours, it'll all be over.

Our strategy was alright but not reassuring and likely to change anytime. The fact that we had to act in Moscow gave us a little leeway.

The phone rang, and Nikolai lifted the handset. The conversation was brief. Suddenly, he turned to me, took me in his arms, turned me in the air like a child and set me down on the sofa. He was happy about the news he received by phone. I only understood a little of the conversation and was waiting for clarification.

"Ana, we've been given a break," Nikolai began. "We don't have to risk going inside the KGB building anymore to get our hands on that list."

"You mean we're going to give it all up?"

"No, we'll get the list in a more accessible place.

"Great! Will you tell me where?"

"All I can tell you is that a copy of the list we're looking for is hidden in a private house's less protected safe deposit box. All this time, I thought someone had to have a copy of the list. That's why I hadn't given up trying to find it using all my resources."

"What makes you so sure that it is true?"

"I have information that the fall of the Berlin Wall has created panic in the upper echelons of the KGB. As a result, some high-ranking officers took the lead and began to place important documents in secure locations. Thanks to these documents, they will have nothing to fear. They can ask for protection from the countries concerned and large sums of money. Our list is among those documents."

"Are you absolutely sure the information is accurate? Is the informant someone loyal?"

A guttural laugh came from Nikolai's throat.

"Ana! Wake up! The only thing that motivated my informant was money. It's the only thing that matters today. People need money to handle their limited options. The struggle is unequal between them and those who have enough money. The larger the sums, the greater the ease. My contact figured that out a long time ago."

"Do I know him?"

"I prefer to keep his name a secret, but I can tell you that my information is accurate. I'll notify Grigoriev of the change of plans, and we'll go on a recon tour."

We drove silently through the city. Wind gusts were blowing down the street, and traffic was becoming sporadic. We have arrived in a neighborhood where opulence excelled. Elegant brick houses lined up on both sides of the street were owned by rich people privileged by the regime. The house we were looking for was set back from the street, surrounded by a one-hectare park. A cement wall surrounded the property, and a narrow road provided access to the driveway.

I surveyed the street and its surroundings. It wouldn't be a walk in the park, but it would be a breeze compared to the KGB building.

CHAPTER 21

For four days, observing and planning were our only realities. Through our binoculars, we examined the house from every angle. Then, we took turns watching the ebb and flow of people, hoping to find a pattern. Many servants were working in the house, which we had to avoid. They were quick to report any unusual activity to prove their loyalty.

We took precautions for the most unlinked situation. Each team member had a specific role to follow to the letter. Driving a cab, Ivan will check the streets and tell us if the coast is clear. A taxi won't attract attention; people are used to seeing them everywhere. After taking possession of the list, Nikolai and I will board the cab.

Grigoriev will be driving a truck loaded with wood on the highway. He would intervene if our mission was exposed and provoke an accident with the pursuers to facilitate our escape.

Sergei will wait by the phone if we need to give him further instructions.

The best time would be in the evening. Visibility was reduced in the evening, but traffic was heavier, a parameter that would work in our favor. We were now ready and waiting for the right moment.

It was a Saturday night, our fifth day of waiting. The dim light of the evening began to cover the city when we noticed that the massive gate of the property was opening, and a black limousine appeared in its frame. Through my binoculars, I recognized Sergei Ostrakov, one of the most prominent high-ranking officers of the KGB. An elegantly dressed woman was seated by his side. I felt a chill run down my spine. If things went wrong, we would have no chance against enemies of this level.

We watched the limo's backlights disappear in the distance. Now, it was all about timing. Nikolai gave the signal to Ivan, who walked towards the cab parked a few blocks away. Stealthily, Nikolai and I began to approach the house.

The world no longer existed. We acted like two predators, following our instincts, ears peeled, trying to discern any abnormal noise. Every time a car drove down the street, we had to hide against the cold ground. When we were about three hundred meters from the house's entrance, a cab passed slowly down the street. For a split second, his headlights went out. We recognized Ivan, who was signaling that he was in position and ready for action.

At the same time, Nikolai and I checked our watches. Standing almost side by side, we crossed the street and moved slowly to our left along the wall. The arrival of a car covered the sounds of the night, but we could no longer be seen from the street. The car lights went out for a split second; this was the last signal with which Ivan informed us there was nothing to worry about in the adjacent alleys.

I climbed up the wall and landed on the other side steadily on my legs. The soft rubber of my boots diminished any noise from the contact with the ground. Not far from where I landed, Nikolai did the same. Everything was quiet. The dogs had yet to discover our intrusion. We pulled out our short-range pistols loaded with carbon dioxide cartridges. The dogs we saw through their binoculars were dogs trained to kill. A gust of wind in the right direction would make the dogs smell our scent.

They took little time. At an increasingly fast pace, several dogs bolted straight to us. As they were approximately fifteen meters away from us, Nikolai and I aimed and fired simultaneously. Our short-range pistols threw tranquillizing darts instantly. Without a sound, the dogs fell to the ground.

So far, everything has gone perfectly, but we are still very far from our goal. We covered our faces with black hoods and began to crawl on our bellies towards the house. Our black attire helped us blend into the darkness of the garden. The light was visible through most windows, and there was still a lot of activity in the house.

Moving quickly, we crossed the garden until we were five meters from the service entrance. The owner did not want to share the main entrance with his servants, whom he ironically called his comrades. They were trusted employees willing to betray anyone to keep their jobs. It ensured them a decent life in a country where most people lived in poverty. Nikolai and I have no doubts about their reactions; it would only take them a fraction of a second to sound alarms. At the same time, there were advantages; as long as they were in the house, they would inevitably be noisy, and the alarm system would not be active.

Nikolai observed the surroundings, a silenced pistol in his hand, ready to pull the trigger if necessary. A light whistle signaled to me that he was in position. I approached the door, feeling my heart racing. The lock was new, which meant it could be bypassed easily.

Holding my breath, I introduced one of the lockpicks into the keyhole and listened to the tiny vibrations of the metal. Slowly, I pulled the pick slightly towards me. The door swung open without any noise.

I put my tools back in their place and signaled Nikolai to come closer. Cautiously, we checked whether anyone was around and then walked into the hallway in front of us.

The sound of the wind suddenly muted. We had to find the safe before the servants saw us. Our rubber boots didn't make any noise on the ceramic floor. It took us a few minutes to check almost every room in the house, which had several bedrooms and beautifully furnished bathrooms.

The owners loved luxury.

Quietly, we walked down a hallway and felt the smell of hors d'oeuvres reaching our noses. We also heard the metallic sound of pans and other kitchen utensils. At any moment, someone could appear in the hallway, spot us, and sound the alarm.

At one end of the dining room, there was a locked door.

"It must be here," whispered Nikolai. "I'll watch the hallway."

I took care of the lock with my tools, and the door opened in less than five seconds. I went in and closed the door behind me. Except for a few paintings, bookshelves covered the walls. A desk and a chair upholstered in dark green complemented the furniture. It was obvious that the cleaning woman had rarely entered this room. There were two empty bottles of vodka in the trash, and cigar butts were filling the ashtray.

Ostrakov must spend much time here to avoid being bothered too frequently. The safe must be here.

I began by looking behind each painting but discovered nothing but the discoloration of the wall, not exposed to cigar smoke. I touched the wood of the shelves and the desk's surface with my fingers. Nothing.

I returned to the middle of the room and cast circular glances around it.

The atmosphere in the room was stifling. I went to sit on the chair behind the desk and opened the drawers. Several files were in a metal organizer: random reports. Minutes passed, and my breathing became forced due to stress.

I returned to the center of the room and once again concentrated on the details on the walls. A picture of a child was on one of the bookshelves in the middle of the library. Finger marks were printed on the frame as if someone had been looking at this picture often enough.

It was irrelevant at first glance. It's normal for a father to look at his child's picture often, I thought, but he doesn't have to move it every time; it's placed almost at eye level.

The words of one of my instructors from the time I was learning to become a Securitate agent popped into my head: *Every detail is essential. The most minor thing could be exactly what you are looking for.*

I looked behind the frame of the child's photo and discovered a small metal rod embedded in the wall. I touched the rod with my fingers. The movement was almost invisible, a tiny variation of light at the edge of my field of view. I felt a shiver of excitement running through my body. I stood up and turned to the back wall. One of the shelves had swiveled and uncovered the location of the safe.

It was a high-tech facility worthy of a high-ranking KGB officer. I knew the Russians were very proud of their safekeeping techniques and had been ahead of the Americans for several years. They used radioactive isotopes and X-ray-sensitive film to see the different rotations inside the safes.

The agents who were forced to use this instrument were exposed to lethal radiation, but that was the last of the KGB concerns. I had prepared accordingly, thinking I had to open the KGB vault. Fortunately, I only needed to use the traditional method here: listen and feel the inner rotation to guess the combination.

I have been unbeatable in this field until now, a quality that will be very useful today. I connected my device. Within two minutes, I had opened the safe.

I took out all the documents inside, kneeled on the floor and examined them, keeping them in the same order I had found.

I found the list in a slightly torn envelope. After photographing the many pages, I pulled the small disk out of the camera and slipped it into a plastic compartment in the inner pocket of my pants. Then, I put another disk in the camera and made another copy. Based on my experience, I had to be vigilant.

Then, I put the documents back in the safe, leaving everything in the same order as I had found it and walked towards the door. I told Nikolai that everything was under control.

"Good work, Ana!" he exclaimed. "You are the best!"

The excitement made him forget where he was, and his voice was louder than it should have been. I signaled him to be quiet but understood his reaction very well. He had reached a mental space beyond fear, specific to the dangerous situations we found ourselves in. Some of the best agents are caught when they let their guard down in those few seconds.

We left the room and walked down the hallway towards

the service door.

I heard a slight air movement, and a door suddenly opened on our right. We barely had time to stick to the wall. A woman with towels under her arm entered the hallway and walked straight into the next room. We promptly advanced towards the exit door, ensuring no one was around.

A cold, cloudy night was covering the streets of Moscow. After crossing the garden, we approached the wall. The dogs' weak whines and growls warned us that the tranquillizing darts' effect had begun to wear off. Glad to have accomplished our mission so quickly, we climbed the wall. It was at this very moment that our illusion of success vanished.

Two police cars blocked the house's exit with their lights flashing. We heard hasty steps and guns clicking.

We remained perfectly still for a moment, trying to understand what was happening. We were desperately looking for Ivan. According to the plan, he was supposed to pass by in his cab every fifteen minutes and give us the signal that he was waiting for us around the corner. He was late. Our plan was simple: quick in and out, and no one gets hurt. But now, with Ivan not showing up and the police closing in, it seemed like a distant dream.

One minute passed and then another, and there was no sign of Ivan. The cold wind was blowing. We looked at each other, beset by the same question: have we been betrayed, or has Ivan had a significant hindrance?

Doubt crept into our minds like dust in an hourglass,

but we fought hard to keep our nerves in check. We were determined to remain calm, even though we couldn't see a way out. We would not let this situation defeat us, even if it meant losing precious time.

"We're trapped!" I finally said.

"Sometimes things don't go as planned," replied Nikolai.

"I know. It is then necessary to revise and improvise."

I didn't know if Nikolai was realizing our precarious situation or if he didn't want to admit that he had made a terrible mistake in trusting the men on his team.

"It was a solid plan, but even the most solid plans can go sideways," Nikolai said again.

"I agree. Yet, I suggested a Plan B. You should've listened to me."

We waited for ten minutes, hoping we were wrong. On the roof of the house across the street, we noticed two snipers ready to fire at any moment. We looked at each other in silence, the tension in the air palpable. There was no need to say anything. We were sure Ivan or someone else on the team had betrayed us.

"Ivan's betrayal gave Sergei Ostrakov time to find a good reason to send the best KGB agents after us. Our chances of escaping are almost nonexistent," I said.

"The bastard! I will make him pay."

"Right now, we need to concentrate and find a solution, if one exists," I said.

We stood against the wall and moved cautiously to a dark corner. We found ourselves in a situation where there was no way out. We could no longer return to the garden because the dogs' yapping would expose us. We did not dare move because we did not know the exact position of the Russian agents. One wrong move, and we could be getting shot at.

Death seemed to dance like a shadow around us. It was killing or being killed.

An SUV stopped about twenty meters from our hideout. Four men went out and came along the wall in our direction. They were armed with AK-47 assault rifles, light, reliable and inexpensive weapons. The driver stood next to the car and looked around with curiosity. He had probably yet to receive a specific order, and his attitude showed he was a beginner in such situations.

I analyzed the calm approach of the armed men. They were experienced agents programmed to shoot and kill. The balance had to be tipped on their side before more assailants arrived.

A torrent of adrenaline poured into my veins, and the only powerful emotion that overwhelmed me was rage. If the system that created me wanted to destroy me, I would not let them succeed easily. They taught me to push myself further than anyone else was willing or able to go. To kill whoever got in my way until I escaped. And this is what I intend to do. As long as Nikolai and I are alive, there is a chance.

An explosion sounded like thunder in the silence of the night. Pieces of cement flew in all directions as Nikolai swerved to his left, narrowly avoiding the bullet. Other shots hit the wall a few inches from his head.

At lightning speed, I pulled out my gun. Following the direction of the shot, I distinguished the barrel of a gun across the street, the shooter drowning in darkness. I pulled the trigger. The shooter fell face down, dead. Other shots hit the wall a few inches away.

Our sudden response to their attack had caught the four-armed Kalashnikov AK-47 men by surprise. They were now only six meters away. Stuck to the wall, with their fingers on the trigger, they understood that the people they sought were not far away.

Every millisecond was detrimental. Without losing any time, I calculated. Every second of immobility was exposing us to someone's line of sight. The car in which the shooters had arrived was about twenty meters away. Nikolai and I had to split up and try to get to it. Under the circumstances, it was our only hope. I nodded to Nikolai, who replied with a squint of his eyes that he understood.

I got up with all the strength in my legs and ran across the street like an arrow. A volley of bullets ricocheted off the asphalt in a loud, tinkling sound. I managed to cross to the other side of the street without being touched.

As I fell to the ground in a dark corner, I heard four muffled detonations. I saw Nikolai cross the street, four Kalashnikovs on his shoulders. All four Russian shooters were dead. Shooting at me as I crossed the street, they exposed themselves to Nikolai's bullets.

More bullets began flying off the asphalt near Nikolai's right leg. Without stopping, he took a Kalashnikov off his shoulder, held out his arm holding the weapon and fired like a madman to cover himself. Arriving a few meters from me, he threw a Kalashnikov in my direction.

"Catch," he shouted.

While grabbing the Kalashnikov, I saw a moving shadow on my left.

"Don't move," a voice said behind me.

A split second later, I felt the barrel of a gun on my head and saw a pair of cold eyes in a dark face. A sadistic smile distorted the Russian features who were pointing the gun at my head.

I realized he was an experienced and skilled man who was used to situations like this one. The silence with which he had moved meant that he was an agile and seasoned enemy. I held my breath as I saw Nikolai's imperceptible gesture to grab his silencer. But I wasn't the only one who saw his gesture.

"Drop your weapons, or I'll blow her brains out," said the Russian, staring at Nikolai.

At that moment, sirens approached, and cars rushed to the front of the house, followed by an SUV filled with armed men. Unintentionally, the Russian glanced in that direction. Taking advantage of his moment of inattention, I hit his jaw with my head. I heard his teeth banging. At the same time, I raised my hand to grab his right wrist and twisted it back. The Russian lost his smile very quickly when I tore his ligaments. I doubled the pressure on the joint. A crack confirmed that the bone had just dislodged.

A groan of pain came out of the Russian's mouth. An

expression of mixed anger and surprise appeared on his face as he fell to the ground. Holding his weapon with two hands for better support, Nikolai shot the man in the heart.

I shuddered at the inanimate body, asking myself if he had been an innocent child, as I had been, who had been forced by the KGB to become a killer. Yet, I wasn't supposed to feel emotions in such situations. A stern voice took over in my head: *you must command your mind. You have no feelings. Get it through your head. It's you or your opponent.*

The wind began to blow very hard, and the sky had cleared. You could see the stars. The moon's glow wasn't to our advantage. We had to hurry to get our hands on a car, provided we lived long enough to reach one. Nikolai stood in the middle of a thick grove with the weapon in one hand and his binoculars in the other. He zoomed in on the surroundings and signaled me to jump the fence.

"This way! Hurry!"

I jumped with agility to the other side and ducked on the ground on my stomach. Nikolai followed me, but his feet slipped on the damp grass as he touched the ground. Unbalanced, he fell to the ground. The two Kalashnikovs fell from his shoulders and made a loud noise by touching the metal fence.

He remained frozen in this atypical position, listening.

I heard furtive steps approaching, and an armed Russian appeared about ten meters from us. He was the image of concentration, moving slowly towards where we were. He'd stop as soon as a branch snapped.

I pulled out my weapon. The Russian was now only two meters away from Nikolai who was awaiting his approach, ready to strike. When he was close enough, Nikolai's right hand grabbed the Russian's throat, while with his left hand, he grabbed his shoulder. Then, he pushed a thumb into the Russian's trapeze, paralyzing his arm and making him drop the weapon. I picked up the gun, and I struck the Russian in the head, who collapsed unconscious.

Time was running out. With every moment passing, we made our escape less likely. We have to take our chances and try to get hold of a car. We run towards the back of the house without stopping to check the surroundings. A few feet behind us, a bullet hit the ground, splattering us with grass.

We both recognized the quiet shot; only a rifle equipped with a silencer made that sound. There was a sniper on the roof of the house. Only our speed could save us.

The silent shooting continued; deadly projectiles were sinking into the grass closer and closer. Finally, out of breath, we reached the wall of the house.

"We must eliminate this sniper," said Nikolai.

"No," I answer him. "A sniper cannot fire an accurate shot while we're in motion. There is still a risk of being hit, but we can get away if we oscillate and maintain our speed. We don't have time to deal with him. We must try to steal a car immediately; otherwise, all our way out will be zero, and the number of pursuers will crush us.

"You're right. Let's go for the car," Nikolai nodded.

We split up to distract the sniper and crossed the other half of the garden as fast as we could. The sniper rained down bullets, slicing through the branches without touching us.

We ran towards the street and leaned against the metal fence, trying to see what was happening. People in plain clothes were walking around, giving orders to men that we couldn't see but who couldn't be too far. Soon, the sniper will inform his superiors that we are alive and nearby.

Our only chance was to get hold of one of the KGB SUVs. There was one just across the street. The driver had stopped the engine and was leaning on the car. We heard the whirring of another car approaching and understood that we wouldn't have time to calculate our next movement. Soon, the street will be filled with KGB people.

"Cover me," shouted Nikolai, sprinting to the car across the street.

In the following seconds, I brandished the two Kalashnikovs, one in each hand, and pressed on the triggers. Bullets hit the asphalt, barely missing the officers who were giving orders.

The attack took them by surprise. All their attention was focused on avoiding the bullets, temporarily preventing them from returning fire. Nikolai crossed the street successfully and headed towards the SUV driver.

The moment he saw Nikolai approach him, the young driver pulled out a gun and pointed it at Nikolai, taking an offensive position. A perfectly useless gesture against Nikolai, who, in a few strides, covered the distance between them and stuck the barrel of his weapon to the man's temple. The driver glanced around as if examining his chances.

"Drop the gun, or I'll blow your brains out!" yelled Nikolai.

The driver let the pistol fall heavily to the ground. He seemed terrified of Nikolai's imperturbable expression.

"Give me the keys!" Nikolai ordered, and the driver complied immediately.

Nikolay took the driver's gun and slipped it into his pocket. He hauled open the door, slid behind the wheel, and put the car in gear. With a masterful fluidity, he reversed, using the gas and the handbrake, back up to the sidewalk where I was waiting and signaled me to get in. I jumped into the passenger seat and immediately noticed the pile of ammunition in the back seat; enough to fight an army.

Nikolai slammed the gas pedal, carelessly exceeding the speed limit. The car leapt and flew down the street, tires screeching. I saw two vehicles chasing us and approaching at high speed through the mirror. Suddenly, I heard a burst of gunfire, and the back window of our car cracked like a spider web.

Police sirens were beginning to sound in the distance. I jumped into the back seat of the vehicle, and a fraction of a second later, the shots of my gun echoed, and a volley of bullets ricocheted off the metal of the car behind us. I aimed, and with a perfect shot, I fatally hit the driver in the chest.

The second car had overtaken us, and a screech of rubbing metal bleared.

"Go for it!" I shouted. "Now!"

Nikolai stomped on the gas pedal until it hit the floor, making the engine roar. The car lurched forward, leaving our pursuers a few meters behind. I opened the door and dropped to the floor of the vehicle, part of my body hanging out, a Kalashnikov in my hand. I aimed at the tires of the vehicle behind us and fired. The car skidded and swerved on the slippery asphalt, lost control and crashed against an electric pole. This gained us a short break, but the sound of the sirens was quickly approaching.

Returning to the main street, we noticed traffic becoming increasingly congested. Something blocked the street further down; maybe it was an accident. Soon, we could see a roadblock, the flashing police lights reflecting off their windshields. The cars were driving bumper to bumper. Officers checked all drivers' and passengers' identities; it was a police checkpoint.

The sound of engines growling disrupted the silence, getting louder and louder. A gunshot echoed, and a bullet hit the driver's window a few inches from Nikolai's head. The shot was too accurate to have been from the police. In the rearview mirror, Nikolai saw two SUVs approaching KGB agents. We were stuck between the police barrier and the KGB agents.

"Drive through the barrier!" I shouted. "Before they blow us up!"

The sound of a machine gun firing accompanied the

roar of the engine. Nikolai pushed the car to the maximum speed and narrowly avoided a tanker.

I thought that at that speed, we could die in a collision, but it would certainly be less painful than falling into the hands of the KGB.

A series of bullets bounced off a traffic sign, meters from our car. Looking in the mirror, I saw the two KGB cars driving side by side as if they enjoyed intimacy. The drivers were pushing the powerful engines to their limits. I turned around and fired at one of the SUVs. The bullets crashed through the side of the vehicle, which skidded, straightened and kept going.

The second vehicle approached us and soon was almost parallel to our car. As the rear window on the driver's side lowered and they got ready to fire at us, I fired, killing anyone inside. The car made a few turns and came to a halt. At the same time, Nikolai slowed down and quickly turned the wheel to the left, trying to force the second KGB car off the road.

To a professional, maneuvers become instinctive. The driver slammed the brakes, and the car rocked on the asphalt until coming to a stop. Unfortunately for the KGB agents inside, a truck coming in the opposite direction hit their vehicle at high speed. Nobody could survive the impact.

I was relieved but remembered that the odds of escaping were very low. Now that they knew our position, other KGB cars would come after us. Even if we managed to lose them, we were still in Moscow. All roads, highways, airports, and train stations would soon be under strict surveillance. No matter what happened, the risk was enormous.

We now merged onto a two-way main road. As we blended into the traffic, we heard police sirens behind us. Soon, we realized it wasn't the police. The cars approaching at a tremendous speed were KGB cars.

Nikolai stepped on the gas, and the car roared. We were driving at maximum speed, and the vehicle began to sway dangerously when overtaking. Our pursuers were in range now, their weapons in action. I had already raised my gun.

"Shoot!" exclaimed Nikolai.

The exchange of fire created complete chaos in the traffic. The panicked drivers were losing control of their steering wheels, their cars shifting abruptly from one lane to another. Nikolai and I were desperately checking the sides of the road to see if Grigoriev's truck was there. Here is where he should be waiting for us with his massive truck. He was supposed to let us pass and then block traffic to give us a chance to escape.

When we almost gave up hope, we saw a large truck stop on the other side of the road. We recognized Grigoriev's truck. At the signal Nikolai gave him with his headlights, Grigoriev replied promptly. He started the engine, and as soon as we passed him, he blocked the road.

Through the mirror, I saw Grigoriev leaving the truck's cab and disappearing between the cars. The traffic froze, and we took advantage to distance ourselves.

For a few minutes, we were alone on the road. Driving

at full speed, we put a reasonable distance between us and the KGB cars. A sign indicated that we would soon pass through a tunnel. There were no adjacent roads, and we didn't know what awaited us on the other side.

After a low-visibility turn, Nikolai braked hard, leaving wide black marks on the asphalt. A gas truck was driving through the tunnel, its cylinder shining in the streetlights. The tunnel was too narrow, and we could not overtake the truck.

"Hurry up!" Nikolai shouted at the tanker driver, who was going fifty an hour.

As if to challenge us, the truck kept its speed. Every second seemed to pass with an excruciating slowness, and my frustration grew. Deep in my mind, an idea began to take shape; as there were no adjacent roads, if we managed to block this tunnel completely, we would have a chance of escaping. Perhaps the tanker's presence was only for our good. I hesitated for a moment before sharing my idea with Nikolai.

"Excellent idea!" approved Nikolai who was driving dangerously close to the tanker.

I climbed out the window and grabbed the metal ladder to the top of the tank. Moving quickly, I launched myself onto the tanker, and I pulled a small hand grenade out of the left pocket of my bulletproof vest. I glued the grenade to the back of the tank using aluminum adhesive. After making sure the adhesive was holding, I stepped forward along the length of the tank and slid onto the front cabin windshield.

Facing the driver, I pulled out my gun and pointed it at his head. The terrified driver lost control of the steering wheel, and the tanker veered quickly into the tunnel wall. I managed to hang on. As I rolled off the side of the tank, the terrified driver jumped to the ground and began to yell at me. I told him to get inside our SUV and be quiet if he wanted to make it out alive. Nikolai started driving at a slow speed, and when we were almost at the end of the tunnel, he stopped the car without cutting the engine. I jumped into the back seat, pointed the gun towards the tanker left behind and fired.

Sparks exploded on the metal, and immediately after the oval cylinder exploded, a roiling fireball and smoke ravaged the tunnel.

Leaning over the steering wheel, Nikolai pushed the vehicle's engine to its maximum. We managed to escape before the tunnel collapsed into a thousand pieces, blocking the only access road.

A few hundred meters further down the road, we dropped off the truck driver and continued on our way.

CHAPTER 22

Despite the cold night, we opened the car windows to breathe in the fresh air. The road became narrower, and the total absence of trees gave the landscape a certain austerity. Dilapidated buildings were lined up on both sides of the street. There was no trace of traffic lights, and the road was dirty and cracked. Only a few kilometers away from Moscow, the grim reality of the communist regime was revealed.

"Will you tell me where we're going?" I asked Nikolai.

"For starters, we'll get rid of this car and get another one. I have contacts in this village. Then we'll go back to Moscow."

He turned into a narrow alley between two buildings illuminated by a dirty light bulb. Garbage bags piled up all over, and the smell was unbearable. Nikolai stopped the car in front of a metal door and asked me to wait for him in the car. He smashed the light bulb with a punch, leaving the alley in complete darkness.

Ten minutes later, the metal door opened, and an old van stopped behind the SUV. At the wheel, I distinguished the face of a countryman about fifty years old, checking his surroundings. Nikolai signaled me to get into the van, and then he transferred all the weapons and ammunition from our vehicle and got in the driver's seat. The countryman had started the SUV and was moving through the narrow alley.

We drove for a long time to escape the area where we had blocked the tunnel. After several detours, we reached the streets of Moscow. The police sirens reminded us that we could be spotted at any moment. Nikolai was driving carefully, avoiding the major thoroughfares of the city. We saw a car driving too fast coming up an adjacent street. Out of nowhere, several police cars chased him, their tires squealing.

"God damn it!" exclaimed Nikolai. "There're cops everywhere!"

He accelerated and took a side street. Ten minutes later, he entered an underground parking lot and stopped the van in a dark corner.

"We'll continue on foot," he said. "It's too dangerous by car."

We took our silenced weapons and some ammunition and hid them under our clothes before climbing to street level. Other than the occasional police sirens, the neighborhood was quiet. The streetlights illuminated just a part of the sidewalks, leaving the rest dark. There was no one in sight.

Nikolai moved forward with the confidence of someone who knew the area, and out of caution, I followed him at a reasonable distance. He reached for a pay phone, lifted the handset and dialed a number. The conversation was brief, and from his satisfied look, I understood that things had gone well.

Suddenly, the sound of a powerful engine resonated in the street, followed by a second engine. I quickly hid behind a tree. Nikolai looked in my direction and signaled me to stay hidden. He barely had time to hide behind a tree when two KGB cars sped down the street. They had followed us, but how?

The cars slammed their brakes and stopped in the middle of the street. Six agents armed with machine guns got out almost at the same time and split into two teams.

Nikolai's shadow was only partially hidden by the tree trunk. One of the agents turned in his direction, raised his machine gun and pooled the trigger. Nikolai narrowly avoided the bullets that hit the tree, shattering pieces of bark. He fired in return, and his bullet hit his attacker in the chest. The agent made a barely audible noise, bent forward briefly and then got back up. I saw the hole in his clothing, but there was no sign of blood, meaning they were wearing bulletproof vests.

I looked around to assess our escape options. It could have been more pleasing. There was no place to hide and only two weapons to fight back. Once again, we had no other choice: kill or be killed.

I calculated the distance from the nearest adversary. I took a deep breath and jumped from behind the tree. Surprised by this unexpected movement, the agent turned in my direction, raising his machine gun.

Just as he pulled the trigger, my knife plunged into his arm that was holding the weapon, disrupting his shot. The bullets hit the ground close to my feet. Pieces of asphalt flew in all directions.

I clenched my teeth and sped up, my body launching into the air as I wrapped my two legs around my opponent's neck. I heard the sound of torn ligaments; I bounced back on my feet and let his body fall lifeless on the asphalt.

Hearing the gunfire, the other KGB agents approached, ready to fire. I lifted the body of the agent I had killed and held it against me. The only reason they couldn't blow my brains out was because they were afraid to kill their colleague. They had no idea he was already dead. They were waiting for the right moment, their threatening faces revealed in the faint streetlights.

I saw Nikolai looking at their faces distorted by rage, being almost sure that he would not have time to react before I dropped dead under their bullets. This was an all-or-nothing scenario.

After a short hesitation, Nikolai pointed his silencer at the head of one of the five agents, fired, and then sprinted across the street like lightning. A bloody hole had appeared on the forehead of the agent he had targeted, and a few seconds later, the agent collapsed lifeless on the asphalt.

A rain of bullets followed in Nikolai's direction. One of the shots hit him, but he was alive, and his distraction had given me time to realize the gravity of the situation.

Taking advantage of these few seconds of confusion, I ran the distance that separated me from one of the KGB vehicles and jumped on the hood. The soles of my shoes clung to the metallic paint, allowing me to climb onto the vehicle's roof quickly. Nikolai had guessed my intentions as my gaze locked on the four agents.

"You're out of your mind!" exclaimed Nikolai. "Those bastards are going to tear you to pieces."

Two officers approached the car promptly while the other two followed them closely. Nikolai seemed spellbound by my extraordinary courage and skill as I launched myself from the rooftop daringly and elegantly, leaving the KGB agents momentarily stunned. My body seemed to defy the laws of physics, hanging in the air as I set my sights on the armed agents below.

With lightning speed, my legs struck the arms of the closest agents, causing their weapons to discharge wildly. Bullets ricocheted off parked vehicles, house walls and trees, creating chaos.

Despite the intense gunfire, I maintained my balance, my determination unwavering. Descending gracefully, I executed a perfect roll upon landing, minimizing the impact and swiftly neutralizing a third agent with a precise move.

Even as a fourth agent lunged at me with lethal

intent, I held my ground, delivering a decisive blow in a breathtaking display of strength and agility, knocking the agent off balance before seizing his weapon with expert precision. With a single, decisive shot, I incapacitated my assailant; his resistance shattered in an explosive finale.

One of the agents had regained balance and was about to intervene.

"Watch your right," Nikolai shouted.

I pressed my back against the vehicle's hood and fired in the agent's direction. I heard cries of agony, which I mercifully ended with more bullets.

Slowly, I lowered the machine gun and then dropped it to the ground. I heard the police sirens, and soon, their cars surrounded the street. It was time to leave as quickly as possible.

I turned away and quickly walked towards Nikolai. Once I was close to him, he gave me a small, admiring whistle.

"I just wanted to tell you that I had never seen an agent of your caliber," he told me. "Especially a woman. The scenes that had unfolded before my eyes were worthy of a James Bond movie."

"I acted in desperation," I told him. "Otherwise, we will be dead by now."

At that moment, I realized that we had another problem; Nikolai's wound was more severe than I had thought. He was breathing hard and getting sweaty drops on his face.

"We have to leave right now," I told him.

Ignoring the excruciating pain, Nikolai removed the blouse he was wearing under his bulletproof vest and wrapped it around his wound to prevent losing too much blood. The sound of police sirens was getting closer and closer. There was a growing sense of urgency.

"We can take one of the KGB vehicles," I suggested.

"No, we don't; we are very close to our destination," replied Nikolai.

Prudently, we start walking. A cold wind blew over the streets, and the night sky looked like a dark void. Eight hundred meters away, I followed Nikolai into a multistory building. The building was quiet, and I started to relax a little. We arrived on the penultimate floor when Nikolai stopped before a door. He knocked three times, and a moment later, a man of high stature opened the door and stepped aside to let us in.

The tiny, cramped apartment smelled of chamomile. A bookshelf lined the wall from the floor to the ceiling, and a piano took up half the living room. A tall, slender woman stood up from a seat in front of the piano and walked up to meet us.

"Ana, those are Mikhail and Katarina Alexandrovich," said Nikolai. "They're going to help us live the country. They have a married daughter in Finland. They're supposed to leave tomorrow morning to visit her. We'll go instead. We have one hour to impersonate them."

The couple had remained silent. They were a little freaked out by the whole thing.

I followed Katarina into the bedroom. After turning

on a lamp, she took a travel bag from a wooden cupboard and put it on the bed. Inside, there was all the necessary arsenal in the art of disguise. I started my transformation and asked Katarina particular questions about her life and her daughter's.

The light from the lamp projected a lustrous shade on Katarina's hair. She was sitting down slightly bent, knees together, hands clenched on the photos of her daughter, showing them to me with nervous gestures. Fifty minutes later, she left the room.

I applied the last touches to my disguise, got the copy of the Stasi member list from the inner pocket of my pants and hid it in my new clothes. I was ready.

I found Nikolai looking at the pictures hanging on the walls. Mikhail and Katarina Alexandrovich had already left the apartment.

Nikolai had changed his appearance and looked like a replica of Mikhail Alexandrovich. When he saw me, a satisfied smile appeared, meaning my transformation was a success.

"Are Mikhail and Katarina your relatives," I asked him, trying to understand the connection.

"No. My grandparents lived in this building. When I was a child, I often played with Mikhail and…"

A banging on the door interrupted him. Nikolai opened the door, and I recognized Grigoriev. He was dressed as a Russian farmer with an Astrakhan hat on his head. He had two suitcases in his hands and two duffel bags on his shoulders.

"Here's your luggage," he said. "Mikhail and Katarina are in the safe house. I'll get them out of the country if things go wrong. You need to leave now. There are roadblocks everywhere. Driving you to the airport as planned would be a bad idea. It's too risky. Please take a taxi."

"I think you're right," replied Nikolai, his voice concerned. "Ana, we should check the contents of the suitcases," he said, turning to me. "We must know what's inside if they stop us at the border."

Katarina packed regular clothing, a pair of brown leather boots, a samovar, and two Russian dolls. I put them back and checked the contents of the small duffel bag: a passport, a plane ticket to Helsinki, a book by Dostoyevsky, socks, slippers, several scarves, and a plastic bag filled with women's toiletries.

"I have to go," said Grigoriev, watching us while smoking a cigarette. "I want to get out of town by sundown. I've notified our contact in Helsinki of your arrival."

"Thank you for everything, Grigoriev. Take care of yourself," Nikolai said, shaking his hand.

"That's what I intend to do. I'll stay hidden for a while and go to Australia as soon as possible. I have a cousin who lives in Brisbane, and he asked me to join him. If you get to America, let me know."

He shook our hands and left the apartment, slamming the door.

"That's why you ignored my insistence on having a Plan B," I said to Nikolai. "You already had one."

"I would've preferred not to involve Katarina and

Mikhail. They're good people."

"I understand."

The morning was fast approaching, and we had to go to the airport through the police roadblocks paralyzing the city.

When the time came, Nikolai called a cab. Seventeen minutes later, we were in front of the building, each carrying a suitcase and a duffel bag. The taxi driver greeted us with a radiant smile that negated his harsh features. He kept talking and lifting his brow eyebrows.

We passed through several police roadblocks without a problem. Our disguises were so perfect that the police didn't even check our documents.

Arriving at the airport, the driver parked the taxi and turned off the engine. We took our suitcases and paid for the trip. The driver gave us the same radiant smile and wished us a good trip.

Standing in the cold, Nikolai and I gazed at the airport lights, reflecting on what awaited us. Even with real passports and a perfect disguise, we could fall into the clutches of KGB agents. They weren't some inexperienced police officers. They were trained agents who could feel our presence before even they could identify us visually, agents that could see through a different physique, a muscle expansion, size enlargement or a modified face contour. To succeed, we must be more innovative than our intelligent and resourceful opponents, which we had wounded by slipping through their fingers several times.

The airport was full of people. We walked into the

crowd and blended in. With every passing minute, we were closer to the moment when our fate would be decided.

Despite the crowd, I could spot the KGB agents trying to blend in with the mass of travelers. Their cold and hard eyes stared at every passenger waiting in line before the check-in counters. They were solidly built and muscular, scanning through the boarding areas, ready to pounce.

The dim morning light and the lights from the airport signs made their faces dismal. In a state of maximum vigilance, I moved towards the counter, pretending to look at the people before me, keeping my cool and staying on my guard without attracting attention. We were waking on fragile ice.

The couple in front of me finished checking and boarded the aircraft.

Nikolai and I approached the employee. I put my passport on the counter. The employee opened the passport, looked at it, then tore the boarding pass and gave me one half. I nodded politely, took my passport back, and moved on.

I halted two meters away, waiting for Nikolai to present his papers. The employee's scrutiny seemed to stretch into eternity. A flicker of nervousness in Nikolai's eyes caught my attention. The employee's gaze bore into Nikolai as if trying to unravel his deepest secrets.

As Nikolai's gaze steadfastly supported the curious gaze of the employee, the latter's eyes finally turned to the passport. He placed the travel document on the counter and handed him his boarding pass.

The airport was still covered in morning fog when the Aeroflot aircraft took off for Helsinki. Sitting side by side at the back of the cabin, Nikolai and I found it hard to believe it was over. A risky and deadly mission succeeded.

"It's finally over!" Nikolai's voice trembled with palpable relief, echoing the weight of our successful mission.

"Let's hope so!" I replied, suppressing the urge to rub my face. The low-quality disguise products were causing an unbearable itch, and the prostheses were stretching my skin, causing a throbbing pain. I was exhausted, physically and mentally.

The low-quality disguise products I had applied to my face were causing an unbearable itch, and the prostheses stretching my skin were causing throbbing pain.

I refused the food tray the flight attendant offered me, claiming I wasn't hungry. I emptied my glass of water and leaned my seat back as much as possible.

With my eyes closed, I hoped my mind would calm down and let me get the rest I needed. But I felt relieved only when the plane hit Finnish soil.

We mingled with the passengers on our way to passport control. Our turn came, and just as I was walking towards the control officer, I noticed a damp spot on Nikolai's coat. Blood had begun to flow from his wound, soaking through the bandages and now through his jacket. I froze. We couldn't fail, not now.

I should find a way to cover the bloodstain quickly. I pretended to slip on the floor and caught myself on Nikolai's arm, covering the blood stain with my arm. With my eyes, I had shown him the reason for my behavior. With an embarrassed smile, I held Nikolai's arm as if I wanted to avoid another fall. The employee waiting for us at the counter and witnessing what had happened looked at us with impatience.

"What is the purpose of your visit to Helsinki?" he asked.

"Our daughter lives here, we are visiting her," replied Nikolai.

"What's her name and address?"

Nikolai gave him the name and address. After checking his statements on a screen, the employee stamped both passports.

"Welcome to Helsinki," he said in a neutral tone, holding out the passports.

Still glued to each other, we walked to the baggage claim area. With my left hand, I took a scarf out of my handbag and threw it on Nikolai's shoulder, completely covering the spot of blood on his coat. His face looked ashen, even with the makeup he had used to personify Mikhail.

"Are you, all right?" I asked him.

"I have very high pain tolerance," Nikolai replied.

We picked up our luggage and left the airport. Around us, people were rushing to find a taxi. A young woman, whom I recognized immediately as the daughter of Katarina and Mikhail Alexandrovich, walked towards us and enthusiastically embraced us. A groan of pain escaped Nikolai's lips.

We followed her into the parking lot, and a few minutes later, we were outside the airport. Sitting in the back of a pearl-gray Volvo, we watched the gray sky through the window. The young woman had turned on the heating in the car, and a lightheaded feeling hit me. It was strange, but now that it was over and our mission was successful, I felt no joy, just relief.

After a fifteen-minute drive, we stopped in front of a random building in Helsinki. The young woman led us down the black and white marble hallway, and I noticed Nikolai was moving forward without hesitation.

He's been here before, I thought. *It must be a safe house.*

I heard the key creak and turn in the lock a moment later, and we entered a cozy, masculine-looking apartment. The young woman pulled a folder from her purse and placed it on the table beside plates with sandwiches and fresh fruit.

"Here are your passports, plane tickets, and information about your new identity. There are spare clothes in the wardrobe."

I couldn't wait to get rid of the clothes I was wearing and my disguise.

"You know where to find what you need for your wound," she said to Nikolai, confirming that he had been here before. "The car will pick you up at three o'clock sharp." She hugged Nikolai gently and left the apartment.

"Do you want something to eat?" asked Nikolai. "I'm starving."

"I'd rather take a shower," I answered. "A long hot

shower."

"The bathroom is the last door on the right."

"Are you sure you can finish the day? You look exhausted."

"Nothing will stop me from getting home tonight," replied Nikolai. "Everything I need is in this apartment. One shot and I'll have enough adrenaline to get as far as New York."

I didn't insist. I was anxious to get to Frankfurt, too. Since I left Romania, I haven't heard from George.

Nikolai walked into the other room to clean his wound and I entered the bathroom and took a long, hot shower.

We devoted the next half hour to transforming into our new identities. I was surprised to find that, other than a blonde wig, the picture on the German passport was mine. Always vigilant, I transferred the copy of the Stasi list into my new clothes. The other copy was in Nikolai's bag.

Fifty minutes later, dressed as businesspeople, we entered Helsinki airport. We passed through customs quickly. Because of our last-minute booking, we were not seated together.

The flight was unbearable for me. The woman sitting next to me was terrified of turbulence, and she kept talking about everything and nothing. She had an irritating voice and leaned into my seat constantly, complaining about the pilot or the temperature.

Relieved to arrive in Frankfurt, I allowed myself to be carried by the crowd rushing towards the checkpoints. Followed by Nikolai, I passed passport control with no stress. Nothing else could happen to us in Frankfurt. Here, we were protected by the BKA, the German Federal Criminal Police Office, our trusted ally in this mission.

We moved away from the crowd flowing towards the airline's offices. A slender man approached discreetly and shook Nikolai's hand.

"Mission accomplished," said Nikolai in Russian.

"Thank God!" answered the man in the same language.

I looked at them, not understanding. Who was this man? I knew the BKA was anxious to get the list and would contact us soon enough, but why send a Russian?

I scanned the crowd and saw two airport security guards walking directly towards us, making me more nervous. In seconds, more security guards were getting closer and watching Nikolai and me as we walked.

Soon, all eyes in the terminal turned and focused on us. I wouldn't say I liked it. I watched the guards get closer and felt the imminent danger: had they discovered that Nikolai and I were travelling with fake passports? Even so, the BKA is supposed to protect us! They should've planned a discreet meeting unless they wanted to contact us immediately! But why cause all this commotion?

Something wasn't right. My heart raced, and a cold sweat broke out on my forehead as I struggled to make sense of the situation.

The questions jostled in my head without me being able to find a logical answer.

I caught Nikolai's eyes and understood he wasn't as surprised as I was. His face was relentless, and his eyes locked on the security guards.

"We have to get out of here," he whispered.

"What are you talking about? We have no reason to run! This is absurd...."

"I don't have time to explain right now," Nikolai interrupted, "but I have to go. You'll get out of this. I'm sorry."

He turned around and dodged through the crowd. His compatriot followed in a hurry. With their guns pointed at them, the security guards were running at full speed after Nikolai and his compatriot.

"Freeze!" shouted one of them. "Police!"

"Don't move!" shouted another.

A loud cacophony of voices followed by screams suddenly filled the airport. Nikolai and his compatriot were pushing travelers, sinking through the panicked crowd blocking the entrance, trying to get out. Airline employees were desperately trying to calm the panic-stricken crowd.

During this chaos, my stress rose several degrees. I looked towards the exit door where the travelers had rushed, trampling each other. That was the last time I saw Nikolai.

Whose side are you on, Nikolai? I asked myself.

I started to understand that he may work for anyone other than the BKA. Did I get crossed? The thought of Nikolai, my trusted partner in this dangerous game, turning against me was almost unbearable. But in this world of espionage, trust was a luxury I couldn't afford.

It didn't matter. I knew where to look for answers to all

my questions. It was intelligent to make two copies of the list and keep one for myself. I had done well being vigilant; this list could be my passport to freedom.

In front of the accusing gaze of the crowd, the police handcuffed me. They picked up my purse and told me to start walking.

A Lufthansa plane took off and faded into the sky. A few moments later, I found myself in a windowless office with only a table and two chairs. The two security guards left me in the room without saying a word. I could hear muffled footsteps approaching, and a young, red-haired policeman walked into the office. He leaned against the wall near the door, slightly moving his torso to show the holster on his vest. It was a deliberate gesture to let me know he was armed.

He was definitely at the beginning of his career. I ignored him entirely and closed my eyes, trying to calm my headache. The wait was short. Two men dressed in plain clothes suddenly opened the door and approached my chair. I gazed at them in silence. Their faces were impenetrable and full of confidence, the mark of trained professionals.

"Please follow us," said one of them, looking me directly in the eyes.

We left the airport and made our way to the outer parking lot. I was about to ask a question when I heard tires screeching to my left. A car with tinted windows had just turned around and stopped before us. I recognized the license plate used for the BKA. I was taken to the backseat between the two men. The car had a third row of seats, occupied by two men with a cold look, visibly armed. They stared at me in silence, and I could see the surprise in their eyes.

I concluded that they probably wondered why all these precautions were needed for a woman.

The driver stomped on the gas, and we launched towards the exit, turning right at the first intersection to avoid the constant flow of buses and taxis going to the airport. Despite the relentless rain, there were many tourists during this season.

Deceptively calm, I knew I had reached a point of no return and forced myself not to contemplate the worst. The more I thought, the more convinced I was that Nikolai had played me and that he had chosen to sell the list we stole in Moscow to the highest bidder.

Some of his words came to mind, emphasizing his belief that people are stuck with limited options without money. He had said that the struggle between them and those who possess enough money is imbalanced. More money, easier life.

While the car was fading into the city streets, I felt exhausted. I had not slept in a while, and all the emotions had drained my adrenaline. I had to force myself to stay awake and alert. Excessive fatigue very often leads to judgment errors.

We crossed the city center, and the car stopped in front of a building in Frankfurt's busiest areas. We entered the lobby, and I spotted numerous surveillance cameras hidden in white boxes across the ceiling. They dragged me into the building's basement and placed me in a highly secure room, finally removing my handcuffs. I had only one explanation as to how I was being treated; the BKA believed that I was complicit with Nikolai, but I did not manage to escape.

The room in which they had closed me was certainly an interrogation room. There were no windows, so you couldn't distinguish between day and night; there was only the intense light from the fluorescent tubes that never went out, and sometimes, that was enough to drive some people crazy. It is a kind of torture used by almost any Intelligence in the world.

Sitting on a white plastic chair, I felt the exhaustion overwhelming me. I got up shakily and took a few steps, trying to remember the vital things necessary in an interrogation like the one I would soon undergo. My answers had to be as short as possible and extremely precise. I had to be unbreakable. Every circuit in my brain was on high alert. Much of my training to become a Securitate agent had focused on resisting the worst torture. My trainer's words came to mind:

Concentrate. Your enemies' reactions will guide you. Get ahead of the questions. Use what works. You have something of the utmost importance to them. They won't kill you before trying to get the information. This will give you time to try and find a way to escape. Otherwise, it would be best if you died without becoming a traitor.

After a time that seemed eternal, I heard the door open

and fresh air creep into the room. A rather old man of average height, slightly limping, came to sit before me. His eyes sparkled with intelligence.

I understood why I had to wait so long. They had this man brought in specifically for this interview. I knew that teams of torture experts wouldn't be able to obtain what this man could simply obtain with his extraordinary intelligence. This meant they had enough information about me to know my resistance level.

"You look exhausted," the BKA man began, his voice carrying the weight of his authority.

"I am," I answered in a light voice.

"Can you tell me why?"

"You should know why!"

I deciphered early shock in his eyes, but a fraction of a second later, his eyes were once again emotionless.

"You can fill in the blanks," he continued.

I began to speak in a calm voice. The minutes turned into half-hours, hours, and several hours. The more I talked and answered the questions, the more I felt that something was wrong. Yet I was only telling the truth. But I wasn't surprised by the BKA's distrust after what happened at the airport. I suddenly wanted to defend myself but decided not to, knowing this wouldn't change anything. I focused on being brutally honest regardless of the consequences.

After what seemed an interminable time, I finished speaking and handed over a copy of the list. The BKA man squeezed his lips together to prevent himself from smiling, which was really reassuring for me.

He left the room with the list and returned twenty minutes later with a tray containing a cup of coffee and a glass of water.

"You have been tested and come through with flying colors. Now I understand why the Securitate is looking for you so badly. No one should have an enemy of your level."

From experience, I knew how to remain unmoved by compliments, but I had to recognize that his words made me feel good. However, a question tortured my mind and remained unanswered. I hesitated for a split second.

"Can I ask you a question?"

"I'm not sure if I'll be able to answer, but yes, you can ask your question!"

"Since the beginning of the interrogation, I have felt like I am missing something. You weren't aware of the assignment the BKA had asked me to complete. Where you?"

I read the disbelief on his face. He stared at me for a while, his eyes betraying a mix of shock and realization before he answered.

"You are truly a skilled agent! Hats off to you! I will try to be as concise as possible. The BKA didn't hire you," he revealed, his words hitting me like thunderbolts.

In turn, I looked at him in disbelief. Was he making fun of me?

"So, you're saying I was recruited by an organization other than the BKA?"

"That's exactly what I'm saying. And we were fortunate to find out."

"How did you find out?"

"A few days after your departure to Moscow, one of our departments tried to contact you through Paul. You were supposed to meet with one of our representatives to summarize your activity with the Securitate. As a result of Paul's information, we realized that you had been recruited by a group that claimed to work for the BKA. They used Paul to get to you, which leads us to believe they have access to internal information, perhaps in the BKA itself."

"I hope you don't suspect Paul!" I exclaimed, standing up from my chair.

"Sit down," said the BKA man with a firm voice. "Yes, we considered that possibility. But we found out that he was innocent. But his contact at the BKA will support the consequences. That's when we passed your photo to all our borders, hoping you'd show up somewhere. The group that recruited you was too confident we wouldn't find out. Their mistake was putting your picture on the passport you travelled with between Helsinki and Frankfurt. We were notified of your arrival in Frankfurt minutes after your passport was deposited at the check-in counter."

"Did Paul's contact tell you who they are?"

"No. During his interrogation, we realized that he acted in good faith and had been played. But the fact that Nikolai works for them tells us much about the group that recruited you. Thanks to you, they failed. Unfortunately, we didn't have time to send a task force to stop Nikolai. You know the rest."

"The crazy part is, I didn't suspect anything. I should

have been more aware…”

“Don’t be silly. We are pleased with the way things turned out. Without knowing it, you’ve done us a huge favor. The list they now have in their hands is no longer of any value to us. Otherwise, it would have cost us a fortune. Your concern now should be your safety. Is there a place you’d like to live? We are ready to do whatever is necessary to grant you this protection and to help you start a new life. With the Securitate and now the Russian mob after you, your fate is almost decided.”

I remained silent for a while. I thought about all the years I had been stuck up in a horrible conspiracy, all leading up to my arrival in Germany. An offer like this wouldn’t come around a second time. I could retire to the other side of the world, hoping to be out of the Securitate and the Russian mafia’s reach. But to what end?

“I appreciate your offer, but you know as well as I do that, no matter where I will be, if they wanted to find me, they’d be able to. To think otherwise would be naïve.”

The BKA man crossed his arms and didn’t make any comments. He knew I was right.

“What I need is a German passport and a place to live. Alone. My presence in Andrei Munteanu’s house could endanger his and his family’s lives. The Securitate will punish all those who are on my side.”

“Is that your final decision?”

“That’s my final decision.”.

“Perfect! I respect your decision even if I disagree with it. You’ll be taken to your new residence in the morning.

We will notify you when your passport will be ready. We will also open a bank account in your name. It'll give you a little independence. There will also be a car for you."

"Can I contact you in case I need your help?"

He took a pen out of his pocket and wrote something on a piece of paper that he handed me.

"This is a phone number in case of extreme emergency. Your code will be "The List." Memorize the number and destroy the paper."

As the BKA man's eyes flickered to his watch, a sudden realization washed over me; my interrogation was over. "Paul will undoubtedly have some questions for me," I said, my voice trailing off as I struggled to comprehend the abruptness of the situation.

"Paul will be instructed not to ask you any questions."

He shook my hand and left the room, wishing me good luck. When he left, a tall woman with a hooked nose and gray hair appeared at the door's opening and signaled me to follow her. She took me to a small apartment on the third floor that was barely furnished and rarely used. The woman said goodnight and left without another word.

Surveying the sparsely furnished room, I felt a wave of exhaustion wash over me. A tray of sandwiches sat on a small table beside a water jug, but hunger was the last thing on my mind. All I craved was sleep. Stripping off my clothes as I walked, I collapsed onto the narrow bed. The sheets, though simple, were freshly washed, and I found solace in their comforting embrace, my sore body finally finding some respite.

CHAPTER 23

The apartment the BKA representative had driven me to the next day was downtown Frankfurt. To ensure my protection, they opted for a place where hundreds of pedestrians pass daily. Without knowing it, the people all became my lookouts. It was impossible to enter the building without being seen by dozens of eyes. In addition, the building was covered in state-of-the-art surveillance cameras.

In the following days, as I settled into my new apartment, bought winter clothes, and woke for hours to familiarize myself with the neighborhood, a sudden wave of loneliness engulfed me. Today, I felt a strong sense of duty to contact George. It was time to join forces with those fighting against the tyranny of the communist regime.

Despite the potential risks, I had a responsibility I

couldn't ignore. I had to visit Paul's family, even though it meant exposing them to the looming threat of the Securitate. They were my only link to George. The evening had descended on the city, and bright signs were trying to seduce the customer. I looked around, satisfied with how the apartment looked, then approached the window. My eyes landed on a young couple kissing on the sidewalk, their affection radiating warmth in the chilly evening. They seemed oblivious to the world, lost in their own little bubble of love. I had never understood it, the intense feeling that made people be attracted to each other like a drug. I never crossed that line. I walked away from the window and checked my watch. It was time to go to Paul.

Twenty minutes later, I stepped out of a taxi on a street parallel to Paul's residence and continued on foot, my senses heightened, scanning for any anomaly in the surroundings. The recent events in Moscow had increased the number of my enemies, and I couldn't afford to let my guard down.

I arrived safely, and Paul opened the door to me. His parents weren't home; they had gone to Hamburg to attend a wedding. Paul was supposed to join them the next day.

He poured me a glass of wine and sat in the living room.

I told him I would like to contact the Organization's members here in Germany. The Organization, a clandestine group dedicated to protecting our country's interests, had been his life for the past decade.

He seemed to hesitate for a moment, but finally, he

replied.

"I've decided to withdraw from the Organization. Next month I will get married. I want to have children and live a quiet life. If I continue with the Organization, I will endanger the lives of those I love."

My mind was a whirlwind of questions, but I kept my composure, waiting to see if his decision was final. The silence stretched on, thick with unspoken thoughts.

"What happened to your patriotism, your sense of justice?" I finally asked.

"Ever since I arrived in Germany, I've put my life on the line to help the cause of my people. I've fulfilled my duty. I know people who left the country and could have gotten involved, but they did nothing. We all have the right to choose our path, and I've chosen mine." His voice was firm, his resolve unwavering, a testament to his determination.

Evidently, his decision was final, and I wasn't surprised. During my years with the Securitate, many agents had migrated to other countries, leaving behind the world of espionage and doing nothing but settle for a good life. Paul was a regular citizen who had decided to help the Organization and risked his life. He has the right to determine what he thinks is better for him and his future family.

"I assume you have a contact for me?"

"George will be your contact. I've briefed him on our situation, and he's on board."

"Did he ask about me?"

"Yes, he asks about you. He wanted to talk to you, but I didn't know when you'd return. Besides, his calls are pretty brief. He left me a number where you can reach him. You have to call him every Wednesday night at eight o'clock sharp. The line will be safe for three minutes.

He finished the rest of his drink and set his glass down. An embarrassed look appeared on his face.

"Ana, I'm sorry…"

"You shouldn't be. As you said, you have the right to protect your family."

A complete silence took over the room.

"All right, I got to go! Good luck!" I said as I walked towards the door.

I was so lost in my thoughts when I walked straight into the deserted street, forgetting that Munteanu's house could always be watched.

With my enemies' connections, it would be easy for them to realize that this was where they had the best chance of catching me. Acknowledging my mistake, I moved down the sidewalk, my narrow eyes swept from side to side, taking everything in.

I noticed an almost imperceptible movement in my peripheral vision, a simple light variation. I was startled. The steps were stifled but real. Stealthily but not enough, two individuals were moving in my direction.

I calculated my distance from them and estimated my chances of getting away. I did not yet know precisely how to proceed. Those pursuing me were indeed armed, and I had no weapons. Plus, I didn't know how many they were.

When I began to run, a whistle rang in my ear, followed by three others. Bullets were being fired. Silencers had diminished the noise. I pretended to go right, then dived to the left to escape the line of fire. A taxi stopped dangerously close to me. I jumped, rolled over the taxi, and started running again.

A bullet grazed my shoulder so close that it tore a piece of my jacket. My pursuers were fast professionals who didn't lose a second. Suddenly, I heard the sound of an engine closing in. Then another one. Keeping up my pace, I jumped to my right and dived between the two cars, catching my fall with the palms of my hands.

Taking advantage of the split second during which, my pursuers had to readjust their view with the bright headlights and the streetlights, I hopped over the fence of the nearest house, quickly crawling over to a parallel street. But my pursuers weren't amateurs. I had gained a few seconds of respite, but footsteps were already echoing behind me.

"They won't give up", I thought. I didn't even know if it was Popescu's men or the Russians. Or maybe even both. It didn't matter. They were equally dangerous.

Straight ahead, there was a bus stop. A few people were waiting patiently, sitting on a wooden bench. I passed the bus stop in a flash, knowing that stopping there would be suicide.

Even in the presence of witnesses, my pursuers would not have hesitated to shoot me before disappearing without a trace.

Light covered the bus stop surroundings, making it more challenging. They caught me unarmed. In my current situation, the dark must be her best friend. A confrontation wouldn't last very long; her only chance is escaping.

As I approached a fork in the road, I saw a fence that was under construction. Metal wires were hanging along the wall. I picked one up and disappeared into the darkness of the garden surrounding the house. I stopped behind a tree trunk and soon heard a tree branch cracking under the steps of one of my pursuers.

I leapt into the air, the metal wire from the fence in my hands. In a flash, I circled the wire around my opponent's neck. I heard a cracking as the wire crossed through cartilages. He tried to free himself, his right hand flying instinctively to his neck to try to stop the suffocation. Under the unbearable pain, he wanted to grab me and drag me to the ground. I pulled the metal wire even harder, and there was another crack. With an inhumane grunt, my opponent collapsed, mute for eternity.

I barely had time to take possession of my opponent's weapon and ammunition when I heard rapid steps approaching in the dark and then the sound of a cartridge hitting the ground. Trying to retreat, I lost my balance and, while trying to regain it, narrowly avoided another bullet fired at me.

There were gunshots speeding through the air, inches from my head, and all my attention was focused on avoiding the shots, temporarily preventing me from returning fire. I squinted my eyes in the dark and leapt as I zigzagged through the trees of the garden. A volley of bullets ripped through their trunks.

They fired at me recklessly, not caring that we were in a residential area and that someone might get hurt. Running with all my strength, my feet barely touching the ground, I could not help but notice that this time, the order was no longer to capture me alive; I had been sentenced to death.

I skirted the house and jumped into the neighboring yard. A roaring engine pierced the silence, followed by the shrill sound of a police siren. I was disoriented, lying flat against the ground, on the lookout for the slightest noise or movement. I had to find something other than running from one yard to another. The problem was that I needed to figure out how many people were after me.

"*I have to find a solution,*" I told myself. "*I don't have to neglect anything and be more perceptive than my opponent. In this situation, what could the solution be?*"

My eyes swept around. On the house's back porch, a barbecue was covered in a black cover. If the propane tank attached to it was full enough, that could be my solution. The only problem was that I had to get there to find out.

Slowly, I stood up and crouched along the walls of the house. The way to the terrace was long and dangerous, but it was my only hope. Footsteps were audibly getting closer. My pursuers were close.

I continued to move forward when the siren of a police car sounded nearby; something had happened in the neighborhood. I knelt, detached the propane bottle from the barbecue, threw it towards the yard, and fired. There was an explosion of impressive power, given that it was only a bottle of propane.

With my heart beating in my chest, I moved away at the highest speed I was able to reach. The explosion will delay the pursuers and attract police attention to the area. By then, I'll be long gone.

One or two seconds later, a bullet crashed into the wall of the house that I had just bypassed. My pursuers hardly seemed to care that the police car was now nearby.

When I started running again, another bullet brushed my head. Residents began to take to the streets, attracted by the explosion and the police sirens.

"*Stop! Reverse the trap!*" echoed a voice in my head.

Instinctively, I pulled the dead pursuer's gun out of my pocket. Pretending to have been hit by a bullet, I let out a desperate cry and fell to the ground. The hand in which I held the weapon was hidden between my body and the ground.

A short silence followed. I felt the pulsations of my blood in my veins. I waited.

Slow, cautious steps approached me, and two shadows stood on the sidewalk. I now distinguished the two shadows who had stopped a few meters away. They exchanged a few words and continued approaching, pointing their weapons at me.

They were now standing nearby, their weapons pointed at my head. They intended to shoot to ensure they had completed the contract they were getting paid for.

I wasn't surprised. Professionals' behavior under certain

circumstances is very predictable, especially when they have received the same training as I did.

Entirely focused, my thoughts clear and organized in my brains, I knew that the only choice I had was to execute my pursuers or to get killed. I was waiting for the right time to attack.

The moment they pointed their arms, my back bent like a bow to free my hand that was keeping the gun, and I fired several bullets in quick succession on both men. Two black holes appeared in the middle of both of their foreheads. My shots had been so precise that the two men dropped on the cement of the sidewalk without making a sound. The coast was clear.

Then, I noticed the growing number of citizens approaching the house where I had set off the explosion. it won't be long before they discover the corpses of my opponents. I pulled both bodies into the shadow beside the fence, pocketed all the ammunition I found on them and mingled with the confused crowd. Unlike the crowd, I walked away towards the street corner, trying to disappear before residents realized I wasn't part of the neighborhood.

My breath was short and I tried to regain my calm. A few minutes later, I sprinted towards a nearby yard after making sure I had yet to be spotted. Sliding from one backyard to another, I covered a decent distance. I kept an eye on the street, looking for any suspicious movements. When I was sure there was nothing to worry about, I left the yard and entered the street.

The air was cold but humid, and the darkness of the

night surrounded me, giving me a feeling of freedom. Like a stray cat, I walked the streets without any destination in mind. All I knew was I had to escape there as soon as possible. Arriving at a crossroads, I noticed that traffic was denser. I crossed the street, hastening my pace with each stride. Ten minutes later, I was sitting in the backseat of a cab.

Taking a deep breath, I settled more comfortably in the backseat. My recent actions could only increase my number of enemies. Whoever wanted me dead would soon know I was still alive. I was running blind, in a labyrinth, without any way out. It was a close call escape in my game of hide-and-seek with death.

CHAPTER 24

I awoke around six o'clock in the morning after a short night taken over by her nightmares. After a warm shower, I dressed and went outside to look for a newsstand. On the third page of the local newspaper, I found what I was looking for. The title of the article I read eagerly was: "THEFT OR SETTLEMENT OF ACCOUNTS."

I breathed a sigh of relief as I realized the press had chosen not to divulge many details about the discovery of the men I had killed.

There was no mention of the nationality of the two bodies or the existence of a third person involved. The explanation in the paper was simple: the two men wanted to carry out an armed robbery, and, by mistake, they had shot at a bottle of propane, producing an explosion. The reasons why they hit each other remained unknown.

"More news will be published after the police reports are released," said the article.

I wasn't surprised. The truth was only known by a small circle who acted in the shadows to prevent panic among the population. Whether or not my enemies would buy it was another matter entirely. All I knew was that I had caught a break.

I walked for what seemed like an eternity, my senses heightened as I blended in with the bustling crowd. It was Friday, and the town center was alive with activity. Instinctively, I scanned my surroundings, a reflex I had been conditioned to have.

In front of a chic restaurant that smelled like delicious BBQ and garlic, I noticed the presence of a Gypsy. A dusty down covered her colorful clothes, sweeping the slippery ground. Her hand was extended to the customers leaving the restaurant, but they were getting into their cars without paying her any attention.

By connection, I remembered the Gypsy women I had met on my way to the border. Her words came to my mind: *Your pain will never disappear entirely, but it will be mitigated. You'll learn to live with it. Shortly, there will be no change in your life, but that won't last long. After a very hectic period, you will go far away from these lands to join the man you love. You will have two children and a life full of happiness.*

I stopped in the middle of the passers-by. Gypsies were very perceptive fortune tellers.

Some people believe the predictions of the gypsies turn

out to be true. It couldn't be true in my case. In my life, there was nothing but emptiness, violence and darkness. Given recent events, I was unlikely to survive. I looked at the sky full of heavy clouds and decided to return home. In the building lobby, a man was frantically checking some envelopes.

Knowing there was no mail in my mailbox, I followed the elevator's direction, followed by the man who had slipped some envelopes into a briefcase. He smiled and began to stare at me. He was so close to me that I could smell his breath. A bell rang, and the light began to blink, announcing the elevator was coming down. The doors opened, and two men beside a brown-haired woman entered the hall.

I had no desire to take the elevator with that man who kept staring at me. I took out my keys and went back to the mailbox. Followed by the man's insistent look, I opened my box and, to my great surprise, found a brown envelope.

The envelope's lack of inscription meant someone had to have come to deliver it. I paused, grabbed the envelope, and went back to the elevator. The hall was now deserted.

I opened the envelope as soon as I closed the door to my apartment. A German passport under the name of Ana Zaicovich was inside. I had dozens of passports, but none with my real name. The BKA had kept their promise. I couldn't believe it. Was this my chance to escape?

I sighed slowly as I gazed at the passport. The irony of the situation struck me. People had risked their lives at border crossings to get a passport like this. For them, it symbolized freedom, the possibility of a better life.

I had never considered becoming a citizen other than that of my country. But I had become one because I had been a pawn in the service of an odious game whose rules no one had explained to me.

That night, I was plagued by a series of restless awakenings. I couldn't recall my dreams, but a feeling of suffocation gripped my throat. By six o'clock in the morning, I was wide awake, my mind racing with unsettling thoughts.

Two hours later, after some weightlifting and a few hundred abs repetitions, my body was dripping with sweat. Half an hour later, I walked through the streets, stopped in front of the elegantly decorated windows, walked into some shops and chatted with the vendors, mastering the almost irresistible urge to hide in the darkest corners. My gaze examined every pedestrian, car and passenger, watching for a face that seemed out of place. The possibility of being shot by a killer at any moment was intolerable. This couldn't continue. I'd go crazy.

It was still light out when I came home. A little red light was flashing on the answering machine. Surprised and worried simultaneously, I pressed the button, and George's voice sounded in the apartment. He had undoubtedly called Paul, and Paul had given him my phone number.

"Hello, Christel! Don't forget that Alex's birthday is in three days, and he'll be very disappointed if you forget to see him. Put just a candle on the cake, not fifty like you did last year. If you can call me, I'll be home around eight."

The silence had settled in the apartment. I repeated George's coded message. I was sure that the BKA was intercepting my conversations, and I was glad that George was being careful. He had spoken in impeccable German, and he could pass himself off as someone with the wrong phone number. In fact, the message said that I had to contact him urgently at eight o'clock precisely at the number he was giving me, using numbers and words in a certain order.

Without a moment's hesitation, I stepped out into the night. The city was a dazzling array of lights, a prelude to the impending Christmas celebrations. But amidst the festive air, a sense of urgency hung heavy in the atmosphere.

With each step, I could feel the anticipation building up. I was getting closer to the public telephone, the only means to reach George. The city was alive with the sounds of Christmas, but my mind was focused on the task at hand.

I thought he uses a burner phone that leads to a false address.

My heart skipped a beat as George's loud and clear voice broke the silence on the other end of the line.

"Hello!"

"Hey!"

"Ah! Finally! I was afraid you didn't get my message."

"As you can see, I got your message, but it was a little late, and I had to hurry so I could call you in time."

"It's good you made it. I have two minutes and twenty seconds before the line can be intercepted. You have to listen to me carefully. Vlad Herescu's life is in danger. I'll give you the details when we have more time. We managed to get him and his family out of the country before the Securitate arrested him."

"Where is he now?"

"He is in Istanbul, a territory known to the Securitate. Vlad alone has no chance of escaping. He needs help. Now it's time to start your revenge against the Securitate."

I swallowed my saliva. I met Vlad several times during my work with George.

"Don't you have contacts in Istanbul?"

"Yes, but we have a problem; those who can help him are asking for too much money. The Organization does not have sufficient funds to pay them. That's why I've been looking forward to your call."

"You want me to go to Istanbul?"

"Yes. But you can't go alone. It's too dangerous. You'll go with Radu Branescu."

"Who's Radu Branescu?" I asked.

"You don't know him. He's been out of the country for twelve years. His specialty is spinning and martial arts. He sells his services to the highest bidder."

"You just said that the Organization does not have sufficient funds! How will you pay him?"

"He volunteered his services. Vlad's wife was his first love."

"Wouldn't Vlad be jealous?"

"He must consider himself very lucky to have Radu on his side. The men that the Securitate will send are very skilled and dangerous. Vlad's life is an insignificant detail to them. They don't care what happens to him or his wife and daughter."

"How can I contact Radu Branescu?"

"He's in Frankfurt right now."

"Give me his phone number; I'll contact him immediately."

I barely had time to memorize the number when I heard several clicks.

"The line is no longer safe," I thought.

"I have to cut the line," George confirmed. "Thank you, Ana! Take care of yourself."

I heard one last click. George had closed the line.

CHAPTER 25

Despite his large build, Radu Branescu had a regular physique. As a trained observer, I noticed the curiosity in his black eyes, which scanned around without missing a thing.

The experienced look of a spy, I thought.

We have met in a parking lot near downtown. Radu stared at me for a long time.

"Something wrong? I asked him.

"I've never worked with a woman," he began. "Especially in circumstances as dangerous as this one. I can't say I approve of George's choice, but I realize I don't have any alternative."

"I don't know if I should feel insulted or shocked!" I replied. "Give me one good reason you couldn't work with me!"

"For starters, you're gorgeous. You'll get too much attention. To succeed in this dangerous game, we must go unnoticed. In addition, a man is always stronger physically," he concludes.

I couldn't believe my ears! Radu Branescu had a visceral distrust of a woman's strength. His masculine ego made him blind to reality.

"To be honest with you, your words are nothing but noise to me," I replied. "We're wasting our time."

He looked at me momentarily, sighed, and then took something out of his vest pocket.

"George contacted me a few days ago, giving me time to make arrangements," he said. "We're going to travel as a couple with Australian passports. Here's yours. We'll have time to work out the details during the flight. Questions?"

"I assume that you have contacts in Istanbul. My only contact is someone who works at the Russian embassy who, under current circumstances, I'm not sure I want to speak to."

"I have the contacts we need. We'll talk about it tomorrow during the flight."

"All right," I replied.

With that, I left him and went home to prepare my suitcase.

I also have to study the picture of the passport she's travelling with. Assuming a new identity had become second nature to her.

On the second day, Radu Branescu was waiting for me in a small restaurant at the airport to work out the last details. When the aircraft got on the runway, I felt that Radu's opinion of working with a woman had slightly changed.

Having only been there once, I didn't know Istanbul very well. Through the window, I looked at the city between two continents, Europe and Asia.

With a population of more than thirteen million, Istanbul was one of the most populated cities in Europe and one of the largest megacities in the world. Founded on seven hills like Rome, Istanbul was considered one of the world's three most important ancient capitals. The ancient names of the city, Byzantium, Constantinople and New Rome, bear witness to its long history.

When Radu's eyes landed on his watch, I realized that he was not only checking the time but also wondering if Vlad and his family were still alive. I gazed at him as he expressed his thoughts aloud:

"I hope they are still alive. "

"Whatever happens," I said, "we'd better keep thinking of our chances of succeeding and the obstacles that may stand in our way."

"You're right!" he replied.

We cleared customs without any problems. Through the window of the taxi that crept dangerously between the cars, I admired the disparity of buildings that made this city so fascinating. Next to a majestic 17th-century mosque were modern buildings and colorful bazaars.

Turkey has had no official religion since the 1930s, although the religious practices of the various groups are still very much present in daily life.

A secular country, Turkey has welcomed an eclectic population throughout its history: Turks, Armenians, Arabs, Macedonians, Serbs, Russians, Albanians, Bulgarians, Jews, Georgians, and Molokans. All these communities were represented in Istanbul, the capital of several empires and a crossroads of peoples and two continents.

There were no similar faces in the crowded streets: blondes with blue eyes, Asians with almond eyes, and Arabs with big black eyes. Next to women who wore a veil were those who preferred more modern hairstyles.

It's easy to become invisible in Istanbul, I thought.

The taxi stopped in front of the Grand Bazaar, and after Radu had paid the fare, he signaled me to follow him.

The Grand Bazaar was crowded with tourists and locals. With its blazing colors and winding alleys, it looked like the land of Ali Baba. I stopped in front of the first table covered with colored scarves, bought one and covered my hair and half my face. Bending my back, a little and changing my walk, I became a random person. I followed Radu into the Grand Bazaar maze, making a point of going unnoticed. You would have had to be an excellent observer to notice the look into my eyes that didn't miss a thing.

After about twenty minutes, Radu Branescu stopped before a souvenir stand. A male salesman immediately approached us and signaled us to follow him to the back of the shop.

A lot of merchandise was stored on shelves, and a smell similar to that of a clothes warehouse filled our noses. The man stopped before a coffee table surrounded by four chairs and signaled us to sit down.

"Ana, this is Mustafa," said Radu.

I shook the hand of the salesman, who began to speak in impeccable German.

"I have some bad news," he said, his voice carrying the weight of the situation. "Vlad and his family were intercepted by the Securitate three hours ago. They are now in one of the neighborhoods along the Bosphorus, in a house officially owned by a Turkish man, Akturk Bahri. Unofficially, the house belongs to the Romanian Securitate. Akturk Bahri is being paid to cover up for them. The power of money has no limits in Turkey."

Just like anywhere in the world, I thought.

"Then, we don't have time to waste," confirmed Radu, reflecting our shared determination. "Call Ambrosio and tell him we'll arrive in half an hour."

We left the Grand Bazaar through an exit different from the one we had entered and took the first free taxi.

"Who is Ambrosio?" I asked Radu.

"He's my contact here in Istanbul. He can help us save Vlad."

Twenty-five minutes later, a tall man with a muscular body opened the door of his house to us. He greeted Radu and then turned to me. While he was shaking my hand, I read the surprise in his eyes.

I thought that wasn't a good start. Like Radu, he has the same distrust of women.

The house was spacious and smelled of mint tea. A

young girl, dressed in very loose panties, tight at the ankle in oriental fashion, brought tea, and we sat at the Turkish table.

"It's been a long time since we shared a tea," began Ambrosio, addressing Radu. "What brings you to my country in the middle of winter?"

In a few words, Radu explained the situation.

"I need your help, and it's urgent," he concluded.

"You know it's going to cost you," replied Ambrosio. "Securitate agents are hazardous. They do a lot of smuggling on our territory, but no action has been taken by the Turkish authorities. They are protected by high-ranking officials who are paid very well to close their eyes."

"You will be paid the amount requested," answered Radu. "We don't have a minute to lose if we're going to find Vlad and his family alive."

"I don't mean to be rude," said Ambrosio, "but there's no room for a woman in all this."

"Ana is not just any woman," answered Radu, to my surprise.

"I agree with you," said Ambrosio, admiring me.

Realizing that his words were misplaced, he continued in a neutral tone.

"Then I have to show you the merchandise."

As soon as he said that, he signaled us to follow him. The small room next to the garage where he let us in contained a veritable arsenal of weapons and ammunition, camouflage clothing, and bulletproof jackets.

"You can get changed here," said Ambrosio, addressing

me. "I have a few calls to make. We'll meet in the garage when you're ready."

I changed my clothes and filled my backpack with ammunition. I had been waiting in the garage for about ten minutes when the door opened. Radu and Ambrosio emerged, dressed in black from head to toe and carrying backpacks. We settled inside a car with tinted windows, left the garage and soon merged into the city's swarming traffic. The cold wind that had begun to blow in gusts did not frighten the people who were invading the city, wandering in all directions without respecting traffic rules. Soon, the darkness would spread in the sky, and sparkling lights would appear all over the city.

Thirty minutes later, the car stopped in front of the Bosporus marina. We remained silent; the engine stopped, and the lights were off until a man suddenly appeared out of the darkness. I recognized Mustafa, the salesman we had met in the bazaar. He led us to a small boat covered with a canvas over the cockpit.

The boat ran through the dark waters, with its powerful engine efficiently responding to the driver's demands. We were barely visible from the shore in the dim light of sunset.

Twenty-three minutes later, the engine slowed down, and Mustafa began to zigzag carefully to slip between two big boats docked in front of a huge house. No light shone in the house, which was unsurprising after Ambrosio explained that the house owners spent their winters in places privileged by the sun and white sand beaches.

Ambrosio's plan was simple: Radu and I had to follow

him because he knew the terrain like the back of his hand. Mustafa remained in the boat, ready to live at any time.

We left the boat, avoiding the elegant walkway, crawling instead on the land covered by the dry grass of the lawn. A fresh wind was blowing through our faces.

We advanced in the dark to a street where houses stood surrounded by large yards. The musical sound of an organ was heard in the street, and we heard several voices in the neighboring house.

We moved quickly, relying on the noise of the elements to cover our movement. Four hundred meters away, we saw the Securitate house's contours and stopped. Streams of light shone in the vicinity of the gigantic house. The vast parking lot was filled with elegant cars, and the stone fence was lined with marble statues. The terrace was dotted with wrought iron tables and pots of plants dried by the temperature. Half covered by a blue canvas, a cigarette boat was docked at the landing.

I admired the house's splendor. It was always the best for the Securitate, and the oppressed paid for this luxury.

We decided to split up to check the house's surroundings and meet at the same point half an hour later.

I started moving in the opposite direction to the water while remaining a few meters from the fence surrounding the land, emerging into the street leading to the house. I advanced furtively, filtering through every corner for a few hundred meters. By the time I had retraced my steps, the temperature had dropped sharply. The town's lights reflected on the low clouds on either side of the Bay.

I turned my attention to the land around the house. The large number of mature trees enabled me to hide behind them without being seen. Perturbed by my intrusion, a night bird flew away towards the neighboring garden. I stopped, realizing that I wasn't the one who had alarmed the bird. There was someone else around. Through my night vision goggles, I distinguished the shape of a rifle with a built-in silencer. Something was threatening in the stillness of the weapon.

Glued to the ground, I waited for a few seconds. After ensuring the guard I was watching hadn't noticed anything, I moved silently in his direction. Sixty seconds later, I stood two meters before the guard holding the gun. Surprised, he raised his weapon to fire. But I was faster than him. I heard a slight groan when my knife punctured his throat. A smell of blood permeated the fresh air of the night when the guard lay lifeless on the ground.

Time was of the essence. The discovery of the guard's body would instantly trigger the alarm, leaving no room for delay.

Checking the time, I realized I had only eleven minutes before the pivotal meeting with Radu and Ambrosio. I moved swiftly to avoid any noise to the far end of the garden. The darkness of my clothing and the moonless night gave me a cloak of invisibility. I could hear muffled voices and whispers to my left, about ten meters away.

Looking between the trees, I saw two Securitate agents with their backs turned to me. They were immersed in conversation, paying no attention to their surroundings.

The tallest one turned slightly, enough for me to see his face. At first, I felt a sense of déjà-vu; the next moment, a chill of dread ran down my spine. My breath caught, and the world around me faded into a blur. There was something unmistakably familiar in the cold, calculating eyes, the slight tilt of the jaw, and the scar that cut just above his eyebrow.

It all came rushing back in a violent, unforgiving wave. I knew this face. I knew it from the nightmares that had haunted me for years. It was the face of the man who had torn my world apart, the murderer of my family. Recognition hit me like a punch to the gut, visceral and undeniable, and I was paralyzed with a mix of terror and fury. Within a second, I was a little girl again. My throat knotted, and I remained ultimately still, holding my breath.

Slowly, I came to my senses, the fog of shock lifting just enough for clarity to seep in. My pulse pounded in my ears, a relentless reminder of the precious seconds slipping away. I couldn't let my family murderer escape, not now, not ever. Sometimes, some moments define everything, moments where the world narrows to a single, unbreakable resolve. This was mine.

With a certainty that settled deep in my bones, I knew I couldn't leave this place without punishing this assassin. My breath steadied, a fierce resolve burning through the paralyzing fear. I wouldn't just survive; I would make him pay for every ounce of pain he had inflicted.

I fell to the ground, gripping my weapon so tightly my knuckles turned white, fighting the urge to fire. My breath came in ragged gasps, each a battle to maintain control. Suddenly, the house door swung open, and six men spilled out, their footsteps echoing ominously in the night. They moved with purpose, heading straight for the vast parking lot.

Engines roared to life as they climbed into their sleek, elegant cars, the screech of tires piercing the silence as they sped away, leaving behind a trail of burnt rubber. Then, I heard a faint buzzing sound, distant but growing louder, cutting through the night like a warning. My eyes darted upwards. High above, a flashing light blinked against the dark sky, drawing closer with every second. Through my night vision goggles, the shape of a helicopter emerged from the shadows, its rotors slicing the air with a menacing hum.

The buzzing intensified, a thunderous roar fluttering the leaves around me wildly. Dust and debris whipped across the ground as the helicopter descended, the force of its approach pressing against my skin like an invisible hand. With my breathing and heart rate steadier, I ducked below the trees and crept toward the meeting point with Ambrosio and Radu. I found them lying flat on their bellies; they were following the helicopter's descent into the parking lot.

"I think we're too late," said Ambrosio. "Your man must be significant for the Securitate if they send a helicopter to pick him up!"

"He's not that important to them," I replied. "There must be another explanation."

"Look! ", blew Radu.

A man emerged from the house, clutching a portable refrigerator to his chest as he sprinted toward the helicopter. One of the passengers reached out, quickly seizing the fridge, and the pilot powered up the engines. The helicopter roared to life, and with a deafening noise, it ascended into the sky.

The buzzing gradually faded into the distance, leaving a heavy silence that settled like a blanket over the scene. We exchanged glances, the same unsettling thought crossing our minds: that portable refrigerator was likely used to transport human organs. Could the Securitate stoop to such a vile source of income? And how did this connect to Vlad and his family? Were they still alive? There was only one way to find out: to enter the house.

We quickly shared the intel on the guards' positions and debated the best strategy. Staying in the shadows, we moved with deliberate caution. We scaled the garden's fence and split up, each heading in a different direction.

As I advanced silently, my senses sharpened to a razor's edge. Moving with the grace of a stalking predator, I navigated through the garden, letting my instincts guide me. The moon, obscured by swiftly drifting clouds, cast fleeting beams of light that danced across the ground. The silence around me felt alive, like a sleeping giant's deep, slow breaths.

Spotting the first guard, I pulled a steel tourniquet from my bag and approached inch by inch. The guard, weapon in hand, was scanning the ground with a dull, methodical gaze. I crouched low, then eased myself onto the ground, motionless and patient, every fiber of my being focused on the movement of his shadow.

A gust of wind rustled the leaves overhead, and the guard let out a long yawn, his eyes fluttering shut for a heartbeat. Seizing the moment, I sprang forward and looped the steel tourniquet around his neck. He flailed wildly, his arms thrashing in desperate, futile motions. I tightened my grip, feeling the metal dig into his skin. He convulsed, his body jerking in spasms before collapsing to the ground with barely a sound. His final breath escaped in a quiet sigh, and he went limp. I took his automatic weapon and turned toward the house, moving with renewed purpose.

But then, a sharp screech of tortured tires pierced the stillness. I spun around, scanning the parking lot. A limousine screeched to a halt near the entrance, and two men stepped out, striding purposefully toward the house. Keeping low, I slipped into the parking lot and crouched behind the limousine, drawing my hunting knife and stabbing into the rear tires. Then, I crawled up and stabbed the front tires, too. After ensuring all four tires were punctured, I hung the knife on my belt and checked the street for noise.

I hoped that Radu and Ambrosio had heard the arrival of the limousine and that they would not be surprised by the new arrivals. I had to make sure they didn't.

Sticking to the shadows, I moved carefully toward the house, avoiding the sweep of the spotlights. As I got closer, I spotted Radu and Ambrosio waiting at the corner of the building. The area was cloaked in darkness, but they stood out enough to make my stomach tense. If I could see them, so could our enemies.

I was about to close the distance when I froze at the sound of footsteps crunching on gravel. I held my breath and listened. Two men, both armed with automatic weapons, were making their way along the wall, heading straight for Radu and Ambrosio. They were now only a few meters away, their movements precise and deliberate. Everything about them; the way they gripped their guns, the controlled pace of their approach, screamed seasoned operatives, not to be underestimated.

There was no mistaking their intent. I needed to warn Radu and Ambrosio fast. Moving quickly but silently, I shifted to an angle where only they could see me. I pulled out my flashlight, flicking it on and off in rapid succession. Radu's eyes caught the signal, a flash of understanding crossing his face.

"Danger on your right," I signaled urgently, hoping they'd react quickly. The situation was dire, and they needed to act fast. But it was too late. In a perfectly coordinated sprint, the two Securitate agents closed the distance, their weapons aimed squarely at the backs of Ambrosio and Radu. My heart pounded. I had to act now. I couldn't afford hesitation. If they raised the alarm, we would all be done.

My mind raced, calculating every possible move and potential outcome. I needed to reverse the trap and neutralize the agents before they could utter a single word.

There was no time for elaborate tactics; every second that ticked by was a second too long.

I took a deep breath, my focus narrowing to a pinpoint. In a fluid motion, I reached for the silenced pistol at my hip, my grip steady despite the adrenaline surging through my veins. I aimed, exhaled slowly to steady my hand, and fired twice quickly.

The muffled pops of the shots cut through the tense silence. One agent dropped instantly, crumpling like a puppet with its strings cut. The second turned, eyes widening in surprise, but I was already moving, closing the gap. I lunged forward, striking him hard with the butt of my gun before he could react. He staggered, and I followed up with a swift blow to his temple, sending him sprawling to the ground, unconscious.

I rushed over to Ambrosio and Radu, who had finally realized the danger looming behind them.

"Let's go," I whispered, urgency lacing my voice.

We couldn't waste any more time. The threat was temporarily neutralized, but we were far from safe. The night clung to us like a shroud, heavy with danger, and we had no choice but to keep moving. We barely advanced a few steps when a sudden noise cut through the darkness behind us; footsteps, too close for comfort. My pulse quickened. We weren't alone.

Radu reacted in a flash, spinning around and driving his knee hard into the intruder's left kidney. The agent doubled over in pain, but Radu was relentless. He followed up with another brutal knee strike to the gut, sending the man sprawling. Radu's hands shot out like iron claws, gripping the agent's throat. He squeezed, and a strangled, animalistic sound escaped the man's lips, a garbled cry of agony.

"Stop," I hissed sharply, barely above a whisper. "We need him conscious. He has information."

Radu's grip loosened, and the agent gasped for air, clutching at his bruised throat. We swiftly bound his hands and feet, gagging him to silence his protests, then dragged him into the shadows, out of sight. Radu's knife glinted in the faint light as he pressed the point under the agent's chin.

"Vlad and his family," Radu demanded, voice cold and unyielding. "Where are they?"

The agent's face tightened in defiance, his lips curling into a mocking smile like a silent challenge. He wasn't going to break easily.

"You have two choices," Radu said, his voice like ice. "You give us the information, and you stay alive, or you die here like your partners. Your fate is in your hands." The agent's expression remained stone-like, but tension rippled through the air. Radu pressed the blade deeper, just enough to draw a thin line of blood. The agent's eyes flickered with pain and fear, his breath hitching.

"I'm losing patience," Radu warned, his grip tightening, the knife biting slightly into flesh.

A grimace of pain twisted the agent's face, and terror flashed in his eyes. Finally, his resolve crumbled.

"They're alive," he rasped, voice strained. "Vlad and his

family are alive. Four Securitate agents are guarding them inside the house."

Radu didn't relent. "Give us the layout of the house." The agent hesitated but knew he had no choice. He quickly outlined the interior, describing the guards' positions and routines. Surprisingly, he cooperated swiftly; Securitate agents were notorious for their toughness. But perhaps the Securitate had underestimated the risk on foreign soil, deploying less experienced men.

We absorbed every detail, binding the agent tighter to ensure he wouldn't cause trouble later. A plan took shape as we covered the remaining distance to the house, moving like shadows against the walls. The house loomed ahead, dark and silent, its windows shuttered. Not a single light seeped through. With weapons drawn and safety switches off, we approached the main door. To our surprise, it was unlocked. I exchanged a quick glance with Radu; something felt off.

We slipped inside, navigating the dimly lit corridor in tense silence, every step deliberates, every breath held. Muffled voices drifted from a nearby room, indistinct but growing more apparent with each step. We moved closer, nerves taut as wires, ready for anything that lay ahead.

At the end of the corridor, we saw several doors and other adjacent corridors. The voices became more distinct now, the timbres of angry men's voices. How many were there? We could not fully rely on the information we had. We had to act cautiously.

Ambrosio cracked open the first door just a few

centimeters, barely enough to see. What we saw made our blood run cold. A woman and a young girl, bound and gagged, were sprawled on the floor, their muffled cries of pain filling the room. On a nearby wooden chair, Vlad sat hunched, barely recognizable beneath a mask of bruises. His eyes were swollen shut, his once-familiar face now a canvas of violence. His body slumped as if he were a broken doll, limbs bent unnaturally, blood pooling beneath him, staining the floor.

His eyes, distant and clouded, carried a single, haunting message: he longed for death's release. Two men loomed over him, their hands clutching tools of torture, dark intent written in their postures.

A faint rustling sound broke through the air. We snapped our heads up, ears straining, but it was too late. We were trapped. The unmistakable click of a weapon's safety being released echoed behind us. I felt the cold, unforgiving press of a gun barrel against my back. My instincts screamed at me to move, and I shifted slightly to my right.

"Don't even think about it," a voice snarled from behind. "One move, and you're done."

Three against us. It felt like a lost cause. One of them dug his heels into the floor and, with brutal force, slammed the butt of his weapon into Ambrosio's left side, then his right kidney. His face twisted into a monstrous grin as Ambrosio crashed to the ground.

I caught Radu's eye. No words were needed. We knew what we had to do: act now or lose everything.

In a daring move, I curled into a ball on the floor, kicked my legs up, and nailed my opponent in the head. My right hand snatched the automatic weapon, and I fired at the agent controlling Ambrosio. He crumpled, clutching his stomach.

I spun back to the one I'd kicked; he was out cold, blood oozing from where his skull met the wall. Radu was a whirlwind of motion, a martial arts master in action. He disarmed his opponent with precise strikes, yanking the arm out of its socket. The opponent's face twisted in pain and fury as he reached for his weapon with his good arm. Radu didn't hesitate, aiming at the knees and pulling the trigger.

Despite the agony coursing through his body, Ambrosio managed to steady himself against the wall, his eyes fixed on the door where Vlad and his family were held. The barrel of a revolver peeked out, and Ambrosio fired, the silenced shots echoing in the hall. One of Vlad's tormentors fired back with a machine gun. Another one, eyes burning with hatred, stepped forward, aiming his machine gun at Ambrosio's neck.

"Do exactly as I say, or I'll blow his brains out!" he yelled at me and Radu.

But before he could finish his sentence, I aimed my gun at his head and fired. With a black hole in the middle of his forehead, he fell back, eyes wide open in death.

Ambrosio thanked me with a nod. We decided to drag the bodies somewhere out of sight, just in case someone might turn up unexpectedly and see them. According to the information we received, only one other agent remained inside the house, and he was supposed to be in the room where Vlad and his family were being kept captives. He must have heard the exchange of bullets in the corridor, and we must act quickly before he kills the captives.

We hid the bodies in an adjacent room, and quickly, we planned what to do next. The two silencers in their hands, Ambrosio and Radu, opened the door where the third Securitate agent held Vlad and his family captive.

The scenario went precisely as we thought. The moment they entered the room, the Securitate agent pointed his gun at Vlad's daughter. Confused sounds were coming from the girl's mouth, and tears were streaming down her face.

"Drop your weapons, or she's dead," the Securitate agent threatened.

"All right, we'll drop our weapons," Radu replied. "But we need to talk!"

"She's going to die, you hear me? Leave this house immediately. There's nothing to talk about", replied the agent, pressing the trigger on his gun.

The bullets hit the walls, breaking the glass of one of the paintings hung on them into a thousand pieces.

As planned, I moved closer to the room's window on the outside. I smashed the window with my gun, stepped over the wooden frame and jumped into the room. Surprised by the sound of the broken glass, the Securitate agent turned his head towards the window. This moment of distraction was enough for Ambrosio, who fired three bullets with deadly precision. The Securitate agent collapsed on the floor.

I approached him. His face bore no resemblance with the agent who killed my family. Where was he? Had he left the house without me noticing? I will find him. But first, we have to bring Vlad and his family to safety.

Vlad's wife and daughter could walk, but Radu and Ambrosio had to grab Vlad by the arms to move him.

We crossed the corridor and left the house cautiously. The night sky formed a dark canopy, and the temperature was low. No one was in sight. Paying attention to the injured, we arrived in the garden and advanced through the trees. When I was sure the path was clear, I informed them of my decision to return to the house.

"It's personal," I added. "Don't wait for me. I'll know where to find you if I'm still alive."

They were surprised, but I didn't wait to answer their questions. I quickly turned back and covered the distance to the house.

CHAPTER 26

I cautiously approached the front door, leaned against the adjoining wall, and listened. The only sound was of the wind coming through the broken window. I moved closer, opened the door, and went carefully down the corridor without making any noise. One by one, I turned the handles of the three doors at the end of the corridor, applying slow and steady pressure. The three rooms were empty.

Looking around me warily, I briskly walked through the adjoining rooms and corridors. The house was huge, and checking all the rooms took me a long time. I focused on the stairs going down to the basement of the house. Walking glued to the wall, I arrived in a cellar as elegant as the ground floor, with luxurious furniture and abstract paintings. No one was there. The murderer I was looking for was no longer in the house. He left without a trace. I should have known. Had he been there, he would have tried to rescue his accomplices and prevent us from saving Vlad and his family.

I was petrified for a few minutes. Why was luck always on the evil side? As I was preparing myself to turn back upstairs, a smell of acid hit me. I smelled it on my way down but hadn't paid attention because I was too focused. But down here, the smell was so strong that I felt tingling in my eyes.

In a near daze, I stopped. I decided to find out where the acid smell was coming from. I looked for adjoining doors I might have missed during my first inspection. There were none. I released the safety of my silencer, approached the wall where the smell was most potent and listened. The minutes passed slowly, and finally, a muffled sound of footsteps indicated a silent activity was taking place on the other side of the wall.

I stood still and continued to listen. There was silence for a few moments, and then I heard distinct footsteps again. There had to be a way inside. I had to find the mechanism that triggered its opening. The pungent smell of acid hits my nose. I moved a few steps along the wall to get a better view.

During my movement, I touched a vase that fell on the floor, and a noise of broken glass occurred. I froze. With a slight buzzing noise, the wall opened, revealing a room that looked like an operating room. Seeing no one, I walked into the room. Very powerful lamps cast their lights on the pristine white surface of a table where the corpse of a child lay. A large incision revealed a thoracic cage that was surprisingly empty; all his organs had been excised. Unbearable odors from freshly dissected corpses mixed with hydrochloric acid came from a bathtub along the wall.

I remember the rush in which the helicopter arrived and immediately departed, on board with the portable refrigerator used to transport human organs. I looked again at the child's corpse, and I understood that the Securitate agents were engaged in organ trafficking. The acid smell proved that the children's bodies, once deprived of their organs, were thrown in the tub filled with hydrochloric acid. After a few days of maceration, the limestone in the bones dissolved and only a bone paste remained. The children disappeared without a trace.

I was frozen by the horror of the scene. The questions were swirling under my crane: Who were these children? Where did they come from? Was somebody missing them? Were they alone in the world like me? Does the man who had killed my family kill the families of those children, too?

And suddenly, I saw him. He was there, a few yards in front of me. With an evil smile on his face, he stepped forward, an automatic weapon pointed at me.

"Ah! But who do we have here? he exclaimed without taking his eyes off me. "You're the whore that Popescu is looking for. I'll give him a nice present when I tell him I've got you. But not until you and I have a little fun. You are bloody beautiful!”

“I’m afraid you won’t like the fun I’m preparing for you,” I answered. “The time has come to pay for your crimes. You’ll never get out of here alive.”

“How dramatic you are! Killing someone is a very nice therapy for me.”

“You’re a psychopath!”

“Enough with this friendly dialogue. It’s time for you to drop your gun.”

His eyes swung a fraction of a second to a point behind me. It was enough for me to understand that someone else was in the basement.

I jumped while turning around, dislocating the arm of the man approaching me from behind. Twisting his arm, I forced him to move forward, using him as a shield against my body.

“Drop the gun, or I’ll blow his brains out,” I shouted.

But I should have known better. Agents like him, whom the Securitate used as assassins, were devoid of emotions. On his face, the expression of surprise was replaced by rage. The staccato of his automatic weapon resonated, and the power of the bullets hit the body of the human shield I held. A cry of agony left his throat, and with his eyes rolling back in death, he collapsed on the floor.

I felt my chest explodes with pain. The impact of the bullets on my flak jacket was so strong that I doubled over.

My opponent looked at me with a victorious smile.

“I think you will never get out of here alive,” he declared, mimicking my earlier words.

Slowly, we aimed our guns at each other's heads. At that moment, I heard steps on the stairs, and Radu burst into the room. With his right hand, he pointed a gun at my opponent.

"Don't move," he ordered. "Drop the gun, or I'll shoot you."

Caught entirely off guard by this intrusion, my opponent became angry. For a second, his attention waned. I used that moment to pounce on him. With rapidity, leaping in the air and spinning, I threw my right leg and struck my opponent unexpectedly. He lost his balance and fired, emptying his weapon magazine in Radu's direction. I felt the burning powder of the projectiles grazing my face.

With my right arm, I sprang up and dove towards my opponent, throwing his gun to the floor. I heard the cartridge hitting the floor while I made my opponent fall with a violent kick behind the knee. He stretched out his arms, trying to grab my legs and pull me down with him. I pressed my elbow against his larynx. He began to suffocate.

There was an audible crack, and, gasping for breath, he tried to grab me by the neck. I leaped back and, in a twisting motion, used a scissor grip around his neck. Gathering all his power, he tried to stretch his left hand on the ground, searching for his weapon. With everlasting force, I tightened the vice. His pain became unbearable, and he started to lose consciousness. He tried in vain to inhale the air he desperately needed, but a lack of oxygen paralyzed his lungs. With his eyes magnified by anger, he tried to get up, punching me. I ducked and, with a quick move, twisted his neck. The effect was immediate. He collapsed softly and stopped breathing.

I pushed the lifeless body away, holding my breath. I wanted to throw up.

I looked up at Radu and felt my blood freeze. The bullets pierced his legs. He had fallen down the stairs, head down, legs apart in an unnatural position. Blood flowed from his convulsed body, and his face was contorted with pain. I knelt next to him.

"Don't worry, you'll be fine," I said, not believing what I was stating.

"I think it's over," Radu answered me.

I felt sweat trickling down my back. I had to find a way to get him to a hospital. And fast. I looked around for tissue to stop the bleeding. As quickly as I could, I cut out a piece of drapery that covered the window. I could sense Radu's irregular pulse. Scared, I began a quick mouth-to-mouth. I stopped periodically and listened to verify if he was breathing.

"Breathe!" I prayed in silence. "Come on, breathe! "

Minutes that seemed an eternity passed during my frenetic attempts. Radu suddenly opened his eyes, took a deep breath, and then choked. I saw how his neck muscles tightened while he was trying to speak. His pulse was very weak.

"Don't move!" I told him. "I stopped the bleeding. I'll get Ambrosio, and we'll get you to the hospital."

"The boat is no longer where we left it," said Radu. "I asked Ambrosio to leave without us. Vlad needed a doctor as soon as possible."

"Stop talking!" I insisted. "I'll find a way to get you to a hospital."

"Ana! Let's face it! We're outlaws in this country. I am incredibly grateful to you for wanting to help me, but I think it is time for you to leave this house and save yourself."

"Save your breath! I interrupted him. "I'm not leaving you here."

I climbed the stairs, jumping two or three steps at a time. A minute later, I stepped into the shadow of the trees and continued along the parking lot. A car was coming. It stopped about twenty meters from the first house on the street.

A woman exited the car's back door on the curbside and walked towards the house. The driver's door also opened, allowing passage to a man hurrying to follow the woman. They both disappeared into the house.

Relative silence returned to the streets. I quickly retraced my steps. I didn't have time to find a better way to help Radu. I could not afford to waste any time assessing the possibilities. I had to accept the one that presented itself with the arrival of this couple.

Back in the house, I unhooked the door from a cupboard, and with the help of several blankets, I improvised a stretcher on which I fixed Radu's wounded body as best I could. Looking at his cadaverous complexion, I thought of the sordid end that most of those who ply their trade go through. Unexplainable deaths are never solved because people who live and die in the shadows take their secrets to their graves.

I walked more carefully than usual, pulling the improvised stretcher. Radu winced in pain at every move. Once I got to the side of the car from which the couple just left, I checked the doors. They were all locked.

I took a look at Radu. He had tried to get up and slipped on the asphalt. Dogs howled as if they were making a desperate call to the night sky. Without wasting any second, I pulled a roll of invisible tape out of my backpack and stuck tape onto the window on the car's passenger side. Then I took off my jacket, wrapped it around my elbow and, with a sudden gesture, broke the car window. The sound was faint, thanks to the tape, which prevented the pieces of glass from falling. I opened the door and reclined the passenger seat to the maximum. With all my strength, I pushed Radu's injured body onto the seat. His survival instinct kicked in, giving him a burst of strength that defied his wounds. The urgency of the situation was palpable, every second crucial in our race against time.

After settling Radu as comfortably as I could, I hotwired the car, set the throttle, and launched the vehicle into the street. Glancing back at the owner's house, I felt a knot in my stomach. Two figures stood out against the window's light. The engine's roar had caught their attention. They would soon inform the police about the stolen car. But I was determined, I didn't have the luxury of time.

I looked at Radu. He had lost consciousness, and his pallor was alarming. The fear of losing him was overwhelming. I had to find a hospital, and fast. The traffic was chaotic, drivers disregarding all rules. I swerved from one lane to another, narrowly avoiding accidents. I wasn't familiar with Istanbul, but I vaguely remembered a hospital near the Great Mosque.

The car was eating the miles while I was trying to control my heartbeat. Radu had regained consciousness and tried to speak, but the sound coming out of his mouth was more like a weak complaint mingled with gurgling. Anxious, I forgot about the danger and accelerated. Feverishly, I tried to remember the exact location of the hospital. Miraculously, the siren of an ambulance sounded. Following the sound, I drove south, and a few intersections later, I saw the hospital in the light of the headlights.

I arrived in a moment of contained effervescence; nurses and doctors were bustling around the ambulance in an energetic atmosphere. The presence of two police officers next to the ambulance indicated that an unfortunate accident had occurred.

With tightness in her chest, I stopped the car next to the ambulance and looked at Radu's face. His face was still waxy, but his breathing was stable. Hopeful, I got out of the car. With a firm grip, I grabbed the hand of the first man in a white coat.

"Doctor, a seriously injured man is in the car. He needs your attention right now. "

The doctor looked at me with black eyes swollen with fatigue. His pupils did not betray any emotion following my words. With a helpless gesture, he shrugged his shoulders.

"We have three seriously injured people in the

ambulance," he said. "Your friend must wait his turn."

"He lost a lot of blood; he is unconscious. It may already be too late," I insisted, blocking his way.

The doctor shrugged and stood on his heels, trying to contain his annoyance.

"All right, make room for me to examine him."

I stepped aside as the doctor opened the car door. He leaned over just above Radu, aiming his light pencil in his eyes. He immediately understood the seriousness of his injuries and motioned for two nurses to transport him inside the hospital right away. Then he addressed me, sounding suspicious.

"Bullets badly hit your friend. You can't leave the premises until you report to the police. There are two police officers next to the ambulance. I'll ask them to join you."

"That's not necessary. I'll join them and I'll make a full report of what happened."

Seeing the doctor's uncertain gaze, I insisted.

"Please, doctor. With every passing second, my friend's chances of survival diminish."

My worried face convinced the doctor that I was telling the truth. He walked away from the hospital with a small groove of concern between his eyebrows. I feigned a walk toward the police officers, and when the doctor disappeared inside the hospital, I swiftly pivoted and made a beeline for the car, my mind racing with strategies.

A characteristic tingling in the back of my neck told me that I was being followed. I carefully glanced back, but I saw nothing suspicious. I continued walking towards the car. The play of shadows and lights in the parking lot prevented me from seeing clearly. I was very close when I saw the first officer leaning toward the license plate of the car the car I had stolen. The car owners reported it stolen, and the police found it. Another policeman appeared about twenty meters to my left. A third was at an equal distance to my right.

While observing them, I noticed that my clothes were bloodstained. Even if I had no trouble getting away without being seen by the police, I would attract attention wherever I went. I walked away quietly towards the hospital. In a corner of the lobby, I found what I needed first: a telephone booth. I dialed Ambrosio's number. His voice seemed surprised.

"Ambrosio," I breathed, relief flooding my senses at the sound of his voice.

"I see you're still alive!"

"You seemed disappointed!"

"On the contrary, I rejoice!"

I explained the situation briefly, and we established a meeting place near the hospital. I had half an hour to get there.

I glanced around the hospital lobby and hesitated for a moment. Should I go out the front door? Given the frequency with which the ambulances arrived, I could sneak out unnoticed.

A breath of cold air told me that the front door was open. Among the employees bustling around the accident victims, I saw two police officers checking the faces of the people crossing. I looked anxiously at my bloodstained clothes. It wasn't unusual in a hospital, but I better be careful.

I looked down the hall, searching for every other possible exit. With a smooth movement, I turned the first door handle on the right. Inside, there was a deep darkness. As soon as my eyes became accustomed to the darkness, I spotted the forms of several beds and another exit on the other side of the room.

I rushed through the two swinging doors, almost knocking over a nurse carrying a tray on which metal medical utensils were swinging noisily. Despite the adrenaline rushing through my body, I continued to walk at the same pace as the people around me. An emergency exit was on my left. I didn't hesitate; I opened the door and ran into the poorly lit corridor outside the hospital. Once outside, I stopped for a moment, trying to orient myself. I closed my eyes momentarily, trying to remember the instructions Ambrosio had given me.

The sound of traffic surrounded me like a ball. The pedestrians were moving at average speed without paying attention. After a few hundred meters, I found where I was supposed to meet Ambrosio. I saw a gray car parked along the sidewalk. I retreated into a narrow passage, sinking into darkness. The window on the driver's side was open, and I saw Ambrosio smoking a cigarette. For a while, I looked around. Nothing abnormal caught my attention. I came out of hiding and joined Ambrosio in the car.

Ambrosio's eyes stayed on my blood-stained clothes. A

question was born in his dark look.

"You'll have all the answers, but first of all, we must get away from here," I told him.

As soon as I had finished my sentence, Ambrosio pressed the gas pedal. He didn't say a word until we arrived at his house.

I followed him into the kitchen, where he poured a colourless liquid into a glass and encouraged me to drink it. A pleasant warmth spread into my sore body. I explained the situation to Ambrosio, choosing my words carefully.

Ambrosio first frowned, then all the muscles in his face stretched out, and his eyes became anxious. When I had finished speaking, he got up and started walking back and forth. Finally, he said.

"You should never have taken him to a hospital. You endangered my freedom."

"Your concern is unwarranted. Radu Branescu is a professional. He'll never reveal your name."

"The Turkish authorities have the means to break him, chemically or physically, to force the information out of him. I'll probably have to leave my country for good."

"Allow me to remind you that if you accepted the job you're doing, you must've known the risks."

Ambrosio let his gaze wander around the room, and his hands tightened on the arm of the chair. When he spoke again, his voice sounded feverish.

"We still have the means to stop the ordinary course of events. We'll have to get Radu out of the hospital."

"No!" I shouted. "His wounds are too severe, and he's

lost a lot of blood. The hospital is the best place for him right now."

"What do you suggest? Do nothing?"

"Radu risked his life for me," I answered. "I'm not leaving this country until I ensure he's safe."

Ambrosio walked back and forth, lost in his thoughts. A minute of silence passed, then another, until he finally started talking.

"I'll be straight with you, Ana. I'm only getting involved in this mess to cover my own back. I have enough money to live comfortably for the rest of my life anywhere. But my love for my country runs deep, and I'll do whatever it takes to stay here.

Here's our plan: I'll use my connections in the hospital to closely watch Radu's health, monitoring him around the clock. The moment he wakes up, he'll be briefed on what we need him to do. Even if his condition improves, he'll have to act like he's still gravely ill. As long as he's under medical supervision, the Turkish authorities can't force him to talk.

We'll need to wait until Radu is stable enough to handle being moved before we make any big moves. In the meantime, I'll find a doctor willing to take the risk and treat him off the books. For now, I'll start by getting the hospital's blueprints." As Ambrosio laid out his plan, a new intensity burned in his eyes. His words were filled with fierce determination, and I could feel the shift, sensing the urgency in his voice.

I thought the danger was like an addiction for people

like us, recognizing the familiar thrill that Ambrosio seemed to chase. It's not just about the mission but the rush and the high that comes with it. And Ambrosio, he's addicted to it, just like me.

"Until then, you'll stay in a hotel," he continued. "It's safer to split up. The wait can be long. Don't try to contact me. I will make contact only when necessary."

For the next few hours, we worked out how the operation would unfold. We slept a little, and the following day, I awoke early. My body was hurting so much that I was grimacing with pain. After a hot shower, I felt better. Following the smell of fried eggs, I found Ambrosio in the kitchen eating his breakfast, and he invited me to share his meal.

"I have news," he said, shaking his pack of cigarettes and lighting one up. "Radu had surgery. He's in the ICU. The police have set up a guard outside his door, which proves that Turkish security will not let go quickly. They want to know why a foreigner got shot in their country. They're getting ready to send to the press the sketch of the woman who brought Radu to the hospital, hoping somebody will recognize her."

"You mean my portrait sketch."

"I mean the sketch of a woman. One of my contacts in the police just faxed it to me."

He opened the suitcase's zipper next to his chair and pulled out a piece of paper. The woman in the sketch looked very little like me.

"As you can see, we're fortunate. No one will recognize

you by looking at this sketch. I don't think the cop who drew the sketch didn't have a good pencil stroke. I think it was the doctor who gave them inaccurate information."

"You mean he deliberately misled them?"

"That's right. The doctor feared he would have to deal with the people who put Radu in that state. In doing so, he has provided us with great service."

He looked at the glowing end of his cigarette and continued in a firm voice.

"I booked you a room in a downtown hotel. The owner is a longtime friend. There is a suitcase in the lobby full of regular clothing. It would be best if you changed to look like a simple tourist.

"Thank you."

"We'll leave the house as soon as you finish your breakfast."

Twenty minutes later, we drove silently through the city streets. When we arrived in the city center, Ambrosio dropped me off in front of a hotel higher than the surrounding buildings.

CHAPTER 27

The room Ambrosio had reserved for me was elementary, furnished only with a bed framed by two bedside tables equipped with lamps and two dressers. A long, narrow mirror pointed to a closet door.

Without hanging my clothes, I put the suitcase inside. I avoided the elevator and rushed down the service stairs when I left the room. The exit door opened behind the hotel, and I walked down three stairs. Garbage containers were lined up in an inner courtyard. An alley was winding up to a rusty metal door.

Immersed in the human mass and the car flow, I made several hotel tours, memorizing every detail that could be useful if things turned sour.

The air was crisp, and the wind was becoming calmer. I needed a car. I found a car rental office, and half an hour later, I was sitting at the wheel of a Skoda. As I crossed the city, I became familiar with the streets that I only knew from maps. I tried various routes and assessed traffic conditions. As I had already seen on arrival, the traffic in Istanbul was a total mess.

The evening was falling in the city when I decided to stop to eat. The restaurant was noisy and overheated, but I was hungry. When the waiter brought out my order, I realized how hungry I was. As dessert, I ordered a honey pastry and a coffee. The thin layers of dough melted on my tongue, and the strong black coffee warmed my stomach.

For a while, I let myself be carried away by the pleasure of having nothing to worry about. At my second coffee, I realized I didn't particularly appreciate that Ambrosio was the only one making the decisions while I had to wait in a hotel room. I quickly decided to go to the hospital and check Radu's condition with my own eyes. I asked for the bill and was soon driving my rental across town towards the hospital.

The street where the hospital was located was quieter than the city center, but there were still a lot of passersby at this hour. I parked the car at a distance that allowed me to see the entrance to the hospital. I had no definite plan and decided to follow my intuition. Hospitals must always be busy in a crowded and chaotic city like Istanbul. It will be easy to slip inside.

An ambulance appeared on the right corner of the street, all sirens howling, and stopped in front of the hospital entrance doors. Uniformed personnel rushed outside, ready to help.

I exited the car and took advantage of the commotion in front of the hospital to get inside. I had memorized Ambrosio's plans so well that the complex network of the vast hospital was no longer a secret to me.

With rapid movements, I moved quickly through the first floor. I put on a nursing gown that I found folded on the laundry cart and walked toward the elevators. Intensive care was located on the third floor. Equipped with a clipboard I had put my hand on while walking, I crossed the hallway pretending to have a specific purpose. Ambrosio's information was valid; a copper-faced guard, who followed me with his dark eyes, was sitting on a plastic chair in front of one of the doors. Radu should be inside that room. Delighted to note that my heartbeat and my breathing were perfectly normal, I left the hospital and returned to my hotel room.

The following days passed very slowly. By car or on foot, I crossed the city end to end, eager to hear from Ambrosio. I never stopped admiring the impressive mosques, their erect towers like challenges against the sky.

A week and a half later, at precisely eleven hours and fifteen minutes, Ambrosio sent me a message. We met in the Grand Bazaar, and he took me to the back of a spice shop. An older man served us smoking tea and then walked away quietly. I was reaching the limit of my patience when Ambrosio finally began to speak.

"They discovered the carnage in the Securitate's house on the Bosphorus," he said, "but they have no leads. As long as Radu doesn't talk, we're out of danger."

"How's he doing?"

"He is out of danger. He underwent several surgeries, and the recovery will be very long."

"Was he interrogated?"

"They tried, but it didn't work."

"What do you mean? They try to torture him?"

"Of course not! They can't do that in the hospital! They will be patients until they can transfer him to a secure location."

Despite my grief, I forced myself to remain calm.

"What's your plan?" I asked him.

"Tonight, at quarter past ten, we will enter the hospital. At half past ten, we will cause an explosion that will break a water primary on the second floor. That will force the hospital administration to evacuate a large number of patients. The unexpected situation will create confusion and disorder. That is when we will intervene. Two of my men will take Radu outside. The two of us will make sure that everything goes smoothly. A false ambulance will be waiting for us at ten forty-five in front of the hospital."

I looked at Ambrosio's strong and rigid face, a face that knows how to hide his thoughts behind an impenetrable mask. A range of wrinkles and greyish hair at the temples marked premature aging. He seemed relaxed during their discussion, which reassured me of his intentions. I decided to trust him. Under the circumstances, I had little choice. Ambrosio had the advantage of being in his country and having all the contacts.

We spent the next few hours perfecting every detail of the operation. In the backpack Ambrosio had brought for me, there was a bulletproof vest, a gun with a silencer, a knife, and lots of ammunition. In a separate pocket were a nurse's gown and a badge. The city was lit like a Christmas tree when I left the bazaar. At precisely nine hours and ten minutes, I started my rental car, and as soon as Ambrosio passed by in his SUV, I followed him.

Halfway to the hospital, I parked my car and entered Ambrosio's. At ten o'clock precisely, Ambrosio parked the vehicle at the intersection of two alleys and signaled me to get out. A middle-sized man approached, and without saying a word, he got into Ambrosio's car and sat in the driver's seat.

Ambrosio and I walked the remaining distance. At the corner of the hospital, we put on the nurses' gowns, fastened our badges and walked inside the hospital after a short exchange of glances. With our heads bent, they pretended to be preoccupied.

On the third floor in the intensive care unit, all was calm. The guard posted at Radu's door had fallen asleep in his chair, his head bent over his chest. There was a smell of chloroform in the air. We saw employees chatting quietly through a half-open door behind the reception desk. Everything seemed in order.

As Ambrosio walked cautiously toward the sleeping guard, a feeling of anguish invaded me. I approached the door where the employees were chatting and listened briefly. Then I looked towards Ambrosio. He was standing behind the slightly open door of the emergency exit. He used his right hand to pull out of his pocket a light and discreet weapon equipped with a massive silencer at the end of the barrel. He waved at me to look at my watch.

The next moment, the explosion erupted. The sound was so loud that it hurt my eardrums. Debris flew through the air, forming a gaping hole in the corridor's ceiling. Instantly, the guard raised his head, his eyes filled with animal panic. He looked around, trying to figure out what had happened. Advancing on his toes, Ambrosio approached the guard from behind and whacked his head with his gun, strong enough for the guard to faint but not strong enough to kill him. Then he caught him under the armpits and dragged him behind the emergency door.

Panicked voices followed by hasty steps came from the corridor. I sprinted and hid behind the first door. Through the gap, I saw three employees. Judging by their panic-stricken gestures and attitude, they did not fully understand what had happened.

The explosion damaged a water pipe, raising the water level in the hallway. After a few exchanges, the staff moved away in haste. I returned to the corridor. It was time to move on to the second phase of the plan. Emerging from their hiding place, Ambrosio's men installed Radu Branescu in a wheelchair and began to descend towards the hospital's exit. Ambrosio and I followed them, ready to intervene if necessary.

As Ambrosio had anticipated, chaos reigned in the hospital. Zigzagging in the corridors, overwhelmed by the number of patients in wheelchairs or on stretchers, Ambrosio and I followed the two men carrying Radu toward the exit. Around us was a cacophony of groans and screams from patients and employees.

At exactly ten-forty-five, an ambulance stopped before the hospital's entrance. After installing Radu inside, Ambrosio's two men disappeared into the street. Ambrosio went to sit up next to the driver and signaled me to get in the back.

"Hurry up, for God's sake!" muttered Ambrosio.

I got into the ambulance. Radu, who had received a hefty dose of morphine, was asleep. The blood had soaked his clothes, but he looked relaxed, oblivious to what was happening around him. With an almost clinical detachment, I changed his bandages.

We drove for almost two hours. Shortly after midnight, we stopped in the circular alley of a brick house. The ambulance's back door suddenly opened, and Ambrosio signaled me to get out. Almost simultaneously, the house door opened. In the sudden ray of light, I distinguished the silhouette of a man in his sixties. With hasty steps, he approached the ambulance and, with the driver's help, carried Radu inside the house.

"Where are we?" I asked Ambrosio.

"Not far from Istanbul. This is a doctor's friend's summer home."

We reached the foot of a staircase and climbed the steps. The house was vast, and the walls were cluttered with photographs of the various members of the doctor's family.

We waited in the hallway, anxious for the doctor's verdict. After a short while, the door opened, and the doctor came out smiling and addressed Ambrosio with a triumphant air.

"Your friend has deep, serious wounds, but no vital organs have been affected. The real problem is the injury to the left leg. I'll come by every day to make sure his health improves. This is a phone number where you can reach me in case of emergency," he said, giving Ambrosio a piece of paper.

"How soon will he be able to travel?" asked Ambrosio.

"Probably in two weeks. But he will undoubtedly need a wheelchair."

I stared at him, not understanding why he looked so triumphant. On the one hand, I felt relieved about Radu's diagnosis; on the other, I was worried about not being able to leave the country earlier. I had hoped that a few days would be enough. I sketched a forced smile and shouted a few words of thanks.

"It is time for me to leave," said Ambrosio. "When the time comes, one of my men will take you to the airport."

A few minutes later, I heard the front door open and close. I was alone with Radu and the doctor.

"I must leave too," said the doctor. "I let you discover the house on your own. You can sleep in the room adjacent to your friend. I left the phone number where you can reach me, if needed, on the kitchen counter."

After the doctor left, I remained motionless for a moment, then went to the room next to Radu's and lay on the bed. Sleep should have come quickly, but it didn't. I couldn't escape the feeling of responsibility and guilt over Radu's condition.

I tried to focus on something positive: the fact that we had saved the lives of Vlad and his family and that my family was avenged. I thought I would feel better after getting revenge on the man who was guilty of my family's death, but I realized that his death could not compensate for the emptiness I felt without a family, an emptiness that I would never be able to fill. Convinced she could not sleep, I got up and walked around the room. Then, I examined the grooves on my silencer and slipped the gun into the nightstand. I went into Radu's room and stood still momentarily, looking at him.

Radu's sleep was restless. He seemed plagued by obsessive dreams that made him moan. Sometimes, he'd make random gestures. When I wrapped his forehead in a cloth soaked in cold water, he raised a small grunt of protest before falling back into a feverish sleep.

I thought that our nightmares were part of us. We must live with the recollection of what we have accomplished. We will never be able to reconcile with the evil that we have done. He will come to haunt us until the end of our days.

I got up and exited the room. As I squinted my eyes to get used to the darkness, I wandered from room to room without purpose. The wooden floor of the house was covered with many Persian carpets. Some walls were decorated with family photos, others with carpets worth a small fortune. I entered the vast garden and quietly closed the door behind me. The only sounds came from the wind, which carried the distant dog's yelps.

A sense of extreme loneliness slowly crept into my mind. My restless existence had been interspersed with moments of solitude but never as acute as tonight. I thought of George and the thousands of people risking everything for a better life and stood still for several minutes. Surreal shadows and ghosts were hunting my mind, images I could never get rid of.

The night imprisoned me, and the wind, which rose steadily, whipped my face and glued my clothes to my body. Panting with cold, I stood up and returned to the room where Radu was sleeping. His fever was dropping; the Turkish doctor's treatment was working. Not having the courage to leave him alone for a long time, I curled up in the leather chair in the corner and covered myself with a blanket.

Gradually, I felt relaxed, and I fell into a restless sleep. In my dream, I was swimming in a deep, black lake. The water was carrying me away and I was trying desperately not to fall into the stillness of the depths. As my strength left me and I thought I would die in those dark depths, I felt strong arms pulling me to the surface and felt the sun warming my body. I opened my eyes. A man with sandy hair and deep blue eyes held me in his arms. I trusted him. A comforting warmth relaxed my muscles, and I drifted into a deep sleep.

CHAPTER 28

Radu's injuries turned out to be far more severe than the Turkish doctor's initial diagnosis, and his recovery took much longer than the two weeks predicted. I blamed myself for his condition and dedicated every moment to helping Radu regain his strength. Christmas and New Year passed, but instead of festive cheer, there was only the oppressive weight of isolation. I felt like I was suffocating, cut off from the world. To quiet my restless mind and manage to sleep, I pushed my body to exhaustion through relentless workouts.

By January 2, Radu managed to walk around the garden using a cane. Though the effort drained him, he insisted he was fit enough for the flight to Germany. Eager to leave Turkey behind, I contacted Ambrosio. He arrived within hours, bringing new passports, plane tickets, and everything we needed for our disguises. He even included a doctor's note explaining Radu's condition due to a fall in the city's catacombs in case somebody at the airport asked for an explanation. "Accidents happen," Ambrosio remarked as if reciting a line he'd rehearsed. "Especially to tourists wandering through Istanbul."

On January 4, as planned, Ambrosio sent a car to take us to the airport. Before we left, I took a last look in the mirror, scrutinizing my reflection against the photo on my passport. The resemblance was flawless. Radu's transformation was so convincing that anyone seeing him in the hospital wouldn't recognize him now.

We set off, the car speeding through the rain-slicked streets toward the airport. As it came to a stop, rain poured down, and Radu struggled to keep up with the crowd surging toward the terminal. Red blotches marked his cheeks from the effort.

Out of habit, I scanned the faces around us, instinctively assessing for threats. A quick glance at my watch told me we were on schedule, but I worried if Radu could keep pace. Sensing my concern, Radu paused to catch his breath, then turned to me. "Whatever happens," he said quietly, "I just want to thank you for everything you've done for me."

"You saved my life," I replied, guilt tightening my chest. "If it weren't for me, you wouldn't be in this state."

We passed through customs without any issues, and forty minutes later, we climbed the aircraft's aluminum stairs, slick with rain. When the cabin door shut, I heard the engines roar to life. As the plane began to taxi, Radu glanced at me, his eyes conveying a silent message: "We're safe now."

Anxious for news, I asked the air hostess for the latest newspapers. On the front page of each newspaper was a photo of the Romanian President, Nicolae Ceausescu, followed by articles saying the same thing in different words:

The death of a dictator – the Romanian revolution.

My lips trembling with emotion, I looked at the photos that accompanied the articles.

It took me a long time to control my emotions and continue to read. The article began with the events which had led to the revolution.

On December 16, a few dozen protesters gathered in front of the house of reformed pastor Laszlo Tokés. Very quickly, other people joined and the protest turned into a compact crowd of tens of thousands of people. The forces of law and order intervene with brutality. The peaceful demonstration soon changes its focus. The crowd began singing anti-Communist songs against the abuses of the dictatorial regime imposed by Nicolae and Elena Ceausescu. The Securitate responded with tear gas and water cannons.

The demonstration continued on December 17, becoming an anti-communist revolution against a regime that has become unbearable. The army is ordered to use force against the demonstrators. Armored transporters run into groups of demonstrators who are targeted by live fire. The demonstration stops. On 18 December, a group of 30 young people carried tricolor flags without the communist badge and sang the old national anthem. The same day, Ceausescu left the country for a visit in Iran. On his return, the situation in Romania deteriorated sharply. On December 20, 100,000 workers entered the city of Timisoara, protesting against the government.

"We are the people; the army is with us."

On December 21, Ceausescu decided to reunite the workers of Bucharest, the country's capital, in Palace Square. He intended to condemn the Timisoara movement.

The crowd began to be agitated, and a protest movement developed. Ceausescu's attempts to calm the crowd are useless. Eight minutes after the beginning of his speech, the crowd shouts: "Timisoara!" and "Change dictator!" Concerned and fearful, Ceausescu interrupts his speech. The following day, the demonstrators invaded the presidential palace. Ceausescu and his wife fled by helicopter from the roof of the palace in the direction of a provincial town. Journalists are stirring up the craziest rumors: Ceausescu is said to be gathering an army to drown the revolt in blood. Several bloody days followed, mysterious snipers shot at the population and there were hundreds of deaths. The demonstrators are being repressed in blood and by mass arrests. Chaos settles in Bucharest. The offices of the Central Committee were vandalized, portraits of the dictator were thrown out, and hidden assassins continued to shoot innocent people. The crowd calls for a government

Overwhelmed by emotions, I closed my eyes and rested my head on the fabric headrest. A myriad of unanswered questions swirled in my mind. Radu, who had been snoring gently since we boarded, shifted in his seat. I turned to him. His face was pale, but his breathing was steady. He was oblivious to the turmoil that had engulfed his country.

A part of me wanted to wake him and share the news, but I hesitated. I feared that the shock might worsen his fragile health. So, I concealed the newspapers and checked my watch. An agonizing half hour later, the plane finally landed.

Thanks to the doctor's note justifying Radu's state of health after a fall in the catacombs of Istanbul, we benefited from a priority passage at the security checkpoint. When we reached my car in the airport parking lot, Radu was exhausted. His muscles, which had suffered from this period of inactivity, could no longer support his body mass, and fever chills were shaking his body. He needed to see a doctor.

We chose a small private clinic in the suburbs of Frankfurt, a place where Radu had been treated before. The staff were discreet and didn't pry. An hour and a half later, Radu was settled in a private room. The doctor assured me that Radu was in good hands. A wave of relief washed over me as I left the clinic and droves home. All I could think about was reaching home and calling George. A mix of joy and frustration filled my heart. The revolution had succeeded, but I wasn't among those who had risked their lives for it. In my excitement, I even ran a few red lights, risking arrest.

As I stepped into the apartment, I noticed the little red light blinking on the voicemail. I dropped my suitcase and hurried to the phone. George's voice filled the apartment:

"Ana, call me at this number as soon as you hear this message. "It was a number with a German prefix.

I picked up the phone and dialled the number. A man's voice, with a solid Romanian accent, answered at the other end.

"Hello!"

"Good evening! I want to talk to George, please."

"Who is this?"

"Ana, Ana Zaicovich."

"One moment."

George's voice sounded on the other end of the line a few seconds later.

"Ana!"

"George! You should be proud of your work; the revolution has succeeded!"

There was a silence at the other end of the line.

"George!"

"Ana... we have lost the revolution."

I tried hard to swallow my saliva. I thought the air seemed thicker in the room, and the walls were getting closer. Endless seconds passed before I came to my senses. I didn't want to ask any more questions. I knew George, and I knew he was telling the truth. I now understood why he was in Germany.

"Give me your address," I finally said.

He gave me the address. I looked at my watch.

"I'll be there at five o'clock," I said and hung up.

The distance between Frankfurt and Bonn is one hundred and seventy-six km. I had time to shower before I lived.

Lost in my thoughts and speculations, I drove at high speed towards Bonn. The road was beautiful, and an hour and a quarter later, I arrived at George's address. After a brief hesitation, I exited the car and approached the door. I barely had time to ring the bell when the door opened wide.

"Ana!" exclaimed George with joy

He dragged me into the hall before slamming the door.

He looked at me for a moment and then hugged me for a long time.

"You really are the most beautiful woman I have ever seen," he whispered. "I missed you so much."

Taken by surprise, I didn't know what to say. I didn't expected this display of emotion.

"I missed you too, George, but I need to know what happened!"

"I understand. Would you like something to drink?"

I became impatient.

"No, George! I don't want anything to drink! I need to figure out what's going on. The revolution has succeeded! Why are you here?"

For a while, George remained silent, and then he signaled me to follow him. We entered a living room with modern furniture. As soon as we were seated, George started talking.

"It wasn't a revolution, Ana. It was a coup."

"What do you mean? All the newspapers are talking about how successful the Romanian revolution was!"

"Not the people revolution. The Russians won. They've been plotting with those who worked for many years for Ceausescu. Those who pretended to be on our side betrayed us. They changed their shirts overnight. They shot Ceausescu and his wife to stay in power. A master-stroke."

While he was talking, I would stare at him in silence, unable to accept the reality.

"And yet, thousands of people took to the streets to

demonstrate! I can't believe they let themselves be fooled after so many years of suffering!"

"The whole operation was a gigantic manipulation," continued George. "The population has been manipulated by internal instigators and by foreign instigators sent by the KGB. The way things went, I'm inclined to believe that other outside powers are involved. Their actions were carefully thought out, the population's reactions were calculated, and all the variables were analyzed and considered in their calculation. I'll try to explain their strategy to you so you can understand that each action served a final plan."

He turned his gaze to the window and spoke with a broken voice.

"After Ceausescu's escape, chaos reigned in Bucharest. The demonstrators attacked the national television and managed to take control of it. Spontaneously, the armed forces fraternized with the demonstrators. Fueled by its desire to eliminate all traces of the communist regime, the population attacked the buildings that had belonged to the communist government. They vandalized the building of the Central Committee and destroyed the portraits of the dictator. A new government was formed, composed of members of the Communist Party. The protesters demanded a government without communists. But they had no idea what beast they were dealing with.

Scenarios have been created to manipulate the population. Hidden assassins appeared all over the city, and they started shooting at the population. There were rumors that they were "the terrorists of the old regime." Television has begun to transmit contradictory information. At the airport, two army units began to shoot at each other, each of them convinced that they were fighting the terrorists. The creation of a provisional government called the "National Salvation Front," established by Iliescu, Roman and Voican, was announced on television."

"Iliescu!" I exclaimed. "But that's impossible! He's a former member of the Central Committee of the communist party! Besides, he finished his studies in Russia!"

"Precisely. The Russians have chosen with great care. We must not forget that Iliescu was a follower of Gorbachev's policy and had shown his dissatisfaction with the drift of the Romanian Communist Party. As a result, Ceausescu dismissed him from the Central Committee on the pretext of his alleged incompetence. It had worked in his favor. In my opinion, Ion Iliescu is certainly the favorite of Russians. All the events that followed the "National Salvation Front" creation prove that the Russians wanted to consolidate their power.

"That's absurd!" I exclaimed.

I had difficulty holding back my emotions, and the astonishment morphed into anger.

George looked at me in silence, not knowing what to say. Then, he continued in a neutral tone.

"After the creation of the "National Salvation Front", other scenarios were fabricated with terrorists to maintain fear. They attacked important places of socio-political life: airports, television, radio, the press and the Ministry of Defense. The demonstrators remained in the streets and areas under siege to protect the liberated institutions. Then, the "National Salvation Front" converted to Western-style democracy and launched to the demonstrators the slogan "Down with communism, death to terrorists." As no one was able to identify the so-called "terrorists", the demonstrators attacked people who were suspected to be members of the Securitate. The soldiers and civilians who got their hands on the weapons were persuaded to defend freedom from "the dictator's henchmen." Mass arrests have been made and thousands have been killed and injured.

George remained silent for a while, his gaze locked in a distant point.

I was in shock.

"I cannot accept this conclusion, George, "I said hesitantly. After listening to you, everything points to the fact that we lost. But it isn't easy to accept that people can be deceived so easily. And you may have been speculating too much to come to that conclusion. Maybe there's still a chance. We cannot so easily give up a cause for which we have fought all our lives!"

"How can you doubt my words?" he articulates, short of breath. Do you think I'd be here if there were the slightest chance of success? I wondered a thousand times if coming this far and being defeated halfway to freedom was possible. And I had to accept the facts: the tragedies that blooded the world are, for the most part, manipulations. And the genocide continues. I saw an angry crowd plunged into the most significant confusion."

He couldn't contain his emotions anymore.

"Our dream was shattered, Ana. The Organization no longer exists. My family, Maria and Avram, are all dead. Once the chaos was created, it was easy to make the unwanted disappear."

Stunned by the news, I could not listen anymore. Maria and Avram were my only remaining family. Their absence left me feeling adrift, with no anchor to hold onto, and a profound sense of purposelessness engulfed me.

George kept talking, but I didn't listen to him anymore. I got up and walked to the door.

George rose in turn and followed me down the corridor. "Ana!" he said in a panicked voice. "Don't go! I have so much to tell you! We can try to forget the past and start a new life. Together. I would do anything humanly possible to make you happy."

I turned around and stared at him with a cold look. I will never be able to forget my past, the tragedy of my family and the tragedy of my people who had been manipulated like a puppet by cold, old-fashioned professionals. How could he talk about a new life a few minutes after he mentioned the death of Maria and Avram? It's about time I told him the truth.

"I'll be honest with you, George. There was a time when I was very fond of you. It would be a lie to tell you that my feelings haven't changed. You deserve more than I can offer you."

I walked to the door and left the house before George could say something.

CHAPTER 29

The temperature had dropped, and heavy, slippery, wet snow was falling on the streets. I got into the car and started the engine. Without realizing it, I was taking turns at high speed, making the tires squeal. At a red light, the presence of a police car brought me back to my senses. I continued to drive, unable to focus my attention on the road. I had believed in so many things that had fallen apart, one by one, like sand castles.

Like the growling of a wild beast, a guttural cry rose from my throat, instead of driving down the street in a straight line, I lost control, and the car turned to the side of the road, towards the sidewalk. I heard the car hitting the sidewalk and instinctively pressed the brake pedal. The car stopped, but I made no move to straighten it.

With my hands clenched on the wheel, I closed my

eyes and felt a profound sadness. My life experiences have shown me how rotten this world is. All that was left in my mind were sad stories of broken people who wanted to give meaning to their lives. After all these years, because the Securitate had tricked me, I had only managed to become their enemy rather than a friend.

Remaining in a state of prostration for what felt like an eternity, I was lost in a world of pain and loneliness. The icy wind was roaring along the street, freezing me to the bone. But as I finally opened my eyes, a sense of determination overcame me. I realized that my life would never be the same again. The future, for now, was like a thick cloud before the rain. But one thing was clear in my mind: from now on, I would be the sole architect of my life.

Gathering all my focus, I straightened the car and drove slowly towards the city center. Exhausted, I decided to spend the night in Bonn. The road soon widened into a prominent thoroughfare lined with rows of buildings, banks, and shops. I reached a beautiful paved square dominated by the construction of a luxury hotel.

In the hotel lobby, everything was quiet. It was supper time, and the guests were either out for dinner or back in their rooms. The concierge handed me the key with a professional smile, and moments later, I opened the door to a spacious and elegant room.

I spent a long time taking a hot shower to warm up my body. As I had no change of clothes, I put the same ones on again and stood in front of the mirror. My faded jeans and black turtleneck sweater were not ideal for dining in a fancy restaurant. But at that moment, I found myself indifferent to my appearance. I approached the window, pulled the curtain, and looked into the snowy landscape, listening to the thudding sound of snowflakes pattering on the window. With a sudden gesture, I ran her hand over my face as if I wanted to chase away my thoughts.

"It's over, I told myself. Finished. I have to accept reality. I have to learn to live day by day."

I left the room and I went to the hotel restaurant.

The restaurant was warm and comfortable, lit by the flames of a massive stone fireplace. The smell of charcoal and wonderfully appetizing smells floated in the air. Despite my emotions, I realized that I was starving. I hadn't eaten anything since morning.

A waiter quickly showed up and handed me the menu card. I ordered mushroom ravioli accompanied by smoked duck magret. Twenty minutes later, the waiter returned, holding the dishes in balance on his forearm.

I ate my dinner in record time. When I called the waiter to order a coffee, I felt someone was watching me. I looked around discreetly. Most of the tables were occupied, and a few were sitting in boxes along the wall.

I caught the eye of a man sitting in one of these boxes and felt an electric shock through my spine, recognizing Matt O'Connor. He stared at me for a long moment, then focused on the beautiful blonde woman beside him. His attitude meant he recognized me but preferred the woman beside him. The night when he tried to help me escape from the Securitate assassins came back in my memory.

I felt a sharp pain in my heart while my gaze remained fixed on Matt O'Connor's sandy hair and athletic build. Realizing the ridicule of the situation, I looked away, the pain exploding in my heart. I found it difficult to accept, but I had to recognize without any doubt that I had fallen in love with this man. From that distant night when he held me in his arms, I had dreamed only of seeing him again, a longing that never faded. That was the reason why he came back so often in my dreams, a cruel reminder of a love that was never meant to be.

Feverishly, I asked the waiter to bring me the bill. I wanted to leave the restaurant as soon as possible. While I was paying the bill, I felt someone approaching my table. I looked up and thought I saw a ghost. I glanced towards the table where Matt O'Connor was still sitting and looked again at the man beside me. Except that one of them had tanner skin, they looked like two drops of water, like twins. I was taken aback, my heart beating uncontrollably. A mocking smile appeared on his face when he began to speak.

"You have mistaken me for my brother. I'm disappointed. I'm Ryan."

Slowly, I came out of her stupor and swung into reality. He was so close to me that I felt his manly scent and the warmth that emanated from his body. Suddenly, I felt an overwhelming urge to run away. I couldn't let this man guess how I felt about him. I pushed back my chair so aggressively that it made a scratching sound on the tile floor.

"Sit down, please," he asked me.

Stunned, I looked at his beautiful, determined face. His whole person emanated confounding assurance and genuine charisma.

"I thought you were a ghost!" he laughed. "But you're real. Do your "associates" know you're here?"

"I won't cause you any more trouble if that's what you want to know," I answered.

"Trouble! You turned my life upside down!"

"What do you mean?"

Ryan cleared his throat with an embarrassed look.

"You were stuck in my memory for so long. I've seen you so many times in my dreams ... and I didn't even know where to find you. I don't even know your name."

"I saw you in my dreams, too," I wanted to say, but I didn't say anything.

I tried to control the emotions that invaded her, but she was unable to think coherently. And when Ryan laid his warm, firm hand on mine, I didn't remove it. For the first time in weeks, I felt safe. We talked for a long time, and I became increasingly aware of my feelings for him as the hour progressed.

Had the restaurant not closed, we would have talked and stared at each other forever. Ryan paid the bill, then drew his face closer to mine and whispered firmly, "This time, you will not disappear."

I felt an iron grip closing on my wrist, and he led me out of the restaurant. Overwhelmed by emotion, I obeyed, feeling isolated from everything around me. The elevator was slow and stopped on each floor, letting people in and out of the building. Ryan smiled at me enigmatically and tightened the grip on my wrist. In his eyes, something enigmatic troubled me and made me forget the distress of the last few hours. As soon as the elevator doors opened on the top floor, he lifted me up like a child and carried me across the hall. When we got into the room, he kissed me softly. His fingers were strong and skillful, and his eyes did not leave me; he observed every reaction he provoked in me. Overwhelmed by the sensations, I shuddered with an almost intolerable pleasure. Without leaving me out of his sight, Ryan slowly increased the intensity of his caresses. His lips followed the same path as his fingers. His eyes were intense, almost feverish.

With Ryan's almost mind-boggling voice in my ear, his fingers slipping with exasperating slowness on my burning body, I immersed myself in a pleasure that I couldn't control.

CHAPTER 30

The dying sun gives the mountains a blue-green hue, and the wildflowers provide a delicious scent. Lying in the grass, I was in a suspension state. Twenty years have passed since my marriage to Ryan. Twenty years of happiness. My gaze embraced the horizon line, where the earth meets the sky. Beyond the horizon is the ocean. Further, there is a small village where members of my family are buried. My mind increasingly blurred their faces, but I will always carry them in my heart.

The scars of the past had stopped hurting me. I had followed the changes in the world as a spectator does for a play. At the cost of thousands of deaths and thousands of mutilated people, democracy is returning to the countries of Eastern Europe. After twenty years, history textbooks and television programs still present divergent views on the Romanian Revolution of 1989. Specific archives and witnesses have disappeared, and the sources are incomplete. In the USSR, fifteen Socialist Republics had declared independence in 1991. It was the end of an empire. The tricolor flag of Russia had replaced the red flag of the Soviet Union. Although the Russians are freer than they've ever been, the rate of poverty remains very high. Many former officers like Vladimir Putin had switched to the new Russian market economy or politics. With him as president, Russia is back on the international scene, regaining its position as a great power.

The silence of the borders has been broken. A new monster is born: terrorism. Plunged into the torment of terror, millions of people have only one lifeline: escape. Risking their lives to escape, they invade the promised land.

Thinking about all those changes, a shiver passed through my body. For a moment, I felt invaded by panic. Are my children safe?

My hand slipped into Ryan's, and I put my head on his broad shoulders. He held me protectively in his arms, exorcising the demons that revolved around me.